A DOULA TO DIE FOR

"Doulas stand in the doorway of life, with their main focus on mothering the mother."

AMY WRIGHT GLENN

1

VIVIENNE ROSE

The glow of a full moon hung over the highway as Vivienne Rose's Tesla purred smoothly along. "It's a marvelous night for a moondance," sang Van Morrison in his throaty voice.

She turned up the volume with the press of a finger and then lowered all of the car windows. Hot dry air brushed against her cheeks. Her hair, damp at the back of her neck, lifted with the breeze as she watched the speedometer rise another ten miles per hour.

A glance at the temperature revealed 112 degrees. But unless you've experienced the feel on your skin and the blanket-heat in your lungs, the number has no real meaning. *Tomorrow's going to be a scorcher.* She hummed along to the song, the moon casting light on the highway ahead.

Only an hour earlier she'd witnessed the lusty-lunged birth of a brand-new baby boy. Both parents, local residents of Palm Desert, sweaty with exertion, radiated joy.

"We're so grateful," the mom had said, clutching her baby to her bare chest. Water from the birthing pool lapped against her body.

Her partner stood to the side, wiping the back of his hand

across moist eyes. "I am so happy we did a home birth. This was the most..." He tried to find words but instead reached over to envelop Viv in a huge hug.

The memory made Viv sigh with pleasure. *No matter how many babies I've helped into the world, each one is a miracle. But this one, after my hiatus, feels very special, more memorable than most.*

She ran her fingers through her hair, tugging on the scrunchy tangled in her curls. A quick glance in the rearview mirror revealed hair amassed around her head. With a tug she pulled all the tangles back into the scrunchy, securing it with her free hand.

As the notes of Van Morrison's song faded, Viv closed all but the driver's-side window. Cool air, produced by the efficient car, wafted over her face. She felt more relaxed after the song and the window-open dry-air cleansing. Assisting with the long labor, with only three hours sleep, required stamina. She felt ready for a cool shower and some rest.

Vivienne pulled off the main highway; she took a right, then a left into her own neighborhood. Cars parked on the side of the road looked eerie in the moonlight. For a moment she thought one looked familiar. A silver-gray Toyota nestled between a BMW and a Ford Ranger.

She continued on, putting the car out of her mind. Braking to a halt at the security gate, she sighed. At this hour no one stood in the small booth on the left to let her through. So she extended her arm out of the open driver's window.

Tapping the code into the pad, the gate lifted, giving her access. She brought her arm inside and immediately closed the window. *Desert Tortoise Estates*, the sign announced on the right. She accelerated her car as the gate made its downward descent behind her rear bumper.

At first she'd refused to live in a gated community. It took her son, Lucas, nearly a year to convince her otherwise. It all started two years ago over coffee.

"I want a smaller house with three bedrooms, but small ones," she complained. "I don't like to dust, but I also don't want to hire someone else to clean." Then she added, "I never want to live in one of those gated communities."

Lucas, having settled into his own career as a Cal Berkeley professor, nodded. "I'll start a search to narrow down your options. I assume Palm Desert is the location?"

"It works for me. My doulas live in that vicinity and I'm used to desert living."

After that, Lucas emailed her links to all of the newer communities in Palm Desert. "Take a look at this one," he'd say.

After several refusals, they arrived at the new community, Desert Tortoise Estates. When Viv shook her head at the gate, Lucas finally lost his patience.

"You're not even looking at the house," he'd complained.

She finally let herself do a tour and had to admit, "This would be nice, except for the gated thing."

He bit his lip in the moment but sent her an email later. "Gates keep you safe, Mom, especially as you get older. I would feel better if you lived in a gated community. Palm Desert is a great community, but as you know, there are a lot of people living on the outskirts who end up getting into trouble. Drugs, alcohol, domestic abuse."

Viv didn't agree right away. But eventually he wore her down with the serious looks and the wrinkles on his forehead over Zoom. She was a sucker for sad and frustrated Lucas.

With one last effort she tried to explain her reluctance. "I'm not a gated community kind of person. I like a nice small house. Easy to maintain. A postage-stamp yard and maybe an enclosed patio for Miss Kitty. But a gate just to get to my front door? That's not my deal."

It had taken a year of back and forth, but finally she noticed that the wrinkles on Lucas's forehead threatened to become permanent. *Probably because of me.* She finally gave in. To give him credit, he paid careful attention to what she wanted in a house and helped her negotiate with the builders. As they signed the paperwork, she could see his shoulders relax.

"You have solar and a swimming pool in your own backyard with a jacuzzi. You pay a bit extra, they will enclose that area with a fence. Miss Kitty has her own private catio. I know a guy who builds specifically for pets. It will be perfect!"

It was the idea of a catio that finally pushed Vivienne from reluctant to excited. Plus when it came right down to it, she just couldn't resist Lucas, this son of hers, tall and handsome and so very smart.

That first night after moving in, she took her wine glass to sit by the pool in the dark. Lifting her chin, she gazed up at the stars. Constellations sparkled in the distant night sky. She had to admit Lucas's persistence had paid off. At first she had trouble imagining living anywhere else but the home she'd raised him in. But after she'd stopped resisting, she'd been able to make the change.

She didn't miss Lucas's father. Oh sure, Laurence had been a good husband, at least while the marriage lasted. Lucas was ten when Laurence finally admitted he'd been seeing someone else for months. "I want a divorce," he'd told her, not bothering to sugarcoat it.

Viv wasn't one to hang on if she wasn't wanted. So she agreed. Opening her arms wide, she released Laurence and her marriage just like that. The only thing she asked for was custody of Lucas and the cash to raise and send him to college.

In his relief to end the marriage, Laurence provided both. He included a lump sum, gave her the house, and promised she could renegotiate if she needed something more. It was by selling that house that she could afford to live comfortably.

Viv knew she'd gotten as good of a deal as she could. So she didn't bother anyone with her sadness over the ending of her marriage. Instead she saved her grief for alone times until after a while, she just stopped thinking about it.

Months after Laurence moved out, Viv emerged from her hibernation to tell her best friend, Tamara. Attending a week-long doula conference, she finally broke the news of her impending divorce.

"I'd have given him hell," Tamara said firmly. "But then I'm not as efficient as you; I guess I never was. You're really something else, Viv. You know what we call you behind your back?"

"No, what?" She dreaded that people would feel sorry for her and treat her like a victim.

"We call you the doula to die for. I mean, you're good at everything. When you had that difficult birth and stepped back for a while to regroup, you settled your own problems and then realized burnout may be a problem for other doulas. So you opened an agency for other birth workers. Right away you got applicants to Desert Doulas. Then you interviewed and got your team together, providing support for all of us.

Viv nodded. "The agency has worked out. Now that we do surrogacies..."

"You're the one who taught us how to get the birth mothers up and back to their own lives after they give up the baby. And you have that emergency phone call hotline. People pester you day and night and you don't even yawn in their ear."

Viv felt relief once she'd told her best friend about the divorce. But she also felt self-conscious as Tamara detailed all of her good points. *A doula to die for? I'm happy my doulas think I'm great. I just hope I can stay in everyone's good graces.*

Unaware of Viv's discomfort, Tamara kept talking. "The reason we all like you is that you aren't one bit stuffy. You drink. You are neurotic about your cat, and you use bad words. And you're the best friend I've ever had. You even let me crash at your house when I need to."

She smiled at Tamara. *She's definitely going on a bit. I guess she thinks I need encouragement.*

Pushing that memory aside, Viv drove slowly down her quiet street. She made a left turn into her driveway. The sensor lights came on. Lowering the visor, she touched the garage door opener. As the door slid open she saw the SUV, which occupied half of the tidy garage. *Tamara must be asleep by now.* Viv parked the car inside the garage, noticing that next to the SUV, it looked small and unimposing. She grabbed her phone and purse before exiting the car.

Viv retrieved her doula bag from the back seat before walking to the door to head inside. The knob on the inner garage door turned easily in her hand. *Tamara always forgets to lock this one.*

A quick push of the button and the garage door closed from behind. Viv stepped inside the house. *Ahhh, air conditioning.* She stopped to fully appreciate the cold air against her face, but her skin prickled. In the dark she dropped her bag next to the kitchen counter. "Tamara," she called in a soft voice. *She probably went to bed.*

Calling again, still no one answered. She stopped calling, listening to a sound in the distance. *Sirens...they're close, maybe near my neighborhood.*

Forgetting about Tamara, she hurried to the front of the

house. Curtain pushed aside, she stared out to the street. Red lights blinked and darted under the dark sky. The flashes bounced off the large boulders from the landscaping in front of the development.

Two police cars and a paramedic van waited on the other side of the security gate. One enormously tall officer stood in the street, holding what looked like a cell phone to his ear.

Maybe he's calling for the gate code?

Another police vehicle lined up behind the ambulance. Lights blinked and a horn tooted. The officer in the street lowered his cell phone and stepped back as the gate began to rise.

Viv let the curtain drop back over the window.

"Tamara," she called out, this time in earnest. "You've got to come quick. There are cops in the neighborhood and it looks serious."

When no one answered, Viv decided, *She's probably taken one of her sleeping pills. I'll check in the guest room.*

2

REX REDONDO

Call me suspicious, but the woman next door arrived at the same time as the cops. Is that just bad timing or did she plan it that way?

I don't want you to think I'm in the habit of spying on my neighbors. It's just that I work odd hours and am pretty private. No swapping cups of sugar or jabbering over the fence. Because once people realize I'm a mentalist, well everything changes anyway.

When she moved in I caught her name by accident. A piece of dropped mail. Vivienne Rose. Nice. I didn't introduce myself though. Put the envelope back in the mailbox to avoid all of that.

But I may have to introduce myself after tonight.

I'm going to step outside for a minute to see if the cops find the right house. I told them her address, 2632 Joshua Tree Way. God it's loud. Those sirens. Do first responders wear earplugs, I wonder? I'm going to look and see. Maybe I can help out, in a neighborly kind of way.

What's that I smell; could it be hibiscus? Smells come to

me unexpectedly sometimes. I can't explain it. Like a warning that something important will happen. The problem is I never know what to prepare for.

Hibiscus, light and frothy, beckoning for me to come closer. But closer to what? Maybe the woman next door.

3

VIVIENNE ROSE

Those cops...they're stopping in front of my house. Vivienne rushed down the hall. *Tamara must be awake by now!* The sirens screamed outside. *They're so close.*

Tap tap tap, she knocked on the door with her knuckle.

No answer from inside the room.

Viv called out, *"*Tamara!*"* and rapped harder.

Opening the door a few inches, Viv looked inside. Her eyes glanced toward the bed. It had been carefully made, the quilt folded back, the pillows fluffed. No sign of Tamara. Her heart beat quickly in her chest as she stepped around the corner.

The bathroom door stood open. No water spots on the shower doors. The bench and shampoos were like Viv left them. A smattering of cosmetics, carefully tidied in a basket, sat next to a fresh washcloth near the sink. Viv recognized Tamara's brand of face lotions. *She's been here...*

A glance behind the door revealed an empty hook. No white spa robe where it usually hung. Viv always kept a robe ready for guests. *Maybe she's gone for a swim and didn't hear me call out her name. Can't she hear the sirens?*

She made her way back to the open bedroom door. The wail of sirens drew her back down the hall toward the front door.

Pounding came next, making her heart race.

"I'm coming," she called out, quickening her pace.

Turning the dead bolt, she swung open the door.

On the other side a woman in a navy-blue jumpsuit held a medical kit. A red cross sat over her left pocket on the front. "Excuse me, ma'am," the woman said. "A neighbor has reported a body floating in your pool."

Vivienne felt her stomach drop.

"We got a report from one of your neighbors," the woman explained again. "He says there's a body floating in your pool." The woman took advantage of Viv's shock to push her way past the door. Heading toward the other side of the living room, she yanked back the curtains and unlocked the glass door. Hot air poured into the room.

Viv's hand came to her head. *Oh no, this can't be happening.*

She swallowed hard and then forced herself to draw closer. *What if it's Tamara...*

Her mouth froze as the words died in her throat.

Viv sat in the guest bedroom chair, staring at the empty bed. Out the window she could see uniformed people efficiently moving around what appeared to be a lifeless body. Tears sprang to her eyes. *How could this have happened to my dearest friend?*

A slight cough interrupted her thoughts. Viv looked over. A female police officer stood in the doorway to the guest room. She checked her anxiety by taking a quick deep breath.

The officer came closer to sit on the end of the bed. She lifted an iPad and leaned forward. "So I assume you had a roommate or a guest who lived with you?"

Viv nodded.

"Okay, ma'am, would you come with me? We need someone to identify the body. Then we have some questions to ask."

Viv glanced over to the bed one last time. When she turned back she noticed that the policewoman observed her carefully. She quickly looked down at her iPad when Viv's eyes narrowed.

The woman stood, reaching into her back pocket. She handed Viv a card. "My name is Officer Farrah. After you identify the body, maybe I could have a look around the house, this room especially?"

Viv cleared her throat. "My friend and colleague was staying here for a few days. She was housesitting. Her name is..." Viv's eyes filled with tears. "Or was," she corrected the tense and then finished, "Tamara Teasdale."

"You think she's the one in the pool?" The officer looked at her notepad. "Would you be willing to have a look?"

Viv didn't answer.

"Or you could come to the coroner's office later for an identification."

She shook her head. "I can give you contacts for her closer family members. I may not be the right person to do the identifying. It might upset them if they're not asked first."

And then she went too far. She knew it as soon as she continued to speak, but she couldn't stop herself. "I don't want to identify the dead body because I'm on call for another birth. I'm a doula. I don't want to internalize the death energy and unconsciously bring it to my next birth. I have to be careful of that, transferring dark energy to a birthing mother or her baby."

Officer Farrah froze. It was as if she saw a spider on the end of Viv's nose. Her eyes flashed. "I have no idea what you're talking about." Having dismissed Viv's words out of hand, her eyes hardened, her lips drew a straight line. Viv felt the other woman's reaction in her heart and gut. *Now that's a hard no. Officer Farrah is all business.*

"All I know is that we have a dead body in your backyard pool and that you have a missing house guest," Officer Farrah insisted.

Viv watched the officer closely. She knew she'd hit a nerve and she wasn't that surprised. Not really. Her work often unsettled people, let alone talking about birth and death energy. *What was I thinking? Talking to a complete stranger about a topic like that.*

"Go ahead and look around," she told the police officer. "If you don't mind I'll stay and watch. I want to protect my friend's privacy; it's respectful and she'd want me to do that. At least I think so."

The officer didn't need another invitation. She stepped past Viv to look more closely at the bed. Pulling back the sheets, she ran her hand over the covers, yanking at the corners, and then peering under the mattress. Then she stooped lower to examine with her flashlight. After a quick look at the nightstand, she picked up a cloth bag with two handles. "Did this belong to Tamara?"

"We all have our doula kits," Viv explained. "We keep what we need close at hand in case we get a call. Some people store them in their car if they're out doing errands. Tamara kept hers by her bed."

"I didn't know that," the officer said, looking less tense. "I don't know a lot about babies, only had one and that was just a big rush."

Viv nodded. "Babies and mothers and families are my business. To be honest, I have no idea what it's like to be a police officer." And then because her confidence had returned, she asked, "Am I a suspect? Is that why you want to question me?"

"Not really. We know that you arrived about the time we did. One of your neighbors told us. Plus you look shocked. That's not something you can fake. At least not when I'm around."

"I didn't actually see the body," Viv insisted. "I didn't even see the backyard. You showed up at my door before I could take a look. I only just discovered that Tamara's room was empty. I expected to find her asleep in bed."

As soon as she said those words, her eyes filled with tears. Then she glanced over at the dresser where Tamara's things had been left. Next to the doula bag, Tamara had also left her purse and her phone.

Officer Farrah followed Viv's glance. She stepped closer to look for herself. "A phone and a purse." She held them up. "Do these belong to Tamara?"

Viv nodded.

"Is she in the habit of leaving them behind?"

"Almost never. We have clients calling us all the time, especially when they begin labor. We have to keep close to the phone. She'd never leave it behind unless there was a good reason."

The policewoman picked up the purse and looked inside. When she was finished, she zipped it up. "I'll take this with me, along with the phone. It will help us identify the body."

Head spinning, Viv took small steps toward the edge of bed and sat down.

I can't believe what's happening. She looked over to the dresser.

Then her eyes caught sight of the photo that Tamara always brought with her. A daughter smiling into her mother's eyes, both of them laughing, taken a few years back...

Viv's throat caught when she realized, *I will never see her again.*

4

REX REDONDO

Even though I stay away from neighbors, I do know what a good one looks like. He doesn't just stand in his upstairs bedroom staring over the fence at cops swarming the backyard next door. I have to do something.

Okay, so I admit, I'm the one who called the cops. Right after I woke up from a dead sleep around quarter to one. I feel that kind of premonition in my spine first. The tingle zips from my tailbone up my neck. Plus Kevin was incessantly barking. Did I mention that?

I didn't want to get out of bed but I did. "Quiet, Kevin," I told him. When he didn't stop, I opened the curtain and looked down. From the distance the moon illuminated the pool next door and I could see a head bobbing to the surface, and maybe shoulders. The rest of the body was submerged.

The word to describe my reaction at that moment? If I need to pick a word, my emotions being all over the place? I felt alarmed. What if my neighbor was swimming in the dark all by herself? I had to make sure that she was safe, right? So I got out my binoculars. I might need to call the cops unless the person starts swimming.

I waited maybe five seconds. The electric current only intensified, up and down my spine. And Kevin just kept barking. "Okay, okay," I told him.

Then I called the cops.

After they assured me they'd be on the way, I took another look. I could see from that distance that the head did not belong to Vivienne. And the head didn't move, nor did the eyes blink. I think it might be her friend the cat sitter. I don't know her name.

They arrive fast; within half an hour the lights can be seen from the street in front of the house. The sirens could have woken the dead. When they stop, Kevin finally gives up and hops on the bed. He rests his chin on his paws.

"Good boy," I tell him. "Don't worry. I've got this."

I get dressed in record speed. Then I head down the hall and out my front door to jog next door. The woman in charge, a cop—tall, taller than anyone else and definitely taller than me—looks like the one in charge. I square my shoulders and step closer, using my professional voice. "So what's going on here, Officer?"

She doesn't even look in my direction. Talking into her cell phone, she turns away. *Okay, lady, I'm going to see for myself.* So I head toward the front door which has been left open. Standing inside I can see straight through to the backyard.

I feel the heat from outside pouring into the house. Struggling to keep up, the air conditioning unit pushes against the heat, working overtime.

People who live in the Mojave Desert know certain things. We know what it takes to stay alive in this area. It's nice for seven months here, even cold on some evenings. But the rest of the time it's survival of the fittest. People who can afford solar and who have state-of-the-art generators for when the power fails, survive the best.

I feel a tap on my shoulder. The tall police officer stands behind me. "Sorry I couldn't answer your question earlier," she says, "but I was talking to the precinct. You're a neighbor, right? Any chance you're the guy who called 911?"

Of course she was gonna ask. I'd be stupid to think I could get away and stay anonymous. But I'm not gonna lie. "I'm the neighbor. I'd like to keep it quiet, you know, with the lady who lives here. I don't want her to think I'm a pain-in-the-neck snoop. Any info on the dead person?" I try to sound casual. Truth be known, I'd love to be her. Not just cop but a detective.

Like Sam Spade, the guy Humphrey Bogart plays in the old noir movie. Clean-shaven. Hard-boiled. Fedora hat pulled over my suspicious eyes.

"But you do snoop over the fence," the cop said in a rational voice. "Otherwise you would not have seen the body. Good thing you did too. The paramedics narrowed the time of death. More tests need to be made, but their estimate is between nine and midnight."

"Did they drown?"

"Looks like it." Mouth shut, she looks at her iPad.

I glance around the living room and then into the kitchen. No sight of Vivienne. Turning back to the police officer, I ask, "So is she okay? The woman who lives here? I imagine it was quite a shock to find her friend in the pool like that."

"How do you know the deceased was a friend?"

Rex, you stepped in it.

"The lady who owns the place—according to my room-mate, she's been away a couple of days. Her friend comes over to cat sit." This interests the cop. She's clearly dying to ask me

18

more because she tilts forward a bit on her toes, and her pupils dilate as if she's on to something.

"Say more," she insists.

I feel my gut twist. "Have you seen the cat? With doors open it might have escaped."

Now a voice comes from down the hall. The officer swallows back her next question. A tingle of nerves runs down my arms.

Was that Vivienne's voice I heard calling? This is a horrible circumstance to meet each other for the first time. Of course the cop will tell her I called in the dead body. Once Vivienne knows that I'm the guy, she may dismiss me out of hand.

Slapping her iPad shut, she tells me, "I'm going to interview the owner of the house. Hang around in case we have more questions."

"Officer Farrah!" one of the other cops calls out.

"I'm heading to the guest room down the hall. Can your question wait?" she yells back.

"Yes, ma'am," he smartly replies.

She takes a minute and opens her notebook again. "I have my report right here," she tells me crisply. "But before I begin, I assume you know your neighbor. Are you close, I mean friends?" She stares at me like my answer may make or break her case.

"As it happens, I don't really know my neighbor. Haven't been officially introduced." I assume a pose of nonchalance; I don't want her to jump to any conclusion.

"I see," the cop says.

Though by the tone of her voice, I'm not sure she does see. But then she recovers.

"When she comes back, I'd like to introduce you to Vivienne Rose. She owns this house and is a close friend and associate of the deceased. Maybe you can help persuade her to identify the body..."

I can hear a door close. Then Vivienne appears from around the corner. My heart stops. She looks small, her shoulders rounded, her eyes red from tears. I watch her walk toward me.

Vivienne gives me a quick glance and then glares at the female officer. "Like I told you, identifying bodies is for the next of kin. I'm on call, waiting for my next birth. I can't be around a dead body." Her voice is firm, filled with authority.

Officer Farrah looks at her sternly. "Does that mean you're afraid to see your friend? That I could understand. But the being around death part? That's the flimsiest excuse I've ever heard."

"Maybe to you," she snaps, "but I know what I'm doing. I've been a doula for fifteen years and it's a vocational calling that I hold very dear. So back off!"

I keep my hands at my sides to resist clapping approval. *You go, Vivienne.* That was a superb bit of boundary awareness right there. She made it clear that she wasn't going to be bullied by the cops. Love at first sight. I hope you feel sorry for me, because there's nothing I can do about it now. Be still my heart.

I reach out toward her, extending my hand. "I'm Rex, your next-door neighbor. I came over to see if there's anything I can do to help."

Our eyes meet, and for a moment her expression changes. Her gray eyes grow wide and then darken. And then if I'm not mistaken, they soften just a little. A flicker of recognition, perhaps? That's what I'm feeling, like we knew each other before, in another life.

She lifts her hand to grasp mine. It feels small and warm; this woman is not easily shaken. Even the discovery of her friend's dead body did not make her hands clammy. Probably because of all those babies she's helped into the world. Nerves of steel.

And then to my surprise, I confess to her in that moment. "I was the one who called the cops." Then I wait to see how she'll react. Instead of recoiling, she looks me up and down.

"Thank you," she says, a slight quaver in her voice. "You saved me from finding Tamara myself. I'm grateful."

I swallow hard. Relieved that she's not mad. In fact, she's grateful. This strikes me as most unusual. I feared that she'd rebuff me once she realized I was the one. But it turns out I'm wrong. Damn, I'm never wrong. I read people for a living. I thought I had this woman figured out, just from observing her over the fence.

But she fooled me. She not only fooled me, I confessed outright; I was spontaneous. I'm never like that. I plan stuff, within an inch of my life. But not with this woman. With her, I just confessed that I'd called.

I stand close to Viv as the officer in charge begins to ask more questions. Her body leans toward me. Then she seems to catch herself and leans away. The officer clears her throat.

"The doors are wide open. Has anyone seen the cat?" I ask what I think will be the most important thing to Vivienne.

"Has she escaped?" She walks back toward the hallway, calling out over her shoulder, "I have to check on my cat first. She may be traumatized by all of this noise."

Officer Farrah nods.

I can look bland. I have that look down pat. I glance up at the ceiling and put my hands behind my back, acting as if I'd just heard the most normal thing in the world. A woman wants to check in with her cat. Not look at a dead body or answer the questions of the police. Not like there's anything wrong with that...

How am I going to stay close to Vivienne Rose? She didn't rebuff me right away. That's good. I know. I'll offer to help out with the cops and everything. Like a detective, I can dig up some intel and share it with her.

Officer Farrah be damned.

5

VIVIENNE ROSE

The police officer's jaw clenched, as if holding back a retort. Finally she cleared her throat to speak. "Okay then, Ms. Rose, go check on your cat. Just so you know? We're not done with you yet. We'll be back tomorrow morning, bright and early!"

"See you tomorrow," Viv said. *I have to check in on Miss Kitty. She's probably terrified with all this noise. Not to mention strangers walking around her house...*

Viv didn't admit this to just anyone, but she usually had a conversation with Miss Kitty before she invited people over. It took several days for Viv to work up to the necessary conversation with Miss Kitty once she planned the monthly doula gatherings. Knowing full well that her cat was overly sensitive, Viv took her time, finally coaxing Miss Kitty down from the top perch of her cat castle.

"So Miss Kitty," Viv began the conversation, craning her neck to see the cat, who had her back to the room. "I have a rather delicate matter to mention to you and I was wondering if you have time to listen this morning..."

The cat met her halfway. Hopping to a lower platform, she sat, her tail wrapped closely around her body. Viv began to carefully explain how she wanted to have the Desert Doulas over for a meeting. She took her time, trying to sound firm yet open to other opinions. When Miss Kitty looked away as if bored, Viv hesitated.

She waited, watching her cat intently. Miss Kitty finally fixed her gold eyes on Viv with a look of disdain.

"I know strangers aren't your favorite. Would you prefer I bring up this topic again after your nap?" Viv asked.

Miss Kitty continued to stare. Then her tail unfurled from her body and began to twitch in the air. Viv knew that was a bad sign. That she may have to give up her intentions. But then Miss Kitty surprised her.

She stepped forward, gracefully jumping to the lowest platform right above the floor. Claws out, she kneaded the carpet with ferocity.

"I can see you are agitated," Viv said.

One last yank and Miss Kitty was finished. She hopped to the floor, coming closer to Viv. Circling her legs, she stopped and leaned in as if waiting for a pet. Viv swooped to pick her up. Holding her close, she walked over to the sofa and sat down.

Viv crossed her legs pretzel style to make a lap for Miss Kitty, who complied by taking a turn and curling between her legs, her face hidden in her furry back haunch. "Oh, I'm so happy that you've given me your blessing." Viv buried her nose in the cat's fur. "No one will disturb you." Her hand caressed the cat's soft fur. "I can assure you that your evening routine will remain uninterrupted."

Miss Kitty's ear twitched.

"Thank you, dear one. I'll call my group right away and give them the good news."

Leaving out the part about Miss Kitty's reluctance, Viv invited her doulas to her home. She never told people about how much Miss Kitty's approval meant to her. She suspected that an explanation of her relationship with the feline may be a bridge too far, as one would say. Her mother, actually. Her mother said that all the time. When she was small and shared her imaginative musings with her mother, she always replied, "Interesting dear, but talking to animals may need to be our little secret."

Bringing herself back to the present, Viv called, "Miss Kitty?" Feeling a presence behind her, she quickly turned. Rex Redondo stood right behind her, smiling. *What is he doing here? Miss Kitty will never come with him hanging around.*

"Miss Kitty," he called imitating her high voice. "I'll help you find her. Miss Kitty?" he called in a high-pitched voice again, still trying to imitate Viv but failing miserably.

For a moment Viv forgot about the cat. She looked at Rex, how he smiled and held himself erect, with a certain dignity. Calling for her cat seemed out of character for such a tightly held presence. *He's well put together and wound kinda tight. But not unattractive.*

Still no meow from the cat. Viv stepped closer to the hallway door. Opening it slowly she stepped inside, waiting for Rex to follow along. No kitty in her usual place at the topmost platform. No kitty on the sofa either.

"This is a great room. You've got screens on that side and a monstrosity of a house for her. Lucky cat." Rex had a slight smile at the corner of his mouth.

Viv explained, "I consulted a special designer and installation expert. I call it the catio. Miss Kitty doesn't like strangers. She has full run of the house but mostly hangs out here." After a pause, she called again softly, "Miss Kitty."

"Meow," came a soft answer. Viv spun around, looking toward the kitchenette.

She pointed to the counter where Miss Kitty peeked around a ceramic canister with the label "Cat Food" plainly printed on the side.

"Get off of the counter," Viv gently chided, not really feeling her words. The cat jumped down to the floor. Viv bent over and scooped her up, holding her close.

Rex began to speak and then stopped. Finally he asked, "What did you call this place again, a catio?"

Viv gave Miss Kitty a quick kiss on the top of her head and then placed her back on the ground. "That's it, a catio." *Is he really interested in my cat or is he trying to keep my mind off of the body and the cops... Curious guy.*

At once she felt her exhaustion, the need to sit down overpowering everything else. She realized a niggle of anxiety underneath her fatigue. *I'd better check the windows.* She walked around the room, checking each latch before turning to Rex.

Scratch, scratch, scratch came from the other side of the room. A three-paneled room divider screened the cat box. Viv saw litter sand sprinkle out from underneath.

She resisted the temptation to talk to her cat and instead thought about Rex. *I wonder when he's going to leave?*

With a sigh she walked to the sofa and sat down. Leaning against the puffy cushions, she closed her eyes and then abruptly opened them again. *He's practically a stranger. Stay awake, Viv!*

He didn't wait for an invitation. He sat on the other end of the sofa. With his legs crossed, he looked the epitome of calm. He turned slightly toward her. Viv sighed and then shuddered.

"All I can think about is the body in the pool," she admitted.

"I suspect you'd like a little privacy. I didn't know if I

should leave you alone right now, considering the shock and all. But it must be unnerving to have a stranger in your house at this time. Do you want me to leave?"

"I'd like you to stay." She felt surprise at her own declaration. *Since he acknowledged it might be unnerving, now I want him to stay. It's kind of nice to have a male presence nearby. Comforting.*

Miss Kitty finally sauntered out from behind the screen. She glanced at Viv but walked straight toward Rex. She stopped to sit in front of his left shoe.

Tail swatting from side to side, Miss Kitty glanced over at Viv and then back to Rex again. Viv adjusted her legs underneath her, the sign for Miss Kitty to come over and sit. Miss Kitty made a decision. She leapt from the floor, landing right on Rex's legs.

"I guess you're her new favorite." Viv was unable to keep the sound of disappointment from her voice.

"Don't worry. She'll change her mind once I'm gone. Cats are like that, aren't they? Kind of fickle?"

"I wonder if Tamara fed her before, you know, before she died..." Viv's eyes filled with tears.

"I can feed her if you want. Just tell me how."

Viv looked him over. "Three spoons of fancy dry salmon, and half a pouch of gourmet tuna on top. She's a picky eater."

"I've got this." He stood from the sofa. Viv took the opportunity to think. *Have I seen him around before? He lives right next door. You'd think I'd notice. Probably been too busy with Desert Doulas to chat up any neighbors.*

She yawned, patting her mouth with her hand and glancing at the wall clock. "It's nearly three o'clock. I need to get a little sleep before I start answering more questions."

Rex stood at the counter, his back to the room. She heard

the clink of a spoon against the pink ceramic bowl. Her eyes began to droop.

She could no longer fight the fatigue. "I'll just lie down for a bit," she called to him. Stretching her legs out on the sofa cushions, she lay on her side, one arm curled under her head. She held her breath and then lightly exhaled through her mouth.

The last sound she remembered was Miss Kitty's meow, as if to say goodnight.

6

VIVIENNE ROSE

Vivienne felt a hand touch her shoulder. The fingers squeezed. She kept her eyes closed, holding onto the last moments of slumber.

"Viv," came a husky voice.

She felt her fingers tingle. The shroud of sleep tiptoed away, leaving an intrusive thought behind. *Tamara is dead. Did she kill herself?*

"Viv," came the sound of her name, with another pat on her shoulder.

She pushed away her thoughts. *Who is shaking my arm?*

Eyes flew open. *Am I dreaming?*

Tamara at eye level stared directly at Viv. Viv sat straight up with surprise.

"You're not dead! Or maybe you're back, like a ghost!"

From her crouching position, Tamara rocked back on her heels. Then she stood, a sheepish grin on her face.

Viv kept talking. "Maybe I'm dead too. That's it. We're in heaven. Now that I think of it, that Rex Redondo guy was here when I fell asleep. Maybe he's..."

Viv took a quick breath to continue. "I don't know why I

trusted him last night. Probably because I was processing the trauma of your death. That must be it. Maybe he's been plotting to kill us both. Like I've seen on late-night TV."

The ghost of Tamara shook her head, looking confused. "What are you talking about? I just got home and found you sleeping in the catio. Have too much wine last night? You met the new neighbor, probably had a few drinks—is that what happened? I'll get us coffee and you can tell me everything."

Viv's eyes opened wider. This was not the voice of a ghost. Very much alive, Tamara's slightly damp hair smelling like gardenia shampoo was a clue. *Ghosts don't take showers.*

"You're supposed to be dead!"

"Meow," came the voice of Miss Kitty. She looked imperiously toward them from her cat castle.

"Have you fed her?" Tamara asked. "Somebody has." She pointed to the empty can next to the sink.

Ignoring the part about the cat, Viv repeated, "You're supposed to be dead." She used her most reasonable voice as if stating a fact.

Tamara looked surprised. "I am obviously not dead. Standing right here. Are you sure you're okay?"

Before Viv could respond, Miss Kitty leapt from the cat castle to the floor. She walked closer to Tamara to make figure eights around her ankles.

Standing, Viv felt a sharp pain in her temple. She touched the side of her head. "I'm a bit off," she admitted. Tamara nodded, walking to the kitchenette to rinse the cat food can.

"We need to talk," Viv said to Tamara's back. "A lot has gone on here. Meet you in the big kitchen in fifteen minutes. I'm going to shower and change clothes."

"Sounds good," Tamara called over her shoulder, reaching over for the cat food canister.

Viv felt relief, a warmth in her chest, her return to reality.

Immediately tears sprang to her eyes. *It's like nothing happened last night. Tamara is alive.* She brushed the tears away with the tip of her finger, closing the door to the catio. Walking to her room, she wondered, *If not Tamara, then who? Who was dead in my swimming pool?*

* * *

The warm water washed over her head. She turned around to pump the shower gel into her hand. After soaping up and rinsing off, she turned the water off and stepped outside the shower onto the bath mat. Reaching for a towel, she wrapped it around her hair before reaching for another towel to dry off.

One look in the mirror revealed dark circles under her eyes. *I only got a few hours of sleep, so that's no mystery.* She rubbed cream on her arms and legs and then got dressed. Remembering her cell phone, she slipped on flip-flops and then stopped to check her messages.

The new baby's family had texted five times already this morning.

Is every twenty minutes too soon to nurse?

Viv sighed. She kept her boundaries ever since she'd navigated burnout a year ago. A life coach had helped her learn to detach from her work. The first boundary was a limit to her hotline call hours. Nine to five, she told all of her new clients. It was well past nine, so she texted back.

It's good for you and baby to nurse on demand for the first several days. I'll call you later to chat.

Not for the first time she realized that her health was

dependent on a good night's sleep and regular hours. If she broke her own schedule, how could she have dependable office hours for her clients? Usually a text, an email, or a quick phone call worked.

She held her phone at her side as she headed from her room down the hall toward her kitchen. Viv found Tamara sitting at the table, a large mug of coffee in one hand and her computer flipped open.

"Is there more?" Viv asked, pointing to the mug.

"I made twelve cups." She closed the lid of her computer. "So tell me why you thought I was dead. Let's start there."

"I'll make some toast for us," Viv said.

With a full mug of coffee and having made their breakfast, Viv sat down at the table. She slid the plate of buttered toast toward her friend. "Have a piece. This is all my stomach can take this morning."

Tamara's eyebrows raised.

"It's not what you're thinking." She took a piece of toast. "I didn't do any drinking last night. I assisted at a birth and then came home after midnight. Soon after, the police showed up at my door. Our neighbor next door called them. He saw a body floating in the pool."

Eyes growing wide, Tamara continued to stare.

"That's the thing. I thought it was you. You weren't in your room. There was no sight of you anywhere. You'd left your cell phone and purse and doula bag on the bedside table. I could only assume you'd gone swimming and somehow passed out..."

"But I can swim. You know that. On the team in high school. Didn't you see right away that it wasn't me when you looked at the face?"

Viv took a long sip of coffee. "Well that's the other thing. I didn't identify the body. I just couldn't. I was so upset. So I told the cop to call your next of kin. Then I blabbered on incoherently about death energy not being good for me. The cop thought I was less than reliable after that."

Viv paused, remembering Officer Farrah's expression. "Actually I may have touched on something else with the cop. I got that feeling, you know, when you inadvertently bring up something in a woman's past that's haunting her."

Tamara nodded. They'd talked about this before. Once a woman heard you were a doula, their birth stories poured out, as if they'd not been able to talk about them before.

To Viv's surprise Tamara smirked. "Just so you know, that kind of conversation happens to you more than me. You're kind of open and a bit less, you know, grounded."

Viv hesitated, feeling herself grow tense. She wanted to push back and disagree. She wanted to say, *I'm grounded and just fine*. But she stopped herself. Grateful because Tamara had walked her through the burnout recovery year, Viv paid attention to her words. *She's just warning me to be careful.*

Tamara shrugged. "You do realize I'm not dead and that you'd have known that last night if you'd just identified the body. Now the cops have called my next of kin. My ex is probably doing a dance right now. No more alimony, which is a pittance compared to yours." She looked around the well-appointed kitchen, her eyes stopping on Viv's. "Not that I'm jealous or anything," she mumbled. "But the ex aside, I'd better call the rest of my family. They will be worried."

Tamara suddenly looked upset with this new realization. Her face was drained of color. She rocked back and forth, as if she were waiting for bad news. Instinctively Viv knew what to do. She'd navigated Tamara's nerves and discussions about the differences between their exes for years. *Change the topic and make it funny.*

"Do you have life insurance?" Viv asked out of the blue.

"Once you're declared dead you can pretend to be your beneficiary so you can collect the money. Then you can escape to the Bahamas, change your name, and come back to get me. I could use a tropical refresh."

The absurdity of Viv's suggestion brought a twinkle to Tamara's eyes. She chuckled. Viv handed her a paper napkin to dab at wet eyes.

"The thought of me lying and getting a new identity?" She coughed, pointing to her throat.

Viv stood up, returning with a glass of water. "Try this." She sat back down. As Tamara took a sip and cleared her throat, Viv spoke again. "So if not you, then who? A random body in the pool or someone I know?"

Tamara looked away. Turning back, she flipped open her laptop. "I'm going to check the news to see if they've reported a dead body in Palm Desert." She leaned closer to her computer.

At that moment the doorbell rang. Viv stood up. "I'll get that. Probably the cops; that will save me a call. I want an explanation before I answer any more questions."

The gravity of the situation hit her full force as she walked to answer the door. The early dizziness had left her, but her chest felt heavy. Mind racing, she kept going over the whole thing in her head, wondering about the identity of the body. *Could it be another one of my doulas? Maybe one of them came by and didn't tell me...*

She opened the door quickly, as another ring of the doorbell echoed in her ears. Her neighbor stood on the doorstep, looking sheepishly at his toes. He glanced up and smiled. "You're up. How are you doing this morning?"

She felt slightly irritated by his pleasantries. Standing there with a smile, dressed in tan slacks and a polo shirt, he looked none the worse for a very late night. *I think he irons his shirts. Plus he bleaches his teeth. They are so white.* "Have you been playing golf?" she asked.

He shrugged. "My neighbor's friend died last night. I'd never do such a thing, in the face of her grief and all. Plus golf doesn't interest me much."

"Come inside." She opened the door wider. "I have something for you to see." He followed her in as she closed the door. "Come on. I'll lead the way. We have coffee."

"We?" he asked, looking around her living room.

"Yes, we."

When they entered the kitchen, Viv swept her hand toward Tamara. "Just in case you need an introduction, this is Tamara Teasdale. She's not dead. Not even a blemish on her from what I can see. It wasn't her in the pool."

His mouth hung open.

Viv held back a smile, enjoying his shock. Then she turned to Tamara. "And this is our next-door neighbor, Rex Redondo. He's the one who first saw the body in our swimming pool and called the cops."

Rex closed his mouth. He'd regained his composure, nodding at Tamara. She stared at him.

"Do I know you?" he asked quietly, his eyes lingering on her as he waited for a reply.

"Nope," she said quickly.

"Are you quite sure?" he asked.

"I am certain."

"Want some coffee and toast?" Viv pointed to the pot and toaster on the counter.

"I'd like some coffee," he said. "Is it okay if I sit down?"

As she passed the table on the way to the kitchen, she pulled out a chair.

Rex moved quickly to claim it. Tamara returned to her computer search, ignoring Rex.

By the time Viv placed a mug in front of him, the doorbell rang again. "I bet that's the police," she said before walking out of the kitchen.

Two cops stood on her front step. Recognizing Officer Farrah from the night before, she nodded. "Do come in. I have news about the dead body."

They walked past her, boots clomping against the floor. "We've got some news for you too," said Officer Farrah. "The body isn't Tamara Teasdale. Our database spit out an entirely different woman."

Viv held up her hand. "Before you say more, I want you to meet Tamara and tell us both. Oh, and our neighbor is here too. You can tell him. We all want to know who was floating in the pool, and I especially want to know how the person got there."

"Right then," the other officer said. "I'm Officer Greg Anderson. Let's go talk. Is that coffee I smell? Can I have a cup?"

"Oh, me too," added Farrah. "And toast. I smell toast. I could use a slice with butter and jam. Can you make that happen?"

"I'm not a short-order cook in a diner," muttered Viv. "But come along. I'll start defrosting some more bread for toast. I must remind you that I have clients waiting for me to call. It's a workday for me."

Viv led them to the kitchen, pointing to two empty chairs. "Have a seat. You can introduce yourselves. I'll be right back."

Her back to the table, she heard chairs scraping against the wood flooring. "Mr. Redondo, how are you this morning?" Officer Farrah asked.

"I'm well," he answered in a businesslike tone.

When Viv returned she set two more mugs of coffee in front of the officers. "Toast will be ready shortly." Then she blurted out what was on her mind. Turning to Rex, she said, "So I'm wondering if our nosy neighbor may have murdered the woman in my pool. After all, I don't know him. We just met last night."

Rex assumed a very bland expression. Then he asked in a dry voice, "Anyone see a bus anywhere?" His neck swiveled as he pretended to look around the room. "I think I just got thrown under."

7

REX REDONDO

She's something else, my next-door neighbor. Not even a warning and Viv forgets that Miss Kitty and I are best friends. And then she dimes me out as a number-one suspect. Remarkable.

I move my eyes away from her so that she doesn't see my admiration. You gotta appreciate a woman who is so up front with her opinions.

I do feel a bit guilty. Not because I killed a woman. I didn't have anything to do with that. That's not what's niggling at me this morning. I admit, I know it sounds strange, but there's just something about that Viv.

Even when she's accusing me of murder in front of the cops, I can't help but appreciate her candor. Not that I'm going to stand for that, being accused. But since I may be a suspect, I think it's only fair that I do my own investigating in this matter. Here's my chance to be a detective. Look out, Bogart.

Once an intel guy, always an intel guy. That's what you're thinking. I'll get Sutton to do some snooping and then we'll put together a plan.

Just so you know, I usually date younger women. The superficial conversations have kind of gotten to me of late. You see the problem with younger women I've gone out with? They think they're interesting, only they're not.

And then once my date knows that I'm a professional mentalist, she wants me to do tricks. Predicting her future like some kind of card reader or psychic. She expects a thrill a minute too, going out to dinner and hitting the hot spots in Palm Springs. I'm almost sixty years old and frankly, every time I step into a nightclub I feel like I'm going to work.

I downplay my profession to every sweet young thing I know. Let's be honest, nothing I do is remotely like magic. I just observe people closely. What better place than a casino, where all kinds of humanity come my way with their needs and desires?

Also, I've got a rock-solid alibi for the cops. I was working last night. My hours aren't like everyone else's.

"Tell me where you were from Tuesday ten p.m. to Wednesday when you discovered the body and made the phone call to the police," Officer Farrah says to me crisply, all business, except for that nervous tell. I saw it right away. Her left eye twitches ever so slightly when she's nervous or excited or both. I'm not her person of interest, but she doesn't know it yet.

I could have played her a bit, just for the entertainment value. Made up some stuff before I told her about my solid alibi. I might have done that when I was younger and more enamored with my own gifts.

Not a gift. Only a penchant for details. I can't say that enough. I observe, a skill mostly shared with card players and some profilers. Some people have told me I'd make a good detective. Maybe that's not so far off.

"My show was from ten to eleven thirty. Talked to some

fans. Took off my makeup. After that I got dinner at the casino and hung out at the bar. I didn't get home until twelve fifteen or so. I came inside, played with the dog a bit, and then went upstairs.

"My dog woke me up with his barking. He was standing in the window so I looked out. I can see the pool from my upstairs bedroom. Saw the body, waited to make sure it wasn't moving, then called 911. I'm not your guy."

I turn to Viv to see how she's taking my precise account. She's sitting with Tamara who I feel like I've met before. But she denied it.

Viv's eyes bore into mine. I wonder what she's feeling right now, this Vivienne Rose, so emotionally self-contained. My feelings are all over the place. My imagination going along for the ride. I don't have to close my eyes to imagine how it would be. My mind just takes over. It's nighttime and...

She turns all the lights off and slips into the water under the stars. Okay, so she isn't wearing a bathing suit. I won't linger here. Maybe a few minutes, that's all. Okay, so I keep imagining. But I don't mean any harm.

There's just something about a beautiful mature woman swimming naked in the dark that's a complete turn-on. She belongs there, her arms sliding through the water, her hair floating behind her. I feel bittersweet when I imagine Viv swimming like that. My throat chokes up.

Let's just say Viv owns herself and her body and surrenders to the water with such grace. At least in my imagination.

Officer Farrah's voice interrupts, her voice gentle but firm. "Which casino?"

"Pair-a-Dice Casino, right up the Palms to Pines Highway, between Palm Springs and that small town called Lily Rock. You know it, right?"

She nods, bringing her small recorder to her mouth. She

speaks the information I told her and then clicks it off. Pulling out a chair, she sits down. In the meantime Viv and Tamara huddle together, sharing their conversation in low voices.

But what's nagging me right now is how familiar Tamara looks. I'm still trying to place her. I've seen her somewhere else. At Trader Joe's maybe, or in town—maybe the casino...

"Mr. Redondo," Farrah says. "I'll call the casino and get the CCTV surveillance tapes. Until then don't leave town."

"Got it." I share my most disarming smile.

She looks at Viv. "I can tell him to stay away from you two, if you feel unsafe."

Viv's eyes drill into mine. I have to force myself not to flinch. There's nothing uncertain about my next-door neighbor. Straightforward and confident. She contains her nerves well.

Her friend is another matter. Hands are folded on the table, her fingers twist inside each other. She's anxious. Her eyes dart from me to Viv and then back to me. She's looking for her balance, maybe even wondering why I'm sitting at the table.

Don't ask me how I know that. I just do.

Turning to Farrah, Viv finally asks, "Have you identified the woman in the pool?"

"Our job includes protecting the woman's identity until family notification." Farrah looks out the window. "It looks like they taped around the entire backyard last night."

A knock sounds from the front door. Viv gets to her feet. "It's nearly lunchtime. I need to get back to my work."

"Will you be leaving the house?" the officer asks right as the doorbell chimes.

"I work from home today," Viv calls over her shoulder.

Left with two cops and Tamara, I see no reason to stop

asking questions. "So you can't tell me who's dead, but do you honestly suspect any of us?"

Farrah turns to Tamara. "Where were you from ten to showing up this morning?"

She speaks right away. "I left the house for an overnight in the desert." She looks toward the doorway. "I attended a free-birth women's circle. We meet every four months to dance and celebrate the new moon. Female stuff." She glares at me as if I'd object, but I haven't said a word.

Farrah clicks on her tablet. "Can you give me the place and times and someone who can verify your attendance?"

"It's not something we advertise. Doulas along with mothers who have given birth are invited. Not open to the public. Pearl Overmann picked me up. You can call her." Tamara slides her phone over for Officer Farrah. "Here's her contact info."

Vivienne returns, followed by three people dressed in hazmat suits.

Farrah immediately takes control of the situation. "I'll take you outside to the crime scene."

She looks back at Tamara. "I wrote down your friend's contact info." She walks away through the living room as the hazmat people follow.

I turn to Tamara with my burning question. "So you went to a desert overnight but left your purse and phone behind?"

Her face flushes. "That's part of the ritual, to cut ties with the outside world. I wasn't driving, so I didn't need my license or anything."

Looking from her friend to me, Viv interrupts, "How about more coffee?" I think she wants to distract me from interrogating her friend. I get that.

Now I do the looking, back and forth between the two women. It feels obvious to me that they're close. They have mannerisms—lifted eyebrows and slight smiles—that they share with each other.

Tamara's gaze drifts down to her hands on the table. She plays with the ring on her finger, moving it up and down. I look away, out the window over the sink. I can see Officer Farrah's hands gesturing. The hazmat people nod. They all huddle around the pool now, staring into the water.

"Any more toast?" I try to sound persuasive. Viv glares at me. I smile at her, my charming *ah shucks, I'm just a boy standing in front of a girl* smile. Like Hugh Grant in that movie... Viv reminds me of a beautifully seasoned Julia Roberts.

I can see she's thinking about how to take my suggestion. Emotion clouds those beautiful gray eyes, from fury to impatience, until finally a slight smile returns to her lips. "You are incorrigible. I know I offered coffee but I have to get to work."

She pulls her cell phone from her back pocket.

"I'll take care of the dishes," Tamara offers instantly. "And I'll show your neighbor to the door."

I see that slight little smile. Viv gets me. I'm the guy who reaches for humor and sometimes falls short. That's me, Mr. Incorrigible.

8

VIVIENNE ROSE

After Viv ushered Rex Redondo out the door, she heard Tamara call from the kitchen.

"Hey, get a load of this!"

Viv closed the door and walked briskly back to the kitchen.

"Give me a minute," she said, glancing at Tamara hovering over her laptop. "I'll get us a refill first." As she took her time with the coffee, she tried to figure out her feelings. *I know I'm not the best at expressing my emotions and that I keep them under wraps. I get in this zone where I set my feelings aside so that I can cope and move on.*

I think my next-door neighbor knows I'm not forthcoming. It's the way he looks at me as if to say, "What else are you feeling?" I'm kind of a mess.

With a sigh she glanced out the window. The patio thermometer already registered in three digits.

She brought the pot back with her, filling each mug. Reading glasses perched on her nose, she looked over Tamara's shoulder to the laptop screen. Video on pause, a familiar face smiled back at her. The close-cropped gray hair, with tanned glowing skin. His black eyes sparkled at the photographer. *Rex Redondo is a man who's used to being photographed.*

Tamara clicked the video to play it. "Today we have Rex Redondo, the Pair-a-Dice Casino resident mentalist here to talk about his family. Of course, all you fans out there know them as Hai-Cam. Say hello, Hailey and Cameron."

The young couple stood on each side of Rex. Smiling toward the cameras, they posed for photos. Hailey gave a small wave.

The Palm Desert news team moved in, a microphone shoved into Cameron's face. "Once we connected the Pair-a-Dice house mentalist with this famous couple, we knew we wanted to interview all three.

"So here we have Hailey and Cameron Steward, that up-and-coming young celebrity couple. For those who don't follow them on social media, Hailey is the actor who starred in the breakaway role of Jessica in the most recent *Vampires for Hire* series. She met her now husband, Cameron, on that set. He's also an actor, having been recently cast in a Netflix sitcom yet to be named. How are you today, Cameron?"

"Okay." He looked away as if bored.

The reporter held the microphone in front of Hailey. "Your social media following has increased to over a million since the box office smash. But there's something more, isn't there, Hailey? A little secret you want to share?" When she didn't respond, the reporter kept talking. "Rumor has it congratulations are in order, that you've recently welcomed a baby boy to your family." The interviewer looked deliberately at Hailey's seemingly flat belly as the camera panned in the same direction.

Cameron frowned and interrupted, taking the microphone in his own hand, moving it closer. "Yes, we're so happy but"—he turned to Hailey—"exhausted from the night feedings." He shrugged at the newsperson, redirecting his dazzling smile toward the camera.

"And you, Rex." The reporter took back the microphone and moved it to the man in the middle. "We happened to catch you with these two at the casino. How is it you know them?"

Redondo smiled, his teeth showing pearly white. "I've known Hailey since she was a baby. She just dropped in to say hello to Uncle Rex." He paused and then added, "Not a biological uncle, just a close friend of the family."

The interviewer pushed the camera closer. "Are you sure they didn't stop by for a reading? For the new baby. Maybe a past life?" he added hopefully.

Rex's eyes narrowed. "No readings from me. Just a friend of the family, offering his support and a gift for the new baby."

The journalist sidestepped Rex by turning to Hailey. "And what's the name for the little one?"

"We haven't decided yet," she said, patting her belly and then resting her hand near her waist.

"Okay, that's a wrap," the interviewer shouted.

When the video ended, Viv stepped back. "So she's saying she gave birth to her baby just a couple of days ago. Good recovery."

Tamara shrugged. "Keeping up appearances, making other new mothers feel inadequate if you ask me."

Viv nodded in agreement. "Influencers and celebrities. How many times have I been asked questions because a client thinks they need to look like the celebrity at a news conference two days after they give birth?" She sounded tired even to herself.

Tamara added cream to her coffee and took a sip. "So did you believe our neighbor that he didn't do a reading on the new baby?"

"Maybe," laughed Viv. "I suspect they were consulting him throughout the entire pregnancy. I bet they paid him handsomely for the privilege."

"Speaking of handsome, he's quite good-looking for an older guy." Tamara grinned at Viv. "Plus I think he has a thing for you."

"He's well preserved. But he kind of unsettles me, the way he watches me so closely."

Tamara nodded. "I noticed that too." She closed her laptop.

Finished with their discussion, Viv excused herself. "I'm going to make some phone calls and catch up on hotline email. See you later."

"Is it okay if I stay an extra day or two?" Tamara asked.

"Of course." Viv stood, picking up the plates and mugs from the table.

* * *

By Friday Viv felt better. Back on her schedule, she'd enjoyed Tamara's company as the police gathered evidence, coming and going.

"By the way, thanks for letting me stay a few more days. After the discovery of the body, I didn't feel like being alone," Tamara said.

"After that scare, thinking you were dead, it was good to keep you around just to make sure." Viv smiled.

"It worked out fine. We have some doula business tonight and then my daughter will be coming over. She's out of a job again. Probably coming home to ask for more money."

"I hope she finds something real soon." Viv looked at Tamara and patted her hand. "I'm also hoping the police will release my pool area sometime today. Maybe they'll even reveal the name of the woman who died." She took a long sip of coffee. "I suppose I'll have to tell our group what happened. They'll want to know why we're not meeting outside under the stars like usual."

Before Tamara could reply, a plaintive meow came from the other side of the house. Viv stood up quickly. "Miss Kitty is calling."

Tamara glanced at her phone. "I'll start my shower and call a few of my clients. Then I have a couple of errands." She stared at her cell phone screen.

"Sounds good." Viv knew when she'd lost Tamara to her text messages. She hurried down the hallway. "Okay, I'm coming," she said, opening the door to the catio.

Out sprang Miss Kitty, her tail waving behind her. She walked past Viv, making her way down the hall toward the living room.

Viv stepped inside the catio and gave a sniff. "Morning cat box pick-up time," she muttered. "I must have the only cat who leaves her business in the cat box, calls out for service, and then steps out of the room while I do the dirty work."

After she finished disposing of the cat litter and freshening the box with new deodorizing pellets, she glanced over the room. *It's time for a morning tidy of the catio.*

Miss Kitty had a bed on the floor, another in the tree house, and a blanket bed at the corner of the sofa. Viv fluffed the blanket first and then folded it carefully. Kitty liked a tidy blanket.

Then she walked to the kitchenette and pulled down a jar labeled cat treats. She put one on the blanket on the sofa, one on the pillow in the bed, and one up high at the top of the tree house. "Just like a turndown service," muttered Viv.

As soon as she'd finished, Miss Kitty arrived at the doorway. "Meow," she said, sauntering into the catio.

"How do you know when I'm done, the exact time to show up and reclaim your sanctuary?"

"Meow," she said, hopping onto the sofa. She bent her neck to sniff the treat. *Crunch, crunch*, as her tail twitched.

Viv shrugged. "Did I at least hear a thank you?" She walked closer to the sofa and fluffed up the fur behind the cat's ears. Miss Kitty began to purr.

"Okay, that's better. I do appreciate being appreciated."

After a few more moments of bonding, Viv removed her hand. Before closing the door to the catio, she saw Miss Kitty jump from the sofa to the carpet to her tree house. Quickly ascending the carpeted pole, the cat stood at the topmost landing, licking her paw.

By noon that day Viv sat behind the wheel of her Tesla. She glanced at her list of errands. *Lunch first*, she told herself. The first in line at Just Desserts, she contemplated her choices. "A tuna salad and a turkey with avocado," she told the clerk. After paying she sat down at a table to wait for her name to be called.

She put her cell phone back in her purse as soon as she heard her name. On the way out the door, brown bag with her lunch in hand, she stopped at the secondhand boutique next door. Out of the Closet Consignments was her go-to when she wanted to refresh her wardrobe. They were known for carrying secondhand clothing cast off by celebrities in Palm Springs.

She stepped inside. "What's new, Jason Knew?" she called out, the pun making her smile. A young man came from behind the counter to give her a hug. He stood over six feet tall, his blonde hair shaved over the ears. Longer strands of hair had been carefully coifed to dangle in his eyes.

"Girl, it's been ages." Jason stepped back from their embrace to look her up and down. "I've got a pair of jeans that will fit you like a glove. They came in two days ago and I said to myself, 'Jay, these would be perfect for Viv.'"

He looked at the brown bag with the Just Desserts logo that she carried by her side. "Is that lunch for me? You shouldn't have. I'm on strict keto and check me out." He stepped back again to pose, one hand on his hip. "Here, let me give you a hint: I've lost weight."

Even though she couldn't tell, Viv liked to encourage him. "You look amazing." She never lied, but she also chose a truth he so obviously needed to hear.

When Jason disappeared into the back room, she looked around the boutique, her eyes zeroing in on a new display of straw hats. She stepped closer as the bell over the door rang, admitting another customer.

Viv took a quick glance. *She's become such a familiar face around here. Two times in one day. I think that's Hailey Steward.*

Large sunglasses covered most of the young woman's face. She might not have recognized the Hailey part of Hai-Cam if it weren't for the tunic top.

Hailey had worn the same shirt to the taped interview. It was the style of clothing that attracted Viv's attention. The top was scalloped at the bottom, made of a stretchy fabric that clung to her tight-fitting yoga pants. A closer view revealed that Hailey's slim, taut body did not look postpartum. Not by a long shot. *If I close my eyes I can imagine a slight baby bump, but it would take a long stretch of the imagination.*

Jason appeared from the back. "Well good morning to you, Mama," he said. "I saw the interview. You looked amazing."

"That's why I'm here. To get some more of these." She swept her hand over the tunic. "I've got two weeks more to wear these horrible tops. After that I can purchase an entirely new wardrobe."

Jason pointed to the back room. "I've got tunics set aside for you already. Five in all, unless you don't want to do laundry. Then you'll have to come back for more to make it for the full two weeks."

"My wardrobe woman hates those tops," she sniffed, waving her manicured fingers in the air. "I only wear them once and then toss them out." Viv waited for Hailey to ask the price but wasn't surprised when it didn't come up. *She can afford whatever she wants.*

Jason went to the back, returning with a stack of clothing. He neatly folded and stacked the tops, then slid them into an expensive bag and tied a bow at the top. *The bag probably costs more than the tunics.* Viv watched as Hailey waved over her head before stepping outside.

Two photographers stopped her as soon as the door closed from behind. Ignoring their questions, Hailey hurried down the street. A limo came from around the corner, pulling alongside the curb. The back door opened and Hailey slid inside. The reporters ran after the limo as it sped out of sight.

"She's so beautiful," Jason sighed. "I wish she were more ecologically aware. Instead of throwing them away, I could take back the tops and sell them again. What a waste.

"I don't suppose," he continued, "that she really likes secondhand clothing, even at my high-end store. I think she likes her followers to think she does, so she makes a point of coming by, hoping to be noticed. That's so very LA."

He neatly folded a pair of jeans and placed them on the counter. "Light wash denim is all the rage for summer," he told her. "These are name-brand and well made. You can try them on here or at home. If they don't fit, I'll take them right back. You know my store policy."

"Thank you so much." Viv took the folded jeans from his hands and put them carefully in her oversized tote. Reaching for her wallet, she slid the right amount of cash across the counter.

"So anything new with you?" Jason's eyebrow raised in a question.

"There's been excitement at my house. I can't say any more right now. But as soon as I can I'll fill you in."

His eyebrows raised. "Really? That sounds intriguing. I won't tell anyone else. You can trust me."

Viv laughed in his face. "Give me a break. You're the worst gossip in Palm Desert. And don't get me wrong, I love that about you."

His lips turned down. "I thought I was subtle and that you hadn't noticed."

"Just as soon as the..." She'd almost said cops. That would only make Jason more insistent. She bit her bottom lip. "You see, I can't help myself. I love sharing with you."

He grinned. "You do, don't you. We're like sisters, Jason and Viv."

She picked up her lunch sack from the counter with a smile. "I'm heading back home. I have to plan my doula group meeting for this evening."

"Have fun with that," he said distractedly as his eyes looked toward the street. "And I could have fun with *that*," he added, his voice filled with double meaning.

She turned to see a handsome man walk up to the window. He stopped to look inside the shop. His chiseled chin and closely cropped gray hair made her gasp.

"That's my next-door neighbor!"

"Well aren't you the lucky one? Maybe I can come over

sometime and get introduced." Jason smoothed back his hair, staring at the man in the window.

"I hate to disappoint, but I'm nearly certain he plays for the other team."

Jason glared at her.

"No one can be certain nowadays," she admitted. "But I did get a vibe."

They both watched as Rex ambled away.

Jason looked back at Vivienne. "Why don't you tell me everything about your bit of excitement. Because I do need to know."

It occurred to Vivienne, once she sat behind the steering wheel, that Rex Redondo was becoming a regular in her life. She'd barely paid attention to him before. First the body, then the news interview, and now shopping at Out of the Closet Consignments. *Is that just a coincidence?*

9

VIVIENNE ROSE

Later that evening Vivienne finished last-minute preparations. Sometimes her doulas brought food, but she usually planned everything on her own.

She gathered all of the single chairs to make a circle in her living room. Her agency consisted of eight women. As a part of their self-care, they met once a month to check in and talk all things baby and birth.

A knock came from the front door. Since Viv kept the door unlocked for the meeting, Pearl came right inside. She carried a covered plate in her hand. "Tamara told me about the body. I figured that's why we're meeting inside this evening." She offered Viv a one-armed hug. "I'll just put this in the kitchen, my mother's recipe for lemon Bundt cake. The secret is in the frosting."

Her bell-like laugh floated over her shoulder as she walked her plate to the kitchen. Before she returned, another woman arrived. Bri Angeles closed the door behind her. She glanced over the room. "Can I help with anything?"

"Just have a seat. We'll grab drinks and food when everyone arrives." Viv smiled.

Tamara walked in next. She raised her eyebrows at Viv before crossing the room to sit down. Viv smiled at her friend. Tamara was her closest confidant. They spent many an hour talking about the personalities of their doula cohorts.

"Have a seat, ladies," Viv announced. "I'm still waiting to hear from Sarah. It looks like it will just be the four of us, unless you know if she's coming."

Bri sat down and opened her planner. "We were going to drive together, but she's not picking up her phone. I do know that her car's in the shop again. I guess there are money issues and they won't release it until she pays the bill."

Tamara nodded. "I haven't heard from her either. Maybe another wrangle with her ex. He's taking her back to court for custody. Says her house isn't safe for a young boy."

"I gave her my attorney's number," Bri said. "Her ex doesn't have a chance. She's doing everything right. Timmy's in school and soccer. Plus she never lets her boyfriends come to her house. They always meet somewhere else."

"That's a good policy for any of us, even without children," Viv spoke up. She often worried about her single mother doulas and their schedules. All-night work required a consistent backup for families. That was one reason she'd formed the agency.

Tamara said, "I told Sarah I'd lend her the money for her car until her next patient paid up. She's also working with a surrogate mom. The baby just arrived and the parents are very wealthy. She'll be able to pay her bills soon enough."

Looks like Sarah isn't coming. I'd better get things going. "We might as well get a snack and some wine. Then we can start with a check-in."

* * *

After their snack, Viv was the first to check in. She explained what had happened. The memory of two nights before left her feeling more like a victim and certainly not like herself. "I'm feeling edgy and exhausted. How can I be both? My legs need to move, my mind is whirling, but my eyes want to push it all away and go to sleep," she explained to the other doulas.

"That's just terrible," Tamara said. The others nodded.

After responding to a few more questions, Viv felt a bit better. *It's good to share with my friends. It doesn't change anything but at least I'm not alone.* Knowing she'd run out of energy to talk much more, she said, "The police will let me know the identity of the person and I'll be sure to follow up with you."

"Let's not dwell on this," Tamara suggested.

"I've already told you what's foremost on my mind," Viv said with a shrug.

"I'll go next." Bri opened her planner. "I'm doing post-partum follow-up with four clients and have been at the birth of three babies this month."

The women stared at Bri, who looked at her book. "I know that's too many. I shouldn't have taken on all of those people, but I need the money. My partner is furious because I don't have any time for us and I'm always tired." She sighed, looking up from her planner. "I'm not sleeping that well when I do finally get into bed."

"Burnout," Tamara said matter-of-factly. "That's why we're here, to be accountable to one another. Lack of sleep and family problems are the direct result of taking on too many clients at a time."

Bri nodded, her hands twisting in her lap over her planner.

"So how can we help?" asked Viv.

"They expect me to be there," Bri admitted. "You all know

that. Families take us in like a part of the family, just like a sister or an aunt. Substitutes are not welcome."

"But they are completely necessary. It's unreasonable to think a doula can just wait for a baby twenty-four hours seven days a week without having something in her own life intervene. Having said that, I'll make sure to follow up before payment," Viv said bluntly.

"After you've made dinners, done laundry, and cleaned toilets," Tamara said sarcastically. "I'm so glad you handle the fees beforehand, Viv. When I freelanced it was the most difficult part of being a doula."

"Thank you, but I'm wondering. Do you still clean toilets?"

"Oh no! I draw the line at toilets. I no longer clean bathrooms, except for wiping down the counter for sanitary reasons. I don't want germs to spread to baby on my watch."

The conversation continued as the other women helped Bri brainstorm how she could take a step back. Preventing doula burnout had become their most common topic at each meeting. Being overcommitted could lead to any number of personal issues or a difficult emergency birth.

Pearl had kept very quiet during the discussion. Once Viv got up to refill her glass, she asked, "Pearl, how are things going with you?"

"As you all know, I had that episode last year. I had to take off three months to get my strength back. I've been very careful this time, only taking on clients with strong relationships."

"Do you ever hear from him?" asked Bri.

Everyone in the group knew who she referred to. "I've taken him out of my phone and I don't initiate any contact."

"Do you drop in on Facebook?" Viv knew she was stepping into personal territory, but it was for Pearl's own good.

Pearl rolled her eyes and then looked out toward the light

cast by the swimming pool. "It would be a good night for a swim," she commented, ignoring Viv's pointed question.

"Except for that crime scene tape," Viv said dryly. Unwilling to be put off, she raised her voice and asked again, "Are you following Dereck's family on Facebook?"

Pearl slowly nodded, her face flushing with discomfort. She bit her bottom lip as Viv cleared her throat. "You know what this means. For your own sake you were to have no direct contact with Dereck, yet you continue to watch him from afar. He's got a new baby and a partner to care for. Plus they have two other children. You're still involved, Pearl. You have to see that."

"I know," she sighed. "But I tell myself it's to see the baby. After all, I was there for the birth and I got to know the mom. I loved her too."

The "too" seemed to echo in the room.

"And look where that got you," Bri chimed in. "Dereck had it on with you right under his partner's nose. She'd just delivered her baby and he manipulated you into that late-night sex. Come on. You know that's what sent you into the tailspin."

During the following silence, Viv stood up. She walked to the kitchen and returned with a tumbler full of water. Stepping in front of Pearl, she replaced the empty wine glass with the water, setting it on the table by her chair. "Here you go. It's hard to hear the truth, but honey, we all love you. We were with you during the fall and the recovery and we don't want you to go down that path again."

Pearl reached for the glass. The other women watched as she took a long sip. When she put the glass back, she said, "You're right. I know you are. I'd hoped to watch from afar and still keep my distance. Neither of them thought to unfriend me, so I took it as permission."

"They were busy with three children, one of them a new

baby. Of course no one thought to unfriend you. Dereck was probably relieved that you left early and who knows about his wife..."

Pearl's head came up. "Do you think Lauren knows about Dereck and me?"

"Does it matter?" came Viv's immediate response. "If you want to keep your professional doula standing, you need to put the experience behind you." *I took a risk with Pearl by not firing her outright. She went to therapy as I suggested and promised to be more stringent about her boundaries. I hate giving up on anyone but I'm still skeptical with her. Having to do it again? I'd probably release her from the Desert Doula team.*

"And make sure you don't take any more overnight jobs. That's the best way to assure your safety and the safety of the birthing family. They are vulnerable and so are you. Birth is a window into all kinds of emotions for everyone." Viv clamped her mouth shut, knowing she might have overdone her warning.

As Pearl processed the information, Viv looked at her silenced cell phone. She noticed a text message from her son as well as the time. "It's ten o'clock. Maybe we should check out."

"Sounds good," Tamara said.

Glancing at the screen again, she saw a call coming in from Officer Farrah.

"I need to take this call." She stood up, walking to the kitchen. By the time she got there, Officer Farrah had already hung up. She redialed.

"Palm Springs Police," came a familiar voice. "Officer Farrah speaking."

"I'm returning your call. This is Vivienne Rose."

"I was about to leave a voice message. We'll come over tomorrow to remove the police tape around nine o'clock."

"Of course. I'll be ready."

"And we have identified the victim and called the next of kin, so we have a few questions for you now."

Viv held her breath. "I realize now that I held back your investigation by not identifying the body. I'm sorry."

"Don't worry," came her surprising reply. "You don't have to beat yourself up over not wanting to look at a dead body. Not everyone runs to the morgue to be helpful. That happens in movies and television, but not in real life."

Viv felt her stomach unclench. She'd been feeling so guilty. "So you know who the victim is?"

"Yep. A female in her mid-thirties. Name of Sarah Esper-anza. She lives in Desert Hot Springs, a couple of towns over. Do you know her?"

Viv gasped. "Are you sure?"

"You know her then?"

"She's a colleague and a friend."

"Can you tell me about her family or work? Any information would be helpful."

"Sarah was a doula, part of my Desert Doula agency. She worked with surrogate mothers mostly. She had the perfect background and was surprisingly good with all of the legal details."

"A surrogate doula. What's that exactly?"

"A person who's contracted to support a surrogate mother until she gives birth and the baby is given to the forever parents."

"That involves in vitro fertilization, right?"

"Usually."

Viv heard the officer sigh. "It's getting late. How about I come over tomorrow and ask some more questions. I'd like to get your perspective before we start our interviews with family and friends."

"I'll do what I can." Her voice sounded tired, even to herself.

"I'll come by tomorrow. Bye for now." The phone went dead.

When Viv returned to the living room her three friends stopped talking.

"The dead person...it was Sarah." Tears formed in her eyes.

"I knew something was wrong when she didn't call me back," claimed Bri. "I figured she had more work, so I quit trying. I can't believe she was really..."

Pearl wrapped her arm around Bri's shoulders. "It's okay, honey. You had no way of knowing." She glanced at Viv, her face contorting with tears. "I can't believe this is happening."

Viv spoke up. "I feel just awful. I mean, why my swimming pool? How did she get past the security gate and into my house and then out to the backyard?"

"Makes no sense," Tamara agreed. Her face looked pale, her eyes wide.

Pearl stood, her eyes puffy from crying. She picked up empty goblets and plates, walking toward the kitchen.

Hearing water running from the tap in the kitchen sink, Viv called out, "I'll put them in the dishwasher later. Don't worry. It's getting late. The washing up will give me a chance to unwind before bed."

Once she said the last goodbye, she closed the door and then rested her back against the wood. Then she walked to the kitchen. Something Bri said earlier ran a loop in her mind. *"Her car's in the shop again. I guess there are money issues and they won't release it until she pays the bill."*

Poor Sarah.

10

REX REDONDO

She stands at attention, waiting for my command. A tall lanky redhead dressed in camo-patterned yoga pants, a tight olive-green t-shirt tied in the front, heavy boots, her hair slicked back into a bun. Eyes behind horn-rimmed glasses focus forward.

"Lieutenant Sutton, I have an important task for you involving a clandestine mission of the utmost importance."

"Sir," she says crisply.

"I assume you've cleared the day for an assignment."

"Yes, sir." I detect the hint of actual enthusiasm in her voice.

"But first show me the photos," I say.

She turns on her heel, taking steps toward her desk at the corner of our high-ceiling great room. She returns with her computer. "Here they are." An open laptop is shoved in my face. I place it on the table. My stomach growls, reminding me of breakfast.

"I want two eggs sunny-side up, with whole wheat toast and fresh black coffee."

"Yes, sir," she says again.

A hint of laughter behind her words, I catch her smirking, breaking with our protocol.

"Okay then, bring breakfast for yourself and Kevin too; we have work to do."

"Bork," comes a voice from the backyard.

"And let Kevin in from outside while you're at it."

"Yes, sir." Then she adds, "Right after I pick up the dog poop, sir."

I never know who Sutton will be. She surprises me every day, with her shifting from one persona to the next, changing outfits, acting out different roles as if she were on stage. She's been my personal assistant for two decades; never a dull moment.

After a short time, I hear pots and pans banging around in the kitchen.

Ignoring the tempting smell of banana bread, I pay more attention to the photos. The series shows Viv doing errands in town. I asked Sutton to follow her yesterday, for her own safety, of course. The photos may not have been necessary. Anyway, first we have Viv shopping at a local boutique, talking to the sales guy.

She leans over the counter, her athletic legs and very nice fanny exposed to the lens. The guy behind the counter smiles at her, his hand waving in the air to make some kind of point.

Three clicks later I see my Hailey walk into the shop. She chats up the same guy, who holds a stack of clothes. Then Hailey pulls her cap over her forehead and steps outside, the consignment store bag hanging from one slim arm.

I'm interrupted by Sutton stepping into the room with our breakfast on a tray. She still wears the camo outfit, only she's released her hair. Strawberry-blonde curls tumble over her shoulders. Without the glasses she looks like a suburbanite coming home from Pilates, not a personal assistant for a mentalist.

"So what do you think?" She places a plate near my right hand. An enormous banana muffin rests next to two strips of bacon and eggs sunny-side up. The muffin surprises me. Not exactly what I asked for. But I'm distracted because she bends down to put a smaller plate of eggs and bacon on the floor for Kevin. Who cares about the muffin anyway.

He sniffs, looking up at her with big black eyes.

"Sit," she tells him.

He remains standing, wagging his tail.

"Not a sit," she reminds him.

His tail droops.

"I didn't say look adorable. I said sit!" Sutton repeats.

Down goes his bottom. She pauses for a moment and then adds, "Okay."

Two slices of bacon and a scrambled egg vanish into Kevin's mouth before Sutton can sit down at the table across from me.

"I like the military persona in the morning. The way you say 'yes, sir' and all. Keep that one."

"Whatever," she mumbles, biting into her own banana muffin. "The photos—"

"They are informative," I tell her.

"You mean you like the ones of Viv, but the rest..."

"Of course I like the ones of our neighbor. But I'm wondering about the crossing of paths with my niece and Viv at a local boutique. That was unexpected."

"What do you read into the situation?"

"It may be just a coincidence. Remember, I'm not psychic. I have no idea why Hailey would be slumming it, buying clothes at a secondhand store, no matter how upscale."

"I was surprised," Sutton admitted. "From across the street with my lens I thought Hailey looked kind of nervous."

"She's avoiding paparazzi since the baby arrived."

"Or at least she's making the pretense of avoiding being noticed. Influencers make that pretense all the time, ducking here and there. But we know from experience that may be a ruse." Her eyes misted over. She began to speak in a low monotone. "Remember that kid in Afghanistan who pretended he was an orphan? We trusted him and then he led us into that ambush."

Sutton rarely talks about our time in the military. The memories are hard for us both. The isolation and the death. It's not something we want to think about, either of us.

I feel Kevin's chin on my thigh. "Hey, good boy." I scratch his ears, still staring at Viv's photo. She's in good shape for a woman her age.

"I don't think we can compare my niece to that kid, but I get your point. She's an actress with a following and she has to be careful. Let's leave it at that."

"She's hiding something," mumbles Sutton, her eyes now focused on mine. "Just like that kid." Her finger points at the computer. "Scroll through and check out the others."

A shot of the limo picking up Hailey is next, then a photo of me passing by the consignment shop. Some more photos of Viv's house, the front door. Nice curb appeal, with a mid-century desert design and spare landscaping. A tall saguaro cactus is the front yard focal piece; the arms appear to be waving at the camera. Artfully placed boulders with river rock give the feeling of a stark desert landscape, smooth and efficient.

My place is the same. Another reason I like Viv. We have similar taste.

"So she had one of her women's meetings last night."

Sutton points to the last photo. "They left around ten. See? I took a photo of each one getting into a car."

"Did you follow anyone home?"

"I had a date downtown," she tells me with a shrug.

I scroll one more time with my thumb and see a selfie of Sutton and a handsome man, both holding a beer. "Isn't he kinda young for you?"

"Like you should talk."

I can't disagree. Since we met, Sutton has seen her share of women, most of them younger, spend the night. I have a thing for twenty-three-year-olds. Come to think of it, we met when Sutton was twenty-three. I look at her across the table. "Weren't you twenty-three when we first met? Funny how we never got together."

She smirks. "You're too old for me. You outranked me. Plus fraternizing is frowned upon."

"Oh, the places we've been." I smile at her, hoping she's feeling nostalgic rather than agitated with the memories of combat.

"That's enough, Dr. Seuss," she grumbles.

The conversation gives me pause for thought. I've lost my zest for younger women. It's been months since I've even gone on a date. Women come up to me after the show and I don't even go out for a drink with them. I sign an autograph and send them on their way.

I'm so fascinated with my next-door neighbor, I've had little head room for anyone else. One glimpse of her at the pool...okay, so maybe a little lust, but definitely more. Maybe there is something to love at first sight.

She only touched me one time, when we shook hands, and I knew—she's the real deal.

As Sutton picks up the empty plates, Kevin lifts his chin from my lap to watch.

She nods toward him. "Okay, Kev, time for our walk." With a tray full of dishes and mugs, she saunters toward the kitchen. Kevin follows right behind.

"Hey, check in before you leave," I yell at her retreating back. I have another assignment in mind.

"Maybe," she says pleasantly.

"I like 'yes, sir' better."

11

VIVIENNE ROSE

The backyard intercom on the wall beeped. Viv pushed the button. "Yes," she said into the speaker.

Because of the security gate, each home had an indoor and outdoor intercom. Electronically connected to the main gate, Viv could greet visitors who did not have the code.

"It's me, Zach, from Pool-O-Rama. I'm here for the weekly maintenance."

Viv momentarily debated telling him about the dead body in her pool. Then she changed her mind. *I'll have to tell him face-to-face.* She pressed the buzzer. "Come on in."

She sat back down in her chair, stretching her bare legs in front of her. Dressed in a loose-fitting sundress, she wore her usual flip-flops and a wide-brim straw hat. The sip of iced coffee felt refreshingly cold on her lips.

"Hello," came his voice after a short while of waiting. She heard the gate to her backyard squeak. Zach came into sight, stopping only to look over the pool area. He looked exactly like a pool guy. Or even a lifeguard, with the tan arms and muscles. He turned to face her. "What happened here?" He pointed to the yellow police tape.

She sighed, wondering how much to tell him. "There was an incident. The police tape hasn't been removed yet."

He made his way across the scorching pavement toward the other side of the pool. She watched as he disappeared around the corner, returning with a long pole gripped in his gloved hands. Dangling at the end of the pole was a net, used to gather debris from the water.

"Is it okay to go ahead and skim the water?" he called out to her.

Surprised that he didn't realize the gravity of the situation, she responded quickly. "You'd better wait on that, at least until the cops take away the tape."

"When will that be?"

"They're supposed to call me this morning. Then they'll come by and you can get on with the work."

He stared toward the side of the house, tugging at the brim on his cap.

"You're new, right? What happened to Greg, my regular pool guy?"

He ignored her question, explaining instead, "I'll return the pole and check the pump and filter. Then I can come back to finish when the tape is removed." He didn't wait for her to answer but walked around the house and out of sight.

Viv looked down at her phone. No texts or missed calls. *I wish Officer Farrah would come get her stuff.*

Zach appeared moments later. "The pump looks fine. The cops must have cleaned the filter. Just text the company when they take the tape away." He closed the gate behind him. The next thing she heard was an engine starting up in front of her house.

She looked toward the catio. Miss Kitty stood in her usual spot, looking out at the pool. "Meow."

***

Once Viv showered and dressed, she finally got a text from Officer Farrah.

> I would appreciate a little clarification.
> Coming by in half an hour to chat.

Half an hour later, Viv opened the front door and nodded toward the kitchen. "Would you like some iced coffee and a cookie? We have some leftovers from our meeting last night."

"Sure." The officer walked inside. "What kind of meeting?"

"My small business, Desert Doulas."

"Do you call yourselves birth workers?"

"You're uncomfortable with that term," Viv instantly responded. "I can hear it in your voice. It wouldn't be the first time I've gotten that reaction."

"Doulas..." Officer Farrah sat down at the kitchen table. "I have to say I've encountered a few midwives in my work. My sister-in-law did a freebirth. She's a lunatic. Are you one of those freebirth doulas?"

"I am not, but I have many colleagues who do freebirth work. It's more popular than it's ever been, and frankly a good option for some birthing mothers and parents."

"I hope I haven't offended you. I'm sorry." Officer Farrah sounded genuinely contrite.

Viv walked to the refrigerator. She knew from experience that women who reacted emotionally to her line of work often had issues in their past. Even a quick mention of her doula work had brought out any number of responses over the years. Usually there was a story behind the reaction.

Over the years she'd learned to keep her personal feelings under wraps, especially when it came to her work. That protected her from saying too much because she never knew what would upset an expectant mother. *Or a police officer who happens to be a mother.*

Viv's response was to educate rather than pry. "Like any profession, doulas come in all shapes and sizes. Many women wouldn't hear of delivering a baby anywhere but a hospital.

"But hospitals aren't the only place to have babies!" she continued. "Birthing people have choices nowadays. That's why doulas have made a comeback. We can accompany people before, during, and after birth. We support their choices."

"But you don't deliver the babies, right?"

"That's correct." She poured a glass of iced coffee and set it in front of Officer Farrah. "Cream and sugar?"

"Both." The officer's eyes softened. "You're right. I didn't feel like I had a choice with the birth of my two. I went to the hospital, got the job done, and came home. It was one of the hardest things I've ever done. And that includes some pretty challenging murder investigations."

"That's exactly what I'm saying. Women give birth and get back up. Rarely do they consider their own well-being or the trauma that's been inflicted upon them and the baby during the birthing process. Most women don't question doctors or the hospitals."

Officer Farrah blinked, then cleared her throat. "I'd like to talk more about this, but I'm really here to ask some questions about the victim. Things you might know as her friend and colleague."

"Of course." Viv sat down at the table. "Sarah and I worked together for over five years." Viv paused as Officer Farrah took out her handheld recorder.

"That's a good beginning," she said. "Just so you know, I have alibis for you and Rex Redondo. And now I've got info on Tamara's whereabouts." She looked at Viv, her eyes widening. "Boy that was something, when you thought the victim was Tamara. It must have been a bad night for you, right?"

Viv knew instantly that Officer Farrah's wide eyes were inviting her to open up and keep talking and maybe give away more information. Though Officer Farrah tried to make her question sound friendly, Viv also knew that everything she said would be carefully recorded. "I was horrified, but now I'm fine," she answered in a firm voice.

Farrah waited but Viv didn't add anything else.

Instead of asking another leading question, Farrah clicked her recorder off. Then she changed the topic.

"The lab is handling the samples we collected around the pool and from the filter. We got lots of information from the autopsy. There's evidence of a head wound; most likely she hit one of the boulders near the pool. She could have tripped and fallen or someone may have shoved her. We searched for blood and fingerprints, but nothing came up. Once unconscious, Ms. Esperanza either fell or was pushed into the water."

"So Sarah wasn't alone."

"We can't say for certain either way. There wasn't any obvious evidence that she had company." Officer Farrah clicked the recorder back on. "We did find traces of bleach around that boulder close to the pool. As if someone cleaned up. Maybe there was blood and they didn't want to leave any evidence."

Viv shuddered. "So there may have been another person."

"That would be my opinion. But it won't take long. We'll find evidence that someone left or took away by accident. It's always the case. And then we keep interviewing until someone gives us new information that we can follow up on."

Viv stood. "Actually I may have something for you." She walked to the living room and brought back a small wicker basket. "I keep this for pool visitors. It has sunscreen, flip-flops, and a deck of cards. People pick out what they need."

Farrah pulled an oversized plastic evidence bag from her pocket. "These weren't by the pool when my team searched. And it was too dark to be playing cards and putting on sunscreen. But who knows. Something may turn up. I'll send them to the lab just in case."

Farrah spoke into the recorder. "Vivienne Rose handed me a wicker basket with potential evidence." She bagged the basket and the rest, taking her time.

Viv remained standing, hoping she'd finish soon.

Officer Farrah looked up. "I have a few more questions. Do you know anything about Sarah's boyfriend?"

"She's been with someone for several months. Sarah moved recently to Desert Hot Springs, a mobile home. That did come up in one of our monthly meetings. We don't pry into the lives of our colleagues unless absolutely necessary. I don't even know his name."

Farrah nodded. "We looked into Ms. Esperanza's past. No arrests. Is there anything she'd be hiding that we should know about, that maybe she talked about at one of your doula meetings?"

"Sarah had been trained as a midwife. She supported mothers who wanted to stay away from hospitals. Mostly freebirths."

Officer Farrah clicked the recorder off. "Like my sister-in-law. The doula showed up with essential oils and a birthing tub. The baby was weeks old before some doc signed off on a birth certificate." She shook her head. "Okay, so maybe not everyone has to give birth in a hospital like I did, but going all willy-nilly and just jumping in a wading pool and popping the baby out in your house..."

"It feels wrong to you," Viv said quietly. "But if you can set aside preconceived ideas, you can at least consider how free-birth may feel like the most natural and healthy way to welcome baby into the world. I don't accompany women who freebirth, but I don't judge them either. I've heard too many stories of unnecessary C-sections and intrusive internal exams to think that hospitals are for everyone."

Officer Farrah's face flushed, as if she were holding back strong feelings. Viv assessed immediately.

Maybe her own births were traumatic.

Farrah wiped her hand over her forehead. "You hit a nerve with me," she admitted. "I didn't see that coming. I may be compromising the investigation with my own issues. I'll try to stay on top of that."

Viv nodded. "It's not uncommon for women who give birth to bury their feelings after the baby comes. And then certain topics bring everything back. I deal with this all the time.

"Mothers move on after the birth because they think it best for the baby, or for many different reasons. Maybe your partner didn't want to listen. Or women in your family weren't receptive to your postpartum concerns."

The officer's eyes looked vague, as if she were remembering.

"I know you have an investigation to work on; how about I recommend a support group—"

"I can handle this on my own," Farrah said firmly.

Viv gave the officer a moment. She looked through the window toward the backyard. The yellow tape had been removed.

"If we're done here, I'd like to call my pool maintenance company back." She stepped away from the table, toward the front door.

Officer Farrah shut down her iPad and stood. "Thanks for

the coffee. I want you to come down to the precinct in the next day or two. It's more likely I'll be able to fill you in better by then."

The door closed with a thud, leaving Viv to call the pool company.

12

VIVIENNE ROSE

Viv sat at her desk, preparing for an upcoming birthing class. Ten expectant mothers had signed up for a month's worth of instruction on pregnancy and prenatal care.

Viv began online teaching after experiencing an emergency home birth. She had to call an ambulance when the labor intensified beyond the midwife's control. An emergency C-section was required. Even though it wasn't anyone's fault, Viv felt bad for the mother. She'd failed to counsel her on the possibility of a C-section early on when they'd put her birth plan together.

Fortunately the baby and mother were fine, but afterward Viv had a breakdown of sorts. Hiding in her house, taking no calls. It took a life coach to point out that she needed a definite routine of self-care to continue her doula work. As a part of that self-care, Viv took on fewer clients and opened her Desert Doula business.

It turned out that her colleagues were enthusiastically supportive. They recommended her online classes to all of their clients. To Viv's further surprise, she liked teaching. In person and online, she'd found great satisfaction in sharing evidence-based birth information, along with good old-fashioned practical advice.

Her home office faced the backyard pool and the fence beyond. The cool air conditioning blew gently over her workspace. Shielded from the reality of the 107-degree temperature outdoors, she turned on her desktop computer and opened Zoom. Eight of her students waited as she clicked to let them in. She greeted each one individually with a nod and a bright hello.

"Meow," Miss Kitty interrupted. The cat leapt from the floor, landing in Viv's lap.

"Time for class," she muttered under her breath to the cat. "I made a space for you." She pointed to a soft blanket placed to the right of the computer monitor, on top of the desk. Miss Kitty eyed it and then swished her tail, refusing to move.

Viv reached into her desk drawer for a cat treat, which she placed on the blanket. Miss Kitty extended a dainty paw to touch the treat. Only when Viv ignored her to talk to her students did the cat poke the treat off the blanket and onto the desktop, finally leaning over to take it in her teeth. With one tentative paw she stepped onto the desktop and then the blanket. Viv could almost read her thoughts. *"I'll sit here because I want to, not because you told me to."*

With Miss Kitty settled, Viv was able to give her full attention to the women. After a few minutes of chitchat, only one student seemed less than okay. The young mother had dark circles under her eyes with hair hanging limply against her narrow face. She spoke in a low voice and averted her eyes from the camera.

Viv knew that some women, especially new mothers, disguised their ill health and emotional issues quite well. She looked at her roster to confirm the woman's name. Running her finger down the admittance form, she stopped at the word

"Surrogate." *If this is her first surrogacy, she may require more support.* Viv circled the phone number. *I can recommend a doula who specializes in surrogacy birthing. Sarah is perfect and I bet...*

She felt a hot rush to her head. She'd forgotten. *Sarah is dead.* She wrote a question mark with her pencil. *I'll have to find someone else.*

By the end of the class, one woman asked, "Is nursing really that difficult? I thought it was natural. Now I'm worried. I mean, do I need to hire my doula for a few extra visits after the baby is born?"

Viv waited for one of the more experienced mothers to reply first. Half of her enrollment included women who had previously given birth, so it was her practice to encourage mothers to talk to mothers before she offered up any answers. Like the time a mother suggested giving her baby melatonin to get to sleep. Viv stepped in right away, telling them medications weren't always the solution and that they needed to check with their pediatrician.

She muted her microphone but kept listening as the women discussed the pros and cons of nursing. Thinking ahead, she wondered if Officer Farrah would text and ask to meet her at the precinct.

Viv glanced at Miss Kitty, whose eyes were closed, completely oblivious to the voices coming from the computer. *How can she be so alert one minute and so unaware the next?*

When she heard a pause in the conversation, Viv unmuted herself to say goodbye to her students. Once everyone signed off, she pushed back her chair to think about the rest of her day. After leaving a message for the young mother who concerned her, she stood, and Miss Kitty kept sleeping.

The doorbell rang. Viv hurried out of the catio to the front room.

One of the perks of being a part of the Desert Doula Agency was having access to Viv's house and pool. She maintained an open-door policy. If a woman needed a day to kick back, away from her own house and family, she was welcome to drop in.

Sitting poolside often brought a moment of quiet to the most difficult day. Viv's kitchen was open for snacks. If more food was required, a quick call for a home delivery worked. Over the past year Viv saw that a swim in the pool suited some people. But most of her doulas, doused in sunscreen, just wanted to rest in peace and quiet.

Up until recently Viv kept a key under a decorative rock in the courtyard out front. That way women could come and go. A couple of months ago, she'd been awakened at two in the morning when she'd heard a voice in her living room. Feeling frightened, she'd popped out of bed to grab a bathrobe.

"Anyone there?" she'd called.

When no one answered, she felt a pit in her stomach. Holding her phone, she punched in 911. Then a familiar voice called out her name, so she dropped the call before alarming the police.

"It's just me," came Sarah's low laugh. "Sorry I didn't call ahead. I had to get away." Once Sarah caught sight of Viv in her bathrobe she kept apologizing. "Oh I am so sorry. I woke you up. It is pretty early in the morning."

"You did give me a start." Viv made her way to the kitchen, knowing she wouldn't get any more sleep. She would spend time listening to Sarah instead.

After that incident Viv adjusted her habit of leaving the key out at night. She asked that everyone text her ahead of time instead. Then if she wasn't home, she'd leave the key. A sound from the front door brought her back to the present.

Maybe I should tell Officer Farrah about my open-door policy for doulas. I didn't mention that. She walked closer to look through the peephole. A stranger stood on her doorstep holding a large brown box. She opened the door.

Viv looked to the street. There was no car running its motor at the curb. *Maybe she's not a delivery person.* Dressed in tight joggers and high heels, the woman stood nearly six feet tall. She wore a white shirt, tied at the waist. A dazzling smile met Viv's frown with an explanation. "Hi, I live next door." She pointed to Rex Redondo's house.

"Oh, I didn't realize he had a partner. I guess we're neighbors then. Would you like to come in? What's with the box?"

The woman didn't need another invitation. She walked inside as Viv shut the door. "This box is for you," she said, putting it down in the hallway. "Mr. Redondo wanted to send you a small token, since the other night was..." she hesitated and then finished, "difficult."

Mr. Redondo. No one calls their partner mister.

"He didn't have to do that." *What can possibly be in that box?* Viv stepped closer, "My name is Vivienne Rose, and you are..."

"I'm Sutton Drew, Mr. Redondo's personal assistant." She pointed to the package. "I have to get going. A busy day ahead. Anyway, let us know if you like the gift." With a half wave, she opened the door and walked outside. Viv closed the door behind her.

She wasted no time. Glancing at the box, she made a quick walk to the kitchen, returning with a pair of shears. Running the blade over one seam, she lifted the lid to find another box inside the box. With some quick scissor thrusts she was able to open the second one. Lifting it up, she read,

"Congratulations! Your Yum Yum Cat Feeder is here! Just pre-measure the food and let Yum Yum do the rest of the work. Your cat will never be without a meal. Batteries included."

Miss Kitty appeared from around the corner. As soon as she saw Viv with the box, she crouched low. "Someone brought you a gift," Viv coaxed her.

Standing up, Miss Kitty stalked her way toward the open cardboard box. She sniffed and then rubbed herself against the corner.

Viv's initial distrust of Rex vanished in a soft laugh. *You knew I wouldn't give back a gift for Miss Kitty.*

13

VIVIENNE ROSE

By the evening Vivienne had answered five phone calls from nervous new parents. Three of the five were about breastfeeding. "Is my baby getting enough milk?" they all asked. The other two were concerned about frequency of nursing. "I can't get anything done around the house," one mother cried.

Viv was the first to admit that body feeding was not for everyone. Yet the emotional response to parenting a baby had a lot to do with how smoothly body feeding would go. She also knew that some women felt disappointed at first when things got difficult. The amount of milk and the time-consuming aspect of nursing made the occasional mother antsy. Some mothers wanted to get baby to a formula sooner than later, just to feel less confined.

One of her phone calls involved lots of tears. Viv had to be patient, waiting for the sobs to subside. "Would you like to schedule a face-to-face conversation? I can meet your baby and walk you through some time-honored feeding routines."

After she completed the calls, Viv sat in her chair close to Miss Kitty. From inside the catio, the room closest to the pool shed, she heard the low hum of the pump. The pool had been filled the day before by one of the crew who wanted time and a half to work on Sunday.

She turned her head to watch Miss Kitty meticulously lick one paw and then rub it over her face. With office hours over, Viv put her phone on silent. As the sun settled over the distant mountain range, the thermometer on a nearby post registered 108. *Time for a swim.*

Once outside she let her kimono drop to the chair. Shoving her hair into a swimming cap, she glanced over to her neighbor's house, eyes traveling to the second story. *That's how he saw Sarah floating in the pool. I hope he's not watching me.*

Sliding out of her flip-flops, she dove into the deep end. The water felt cool against her skin, bringing a smile to Viv's lips. One arm after the other, her body skimmed over the water's surface. She tucked her chin and took a quick breath to the side before turning her face back into the water. The words of her first swim instructor came to mind: bubble, bubble, bubble, breathe.

With a relaxed crawl stroke Viv did her laps, from the shallow to the deep end and back. Her hand would hit the gutter, then she executed a quick flip turn to face the opposite direction. Breathing every third stroke, her muscles ached but she kept going. *Only four more laps. Then I'm done for the day.*

When she was done, she pulled herself out of the pool and slipped her feet back into the flip-flops. Steam rose from where the water hit the concrete. She lifted off her cap and then leaned to the left to shake water from her ear.

By the time she shook water from both ears, she realized, *This is the first time I've taken a swim since Sarah.* Her eyes swept the pool, stopping at the sound of the gurgling filter. She sniffed the slight smell of pool chemicals wafting above the water's surface. The exercise and the clean smell restored her sense of confidence.

Sitting on the side of the chaise lounge, she glanced at her phone screen. A text from Tamara was there from just a couple of minutes ago.

> How about we meet halfway for a drink?
> Casino bar in an hour?

Viv liked The Roadkill, the bar and restaurant attached to the casino. They served a good burger and a grilled seafood special now and then. Though noises, beeps, and bells from the casino could be heard from inside the restaurant, Viv didn't mind, so long as she didn't actually enter the main floor where the gamblers played.

"I don't gamble," she'd remind people who invited her to join. "Slot machines make me jumpy," she'd add, hoping to avoid sounding too judgmental. She'd had experiences in casinos as a child with her parents, which left a lasting impression of the noise and confusion. Since The Roadkill didn't overserve their customers, she felt at ease there, as long as she didn't have to walk inside the actual casino.

For the past several months the bartender smiled every time she walked in. Viv always ordered an iced gin and tonic with a squeeze of lime. She thought the fancy margaritas, what The Roadkill was known for, were too salty. Without a pause she texted Tamara back,

> See you at eight

Kimono and towel in hand, she walked inside the house. The cool air hit her face as she slid the door closed. *Brrr.* She wrapped the towel around her shoulders. Then she heard a faint meow come from the catio. *Why doesn't she just come to find me instead of yelling from the other side of the house?*

Viv knew the answer. Her cat expected a timely dinner of

salmon nibbles right at six thirty every evening. Miss Kitty had a very accurate internal clock.

"I'll be there in a minute," Viv called out. After she showered and wrapped herself in a bathrobe, she blow-dried her hair by finger-combing her waves away from her face. Then she applied a lightly tinted skin cream with a fresh lipstick. No mascara or eye shadow. She'd simplified her routine when she turned fifty.

Entering the catio, she found Miss Kitty standing on the arm of the sofa, her tail twitching in the air. "I'm not late, don't act so impatient," Viv told her. "And remember I have a new toy for you. An automatic feeding bowl from our next-door neighbor."

She filled the feeder with dry food. Knowing the dry food would only satisfy the cat in between her regular meals, she placed it by the door leading to the pool area outside. She returned to assemble Miss Kitty's usual meal.

Miss Kitty leapt from the sofa, trotting softly across the room to sniff her wet food. Then she walked to the new food dish to disdainfully stare before sashaying back to her regular fare.

"I know," Viv admitted. "Getting used to something new takes some time. But you may like it once you've tried it." She realized as soon as she'd said the words that the same could be said for the sender, Mr. Rex Redondo. Rex would also take some getting used to.

Leaving the cat to her dinner, Viv walked to her bedroom. She chose light denim jeans and a tank top. Then she selected a brightly colored kimono to wear over the top since the air conditioning at The Roadkill required another layer.

Life in the desert meant being prepared for extreme temperature shifts. It wasn't just going from outdoors to indoors and vice versa either. Like the time her car quit on the

Palms to Pines Highway and she had to call for roadside assistance. Without air conditioning inside, the car was suffocating. Standing outside in the sun, she could barely take a breath.

The kid who showed up—Brad May was his name—left her with bottled water to keep in her trunk. He'd been driving back to Lily Rock and stopped when he saw her car stalled on the highway.

"You gotta have water in your car at all times," he'd warned. "The desert will get you one way or another." He'd started her car so that she could make it back to Palm Desert to the repair shop.

Not quite ready to leave for The Roadkill, Viv turned on her television. Hailey and Cameron Steward were being interviewed by a reporter who thrust a microphone in Hailey's face. She'd dressed in a sequined tunic top, one Viv recognized from Out of the Closet Consignment. It billowed over her thin frame and her skinny white jeans.

"The baby weight is just melting away," she said, batting her eyes.

"She's back to her old self already." Cameron put his arm around her shoulders, looking adoringly into her face. The reporter turned her back to the couple to face the camera.

"And there you have it, folks. Hailey and Cameron Steward plan to get back to work in just a couple of weeks. They're keeping the baby's gender a secret though. I tried my best to get them to spill but no luck." The reporter shrugged as if to say, *what can you do with these celebrities nowadays?*

"But you gotta admit," the reporter added, "Hailey is already back to her fighting weight. It's only been two weeks."

Viv picked her favorite pair of white leather sandals from her closet. The low heel and cushioned sole felt comfortable. The pearls decorating the brown strap over her toes made the sandals stand out, giving them an "I can walk anywhere and still look cool in these" kind of vibe.

During her year of reframing her life, she'd learned many ways to make things less complicated. Desert Doulas was only the first step. Her lifestyle came next. Viv was aware that other women stopped to look at her, and men too, even at her age. Not because she was thin and in shape but because she looked confident and happy and in tune with herself.

On the way to the garage, Viv stopped to think. *I haven't seen my house key in a few days.* She rummaged in her purse and came up with a key dangling from a chain attached to a saguaro cactus charm. *I have my key, but what about the spare?*

Under the rock outside... But when she stepped out the front door and lifted the rock, it wasn't there. She felt puzzled but knew it was time to leave to meet Tamara. *Better get going so I won't be late. I'll look later.*

On the drive toward The Roadkill she pushed her concern about the key to the back of her mind. Instead she thought about Hailey Steward. If anyone watched that interview, they'd think it was normal to be skinny after you've given birth. *I bet I'll have at least one call tomorrow. A new mother crying because she saw the interview and she's still carrying baby weight.*

Viv arrived at the crowded casino parking lot and found a parking space near the restaurant. On her walk across the hot blacktop toward the restaurant, she noticed a familiar face smiling at her from an enormous billboard. She read the lit-up advertisement: *World renowned mentalist, Rex Redondo, here nightly. He knows more about you than you know about yourself.*

14

VIVIENNE ROSE

People filled the booths and tables at The Roadkill. Viv noticed Tamara right away. She sat at the bar, where she'd saved an empty stool. Viv slid next to her as the bartender asked, "Gin and tonic, right?" He went to get her drink without waiting for a reply.

Viv smiled at her friend as the drink was placed in front of her. "I'll put this on the tab," the bartender said.

Tamara held up her beer glass for a toast. "Cheers."

"Cheers to you," answered Viv, taking her first sip.

"You look amazing." Tamara put her glass down and stared at Viv's straight-leg jeans. "I'm thinking the skinny is out."

"Skinnies were never in for me." Viv drank through the short straw as her eyes moved upward, taking in the shelves and the mirror behind the bar. Her eyes froze as she watched the reflection of a woman in the back booth. The woman's thumb moved with rapid strokes, scrolling on the phone.

Viv nudged Tamara. "Check out that woman over there. She looks kind of familiar. Do you know her?"

Tamara's eyes looked up and then focused. "Nope, I don't know her. But that's quite an outfit she's got on. She's taken feathers to a whole new level. I'm surprised no one else is staring at her." Tamara looked around the room.

"This is a casino. She actually fits right in." Viv watched as the woman nervously patted down the hair next to her right ear. Her long bright-green manicured fingernails combed through the back of her hair. The feather headband reminded Viv of a recent production of *Hair* the musical. She'd gone with a few friends and seen a lot of interesting people, including several with similar hair ornaments.

Some people never make their way out of the sixties. She leaned over to whisper into Tamara's ear, "Check out the leather halter top. I can't see what she's wearing for pants. Do you have a guess?"

"Pleather," Tamara said at once.

"And knee-high black boots?" Viv guessed.

"So are we talking call girl?" Tamara mused.

"Not unusual for a working girl to hang out in a bar inside a casino," Viv said immediately. "I once had a doula client who was a sex worker from Palm Springs. When she got pregnant, she called me. After delivering a healthy baby boy she stopped her work. Got a law degree and lives in Chino now. We're Facebook friends." Viv took a sip from her straw as Tamara smiled at her.

Viv noted her tired eyes. "It's so good to see you. Everything okay at home once you got back?"

Tamara let out a long sigh. "My ex wants me to float him some cash. My daughter needs fall tuition money. I may have to get another job to support what Ace likes to call 'the doula hobby.'"

"Why do people think being a doula is just a hobby? Your ex never saw the light on that topic, did he?"

"That's why we're divorced—at least one of the reasons."

"Are you going to give Ace money?"

"I'll give him some. Never as much as he wants, but enough to keep the line of communication open. The last time I said no, he disappeared and Heather was heartbroken."

Heather was in her mid-twenties, a younger version of her mother.

Viv took another glance in the mirror. The woman in the back booth was now using rapid-fire thumbs to text. Viv turned back to Tamara with a question. "So since the death, I've misplaced my house key. Have you seen it?"

Tamara looked perplexed. "You mean the one with the small tortoise on it that you got at the hardware store?"

"That's the one. I only have two keys to the house. Mine is the one with the saguaro charm, and the extra key has a tortoise. It's the one I left outside for you before the..." Viv didn't say death, just took a sip of gin and tonic instead.

"Oh, I left it on the table by the pool basket." Tamara's forehead wrinkled as if she were thinking.

Agitation bubbled up in Viv's stomach. With a killer on the loose, a misplaced key worried her.

"Maybe the cops found it," Tamara added quickly. "You can ask Officer What's-Her-Name when she calls about that interview."

"Now that I think about it, how did you get back in the house if you left the key inside?"

Tamara reached for a handful of peanuts. "I took your spare garage door opener with me in my back pocket. My car was parked in your garage, remember?"

Viv nodded. "That's why I expected you to be home. Your car was there. But then the cop—"

"I know, honey. You don't have to go over it again. Just have another sip of your drink and put it all behind you."

Viv frowned. "Officer Farrah hasn't gotten back to me. I was under the impression when we spoke that she had more questions. We talked a long time about Desert Doulas, especially about Sarah. She didn't get to finish her interview."

"She hasn't called you yet?" Tamara's voice sounded puzzled. "Well anyway, back to the key. Remember the time you lost it before?" Tamara patted her hand. "You left it in the catio. Miss Kitty must have played with it and shoved it under the sofa."

Viv laughed. "I do remember. Since then I've tried to be very careful. I had the door lock changed and then had a duplicate made for the house. So now I keep one key in my purse just in case the electricity goes out and I can't get into the garage." She looked into the mirror, then back to Tamara. "I suppose I can have another new lock installed. It's not cheap!"

The bartender stood in front of Viv. "Do you two want dinner now? The mentalist show starts in less than an hour."

He must assume we're going to the show.

Viv held up a finger to silently ask the bartender to wait while she spoke to Tamara. "I have an idea. We're in time for Rex Redondo's act. We could stand in the back, the cheap tickets, to see his schtick."

Tamara took the last gulp of beer. "We could have a quick burger first."

"Great idea." She looked up at the bartender. "Make mine rare with mustard, lettuce, and tomato."

"Same for me but add a slice of cheddar," Tamara said.

Viv placed her card on the bar. "I'll pay now so that we can get to the show."

The bartender took the card. "Got the order. It will only be a few minutes."

Tamara smiled gratefully. "Most of my money has gone to Ace and Heather. Thanks for the treat." Her voice sounded heavy with resignation.

As they waited for their burgers, one by one people came by to pay their tab and head toward the casino entrance.

"Email or paper receipt?" The bartender placed two huge hamburgers in sesame buns in front of the women.

"Paper is good."

He ripped off the receipt and handed it to her.

"So how can we be sure we can stand at the back?" Tamara took a bite of the burger while Viv answered.

"Once we're done, everyone else should be seated. They'll release the standing room only. Then we show up at the box office. They often let people stand in the back for half price."

They ate in silence, giving Viv some time to think about her closest friend. *I have it so easy. Enough money for what I want and a job that I love. My son is independent. The most demanding person in my life isn't even a person, she's a cat.*

Viv slid off the stool first, followed by Tamara. "Gosh, that tasted good," she remarked as they made their way toward the exit. Out of the doors into the parking lot, Viv blinked back the dryness of the heat. Tamara led the way toward the box office. She nearly bumped into a six-foot-tall poster of Rex Redondo with his cheeky grin.

"He's good-looking, I'll give him that," Viv said.

"He looks like a used car salesman with that smile. And so sure of himself." Tamara smirked.

Viv took Tamara by the elbow. "So let's have some fun and see if he's the real deal."

They walked side by side toward the box office.

15

VIVIENNE ROSE

Standing in the back of the crowded theater, Viv leaned her back against the wall. Tamara stood next to her, eyes surveying the room. "Lots of people here," she commented.

"Have you ever been to one of these shows, you know, with a mentalist?"

Tamara raised her voice to be heard over the crowd. "Are mentalists the same as magicians? I mean, will your next-door neighbor be pulling rabbits out of hats or slicing people in half in his magic black box?"

Viv grinned. "Since I've never seen the show, I'm not sure. I've been to a few here at the casino over the years. You know, girls' night out kind of stuff."

"He's worked here on and off for years," Tamara said. "I've seen the posters at least."

The curtain began to rise as loud applause filled the room. When the noise died down, Viv leaned over to speak in Tamara's ear. "I heard him say he was retired, but apparently he changed his mind..."

"Overnight." Tamara's mouth twitched.

"Ladies and gentleman," came the voice from the loud-speaker. "Please give a warm welcome to Rex Re-don-do!"

Out came her next-door neighbor, looking debonaire in a three-piece gray suit and a beautiful cobalt-blue necktie. He stood before the audience, arms at his sides, taking a deep bow. From the back of the room Viv could see the sparkles cascading from the shoulders of his suit coat. *Did they sprinkle him with glitter?* He rose to his full height, looking much taller than in real life, and looked over the audience with a huge smile on his face.

He's bathing in the admiration. I wonder which one in the audience he'll pick first. Viv shrugged. "This should be good," she told Tamara.

Her friend's unwavering glance followed Rex Redondo as he stepped from the stage, standing in the main aisle, closer to his audience. His right arm stretched out.

"My assistant, Ms. Sutton Drew!" He lifted his right arm as applause filled the room. The spotlight looked over the aisles, finally stopping on the figure of a tall thin woman holding a microphone. Viv recognized her immediately as the person who brought the package for Miss Kitty. *Hey, wait a minute. That's the woman who sat in the back booth of The Roadkill.*

Sutton had changed into a skin-tight cobalt-blue dress, which matched Rex's necktie. The dress stopped mid-thigh, revealing toned tanned legs. Her hair lay against her shoulders, soft waves of red-gold. Long red nails gave a look of sophistication to her otherwise overly dramatic attire. *I wonder if she uses those press-on things? Her nail polish was green just a couple of hours ago.*

"She's really something," Tamara muttered in Viv's ear. "Do you think they're a couple?" Her eyebrows raised.

"I think she lives in his house," Viv concurred. "She came over with a gift earlier today."

"What kind of gift?"

Vivienne giggled. "Not what you might think. An automatic cat food dispenser for Miss Kitty."

Tamara laughed. "Not what I expected you to say." The applause grew louder as a woman in the middle of the theater stood. The spotlight found her as Rex Redondo began his reading.

"You've recently lost a loved one." His gentle smile exuded kindness. He leaned toward her. "I know you're worried about him, his name is..." He held a finger to his temple as if he were thinking. "Begins with the letter..."

The woman's eyes widened, as if she were willing Rex to get it right. Lifting the microphone toward the woman, Sutton also looked hopeful.

"The letter H," came Rex's resonating baritone.

"That's it! H!" All eyes locked onto Rex. Except for Viv's. She glanced around, wondering how he managed to keep everyone so interested in the name of a dead loved one. *I don't get why people come to these shows.*

Rex pointed to the woman. As all eyes looked to where he pointed, Viv saw him glance at a watch on his wrist. "Harley is the name I'm receiving."

"That's my brother!" came the woman's excited voice. "Is he here? Does he want to talk to me?" Tears ran down her cheeks, while Rex placed his finger on his temple and closed his eyes.

"I feel his presence. Yes, he's here." His voice shifted to a whisper. He held his outstretched thumbs and forefingers to both sides of his head. Silence filled the room as the audience fixed their eyes on him, waiting for his next words.

Viv turned to Tamara. In a loud voice she said, "Great show, don't you think?"

At that moment Redondo's eyes flew open.

Did he hear me?

He dropped his hands, staring at the back of the auditorium. "I know you are with us, Harley," he announced in a commanding voice. "Please know, I mean no harm." Then he closed his eyes again, holding his hands folded in front of his waist.

Tamara hissed in Viv's ear, "Everybody has to make a living somehow."

Rex's eyes flew open as he spoke directly to the woman in a soothing baritone. "You can stop crying," he told her. "Harley wants you to know he's sorry about the money."

The woman did a small jump. "He took all of my savings. I couldn't find any of it before he died."

"Don't worry," Rex repeated. "He says there will be more money coming and that he's sorry he left you so soon. But he'll be watching over you from..." Rex's finger made a slow ascent as he pointed to the ceiling. He held his hand up as the audience began to applaud.

"Did he just tell her that ol' Harley is now in heaven?" Tamara whispered loudly.

"That was the implication." Viv kept her eyes on the woman in the audience. Leaning over, she tried to see what was on the gold chain around her neck. "Here's what I think. I bet she's wearing a cross and that's how he knew she'd be a believer." She took Tamara's elbow. "I've seen enough. Let's go."

"Excuse me," she told the people to her left. "We have to leave." Avoiding stepping on toes, she slid her way to the aisle. Tamara came close behind. Pointing to the exit sign, Viv took one last glance toward the stage.

Rex's eyes followed her. She hurried to step closer to the exit as Sutton marched up the aisle toward her, the spotlight following right above. Sutton in the role of assistant waved at the audience.

"Just a minute," Redondo said. "A skeptic in the audience is leaving." The crowd began to shift uncomfortably.

His voice took on a more cajoling tone. "Please stay, just for a minute. I understand your doubts, but I have something for you."

Rex moved up the aisle, coming closer to where Viv stood. The people between them looked at her and then back to him. The spotlight stayed on Rex.

His assistant touched Viv's elbow, walking her past the seated people and bringing her closer to where Rex waited. Drawing closer, she noted his pancake makeup, the dots of perspiration on his forehead. Eyeliner emphasized the shape of his eyes. His eyebrows had been thickened with a dark gray pencil.

Overwhelmed by everyone's attention, Viv didn't resist. She smiled at Rex as if daring him to continue.

He's a charlatan, probably doesn't even know the truth. He's played people for so long he gets confused himself. What could he possibly know about me that he can pretend to read?

16

VIVIENNE ROSE

Viv glared at Rex. He stood so close she could smell his woodsy aftershave. She clenched her jaw, sending him another scowl. *I feel sorry for the people who come here. They have emotional needs and he's making money off their pain.*

More beads of perspiration stood on his brow. She detected a slight tremor in his right hand, which he held theatrically in front of him, fingers spread slightly apart. *Come on, buddy. You stopped me from leaving. What are you up to now?*

Speaking in a calm voice, he lifted one hand in the air, palm open, as if offering her a blessing. Had she been a churchgoer, she might have relaxed at this point, falling under the spell of his magnetism. But Viv had no experience with healings, nor was she the kind of woman to give up her inner reserve to play along. Never one to respond to the overtures of people wanting her approval, she stood her ground.

"I believe you've forgotten something..." He spoke quietly. "Something you've been missing and were worried about. Something no one else would know about except you, and maybe your friend." He nodded toward Tamara, who stood at the other end of the row away from the spotlight. Her eyes opened wide with anticipation.

Slipping his hand into the pocket of his jacket, he palmed an object. Holding his closed hand in front of her, he lifted one finger at a time.

"Your key." He smiled, opening his hand fully. "The one you thought you'd lost." She heard the crowd gasp as they waited for her affirmation. The tortoise charm glinted in the spotlight.

She leaned toward him, staring at his open palm. Snatching at the key, she gripped it in her hand. A shudder ran down her spine as someone in the audience called out, "Well, is it your key?"

Viv's eyes narrowed. *I can expose him as my next-door neighbor or I can play along just to get this over with.* "Oh my goodness," she said in a high voice, deliberately sounding fake. "It *is* my key. How clever of you to find it." She turned to the audience holding the key in the air. "He must be for real. How else would he have my special key on the tortoise chain?"

The audience cheered as Rex grinned. She dropped the key in her bag and turned on her heel. Moving past the knees of the people seated, she grabbed Tamara's hand. Only when the exit doors closed behind them did she stop to take a breath.

Tamara stared at her, eyes wide. Viv stared back, shrugging.

"So he had my house key," she said flatly.

"But how did he get it?"

"Probably picked it up that night he was over."

"Did he just steal it and then bring it tonight? He didn't know you'd be here to see his show. Kinda creepy!"

That one stumped her. She hadn't thought that far. "I

don't know how he knew that, but I do know that I'm having the locks changed first thing tomorrow."

"You can't be too safe nowadays," Tamara said, glancing toward Viv's purse. "You're certain it's the right one?"

"I'll try it in the lock when we get home."

17

REX REDONDO

Okay, so I had her key. Not sure why I even picked it up that night. With the cops circling and her deep in conversation, I saw the key next to a basket by the door. Okay, be honest, Rex. I wanted to know about Viv and holding her key would give me insights, both visual and auditory. At least that's how it's worked in the past.

Then Officer Farrah said something so I put it in my pocket. A habit I have. It's a thing we mentalists do. I knew it was wrong.

They call it psychometry. I pick up objects and work on stories to go with them. I'll hold the object and sense a vibrational imprint. Winding a story around an object makes my read more accurate. As I talk I watch a person's eyes and micro expressions for clues if I'm getting close to the truth.

All right, I'm feeling on shaky ground here. The moment I looked into her eyes I just felt like we knew each other. My memory started swirling and I found myself wanting to take care of her.

Sutton told me a month or so ago that a lot of women were coming and going next door. I didn't think a lot about it then.

Sutton also told me about the spare key under the rock next to her front porch.

In my defense I didn't bring the key to my show intentionally, I happened to have it with me. So maybe I was keeping it as a charm, just to hold on to something of Viv's. Did I just admit how crazy I am about her? Like a schoolboy. That's me.

Just so you know, preparation for my show includes some recognizance on Sutton's part. She sits in a back booth at The Roadkill and listens in to conversations with a special earpiece. She watches people. Experienced at seeing who she thinks will have a drink and then move on for the performance, she tunes in with her earpiece and then texts me random information, what they look like, and names if she can pick them up. Like what people are talking about. If they want to trick the mentalist. I love that one. We've always got a back-at-ya response to those people.

Anyway Sutton noticed Viv and her friend right away. She heard them talk about the missing key. And since I was the one who borrowed it without asking, I knew the perfect way to get it back to her. A surprise, if you will, for her and the audience.

I was taking a risk. I mean, Viv could have just walked out, which is what she tried to do. I wish she'd have stayed until after the show. We could have gone out for a drink and I could have apologized.

Wasn't she amazing at the show? It was all I could do not to run after her, to tell her how fantastic she was, playing right into my number. Tongue-in-cheek, I could hear her inner voice taunting me. "You're just a big silly fraud," she seemed to say. Her doubt just egged me on.

Most people are so mesmerized by me, they fall right into my spell, hoping what I say is true. They make their experience fit my impressions. But not Viv. She held her own, sized up her situation, and then ad-libbed. The key had to be a surprise. But she didn't overplay it. Impressive.

She told the audience the truth in tone of voice, that hint of sarcasm underneath...

She doesn't take me one bit seriously. What a turn-on. You gotta love that aplomb in a woman. She's just...amazing!

I take a makeup wipe from the box in the corner of my makeup table. Left eye first, then the right, then my eyebrows, and finally the rest of my face. With all my makeup now gone, I am exhausted. This is a young man's game.

And I have another problem. As exciting as Viv is, I'm pretty certain after the stunt I pulled tonight, she'll never fully trust me.

18

VIVIENNE ROSE

As soon as the hostess escorted her onto the patio, Viv spotted Pearl Overmann. She sat in the corner at a small round table. The seat across from her was empty.

"I see a friend over there," she told the hostess. "Give me a sec and I'll ask if I can join her." She walked past the crowded tables, stopping at her friend's table.

"Oh my gosh, I'm so happy to see you!" Pearl stood and gave Viv a hug. "Sit down...unless you're waiting for someone else."

"I'd love to sit with you. I'm only here for an iced tea and to make a few calls and catch up on email. Thought I'd get out of my house for a bit." She waved at the hostess and pulled out the chair. A few minutes later a waitress arrived to take her order.

"What will it be?" she asked in a soft voice.

"Maybe one of your blueberry muffins with the streusel topping?" Pearl said.

"Anything else?" The waitress tapped her iPad. "We also have a fresh pumpkin spice muffin with streusel topping. We're already baking for fall."

"Now that sounds perfect," Viv said immediately. "Bring on the pumpkin spice."

"I'll take the same instead of blueberry," added Pearl. "And a refill on this iced tea."

By the time the waitress returned, she balanced two oversized muffins and a glass pitcher of iced tea with lemon and orange slices floating on top.

Viv took her glass and reached across the table to toast with Pearl. Clinking the side of Viv's iced tea, she said, "It's not about the incense," and then Pearl added, "but about the common sense."

Both women laughed. Since becoming doulas, they'd adopted the saying and made it their own. One of the myths they learned to dispel was that doulas worked as spiritual guides using crystals and incense, rather than offering practical suggestions to improve the birth experience.

Viv spoke first. "So what brings you to Just Desserts this morning?"

Pearl looked over her shoulder. She put her glass down on the table, lowering her voice. "I was going to tell you eventually," she began. "But since you showed up unexpectedly, maybe it's a sign that now's the time. I'm in trouble, Viv. Big time. I don't know what to do and I need help."

Pearl's brown eyes filled with tears. She blinked and then brushed the wetness from her cheeks.

Viv inhaled quickly, waiting for the rest of the explanation. Running a doula agency had taught her that patience. Sometimes pausing gave the person permission to speak more truth.

Other than crying, Pearl looked her usual competent self. She wore her nails short and evenly clipped. Hair tied back in a ponytail, gray mingled with blonde. On the surface Pearl looked the same as always. Except for the circles under her eyes, a clue that something was not right.

Viv knew that most people appreciated Pearl's calm demeanor. All of her clients raved about her competent doula work, how she created a sense of ease and comfort for them during such a stressful time. In their monthly meetings, Pearl often waited until last to speak. If time ran out, she'd smile and say, "Maybe next time."

Viv was not too proud to admit that a big part of her doula practice's success was due to Pearl's competence and attitude. Until a year ago when everyone saw Pearl's life disintegrate, all because she got involved with the partner of one of her clients. During a postpartum evening visit the baby's father started up a conversation and one thing led to another...

If word got out about Pearl, Desert Doulas would be finished.

"So when we had our meeting a couple of days ago, I wasn't entirely forthcoming." Pearl's voice caught in her throat.

Viv nodded for her to continue.

"I've been following Dereck on Facebook. Then he messaged me out of the blue. I wrote him back and we kind of got together."

"How long has that been?" *Keep your cool, Viv.* All of her patience gone, she asked another question before Pearl had answered. "How long has this been going on?" Her heart began to thump.

"A few weeks...okay a couple of months. Maybe three." Pearl's eyes shifted to the right. Her face flushed. "I feel just terrible, but he came after me. I unfriended him after he tried to talk to me the first time. Then he made up a false Facebook profile. I thought he knew another friend of mine, so I accepted his friend request, and then later he messaged to explain."

Pearl sighed. "So he kept pestering me to meet up with him. He said he loved me and wanted to be with me."

Viv kept her focus on Pearl's face without speaking. *I'm afraid she's falling down the same rabbit hole again, reconnecting with him. She's making this his fault and not taking responsibility.* She shifted in her seat, the anxiety making her squirm.

Pearl looked up and then down. "Aren't you going to say anything?"

"I'm listening for now." She took a sip of iced tea.

"So I said okay, you know, about the meetup." She took a deep breath. "And we ended up in bed. Just the once." She looked into Viv's eyes. "Okay, more than once."

More tears flooded Pearl's eyes just as her phone pinged. Viv looked to the phone to see Dereck's name flashed on the screen.

Pearl picked it up and silenced the call. "He wants to meet me here."

Viv drew her words out carefully. "So he wants to have lunch with you in the town where his family lives, including his wife, other children, and a young baby—"

"But you've got to understand," interrupted Pearl. "He wants to come clean with his wife. He thinks he can explain to Lauren that this—our relationship—happened unexpectedly and that he wants to provide for their kids but that he wants a divorce."

Viv let Pearl's words settle. She took a deep breath, staring at the muffin the waitress had placed in front of her. *If something like this gets out, Desert Doulas may be over for me. People would be afraid to place their trust in our services.*

"This is not what I ever expected would happen to me.

Getting involved with the father of a new baby. I thought I was level-headed and knew what to do." She dabbed at her eyes.

"Have a bite of muffin," Viv offered. "We're gonna sort this out together. But first, text him and tell him you cannot meet at the cafe. It's ridiculous. It's as if he wants to get caught. If he's seen and someone tells Lauren, then it's all out in the open. She'll kick him out, saving him the problem of abandoning his family."

Pearl's eyes widened. "Do you think he's deliberately sabotaging his marriage, using me as an excuse?"

"I don't know for certain," Viv admitted. "But Dereck would not be the first man to make a mess, leaving it for the women to clean up."

Pearl picked up her phone. She tapped in a text and hit send. "I'm not going to wait for a reply." She slipped the phone into her purse.

The waitress walked past, and Viv called out, "Could we have the lunch menu? I think we'll be here for a while longer."

"Be right back," she said.

Viv reached across the table to take Pearl's hand. She spoke in a low voice. "You feel guilty for a good reason. But let's not forget. Vulnerability is a sign of doula burnout. You know it happens frequently due to the nature of our work. We're always on call. We come at highly sensitive times, when a family has a baby. Clients can be very needy and at times demanding."

Pearl nodded, biting her bottom lip.

Her chest tightened. *What can I do? If I come down on Pearl she may stop talking to me; then I'll be even more in the dark about my doula's behavior. Better keep it lighthearted until I figure out what I need to do to save Pearl and my company.*

She took a deep breath. "So you're not immune to vulnerability. Dereck was attracted to you. Unlike his wife, you're competent and independent. Let's figure a way out and then we can talk more."

Pearl nodded. "I do feel better now that it's out in the open."

And I'm left feeling horrible. How is that fair?

The waitress arrived with two menus. Before she could set them down, a loud voice came from the entrance. "I want to sit right there."

Viv glanced over. A tall man dressed in a tank top and shorts with worn sandals glared at the hostess. His strong arms, tanned and muscled, accentuated the belligerent stance, arms folded in front of his chest. He nodded in their direction.

He brushed off the waitress to stride across the cafe, heading straight toward their table. "Why didn't you take my call?" His voice sounded rough, intense with anger. He placed a threatening hand on Pearl's shoulder.

Viv stood. "Hello, my name is Vivienne Rose. I'm the owner of Desert Doulas." She stuck out her hand. He glared at her. She'd deliberately misdirected his anger with her introduction, hoping a public outburst was not his plan.

Viv continued. "Grab another chair. We're just ordering lunch. I know I spoke to you on the phone when you were looking for a doula. How are baby and mother doing? Maybe I could stop in for a visit just to say hello."

Dereck's entire body deflated, as if pricked by a pin. He dropped his grip from Pearl's shoulder. His face flushed as he looked at Viv more closely.

He'd started to cause this scene, but Viv had taken control, directing his energy away from Pearl. She handed him her menu. Fortunately a man from a nearby table called over, "I have an extra chair." He pulled it over to their table and went back to his own.

"Sit with us," Viv told Dereck.

With a huff he sat down and then slumped back in his chair. He no longer looked quite as imposing. More like a moody teen than a man about to upend his family.

Viv wanted to ask him to take off his cap, but she decided it would only make things worse. She looked him over and then realized, *He's wearing his hair pulled back in a scrunchy. Why do man buns irritate me so?*

The waitress arrived to take their order, smiling at Dereck. "What will you have, sir?"

"A burger and fries with a large piece of your chocolate cake."

The waitress nodded. Viv ordered a chicken sandwich. When Pearl didn't pick up the menu, Viv intervened. "Make that two chicken sandwiches."

Pearl's demeanor had changed. She looked frightened, her hands under the table, avoiding Viv's gaze. The waitress returned with a fresh pitcher of iced tea.

"Ready for refills?" she asked.

19

VIVIENNE ROSE

While all three sat in silence, the waitress left their orders on the table.

"I'm not hungry. You can have my sandwich," Pearl muttered under her breath. Then she stood and grabbed her purse, heading toward the front of the cafe.

Dereck made a move to follow her, but Viv intervened. "Let her go," she told him. "By the way, how is your new baby?"

He scowled, glancing toward the exit where Pearl's back was still disappearing from view. Phone in hand, he nervously punched in a text. Once he hit send, Viv kept talking.

"New mothers can be depressed. How is your wife doing?"

He pushed against the table, ignoring her question.

"Sit down, Dereck," she said with authority. "You're not going after my doula—unless, of course, you want me to make a police report. It feels more like harassment, not so much a mutual attraction."

When she locked eyes with him he humphed, sitting back into the chair. "You can't arrest a guy for finding someone attractive. It's mutual."

Unfazed, Viv responded calmly, "Nice try. Nastiness

doesn't get under my skin, nor does toxic masculinity." She held up her phone. "I have the Palm Desert police right here." *The longer I keep him talking, the more of a chance Pearl will have to get away.*

"You can't threaten me!"

Viv smiled. "Looks like I just did."

A man dressed in a suit and open-collared white shirt stood in the doorway between the outdoor and indoor cafe. He stared straight at their table.

When Viv gave a slight nod, he walked over.

"I'm the Just Desserts manager. Is everything okay over here?" He had that bland expression people get when they know full well everything isn't okay.

"My lunch companion is having a bad day," Viv explained. "But I think he's better now. Isn't that right, Dereck?" She turned to him as if requiring an answer.

"I want my bill," Dereck said loudly.

Now it was Viv's turn to stand. "Thanks for offering to pick up our tab." She flipped her purse over her shoulder and made her way to the exit. The manager stepped aside as she passed by.

Once she sat in her parked car, Viv decided on her next step. *I'll call Pearl later to check up, but right now I'm going to make a visit to the Palm Desert police.* Starting her engine, she put her car into gear and backed out of the space. *I still haven't heard from Officer Farrah.*

Arriving ten minutes later, she pulled into a parking space in front of the adobe police precinct. Once inside the door, a uniformed cop greeted her from behind the desk.

"May I help you?"

"I'm here to see Officer Farrah."

"May I ask what is the nature of your inquiry?"

"They found a dead body in my backyard. Officer Farrah

wanted me to come in to answer a few more questions to help with the investigation. I haven't heard from her, so I thought I'd stop by."

"Sit down over there and I'll ask the chief." She pointed to a row of chairs against the opposite wall.

Viv sat down and looked at the photos on the wanted board. In a few minutes the woman called out, "He'll see you now."

At that moment an officer came in the front door grasping the elbow of another man who looked familiar.

"You can stay in holding while you calm down," the police officer warned. "I'll be right back."

Viv blinked. She knew she'd seen him, but she couldn't remember when and where. He wore flip-flops and sloppy shorts with a t-shirt. He looked very tan and thin, his arms muscled, an LA baseball cap pulled down over his eyes. He slumped over in a chair, staring at his knees.

Her eyes grew wide. *That's the guy who serviced my pool.*

She stood up, walking toward the front desk. "Is this the way?"

"Yes, the chief is the first door on the right. He's expecting you."

Once Viv was in the hallway she followed the sign with the arrow reading "Chief." She knocked and peered through the narrow glass panel.

"Come in," came a deep voice. She opened the door.

He sat behind his desk. "Ms. Rose? Have a seat."

She sat down facing the chief across his desk, her back to the door.

"Would you mind shutting the door?" he asked.

She got up and complied, then sat back down. "I'm Vivi-enne Rose and I've come to talk to Officer Farrah."

"That's what I've been told." His voice sounded tired. "I'm

sorry to say we haven't gotten any further on the investigation. You see"—he leaned over to look at her more closely—"Officer Farrah has taken a leave of absence. Right after she interviewed you the other day. Anything to say about that?"

Somehow she wasn't surprised. The officer seemed unfocused when they'd last spoken. Viv shook her head.

He tapped the desk with his fist. "She didn't tell me the problem, but she mentioned something about her personal life." He cleared his throat. "But Officer Farrah left a message for you. Something you said started her thinking. So now I'm down a good officer."

Then he added, "This may be awhile, until she comes back." He scowled.

Viv looked around the desk for a name. "Captain Waldo Wilson." She cleared her throat. "I know you blame me for Officer Farrah's decision. But I do appreciate you sharing her message. Of course I wish Officer Farrah the best on her journey, but I do want to know what you're doing about the investigation.

"A woman—a colleague and my friend—was found dead in my pool," Viv continued. "Surely you have another officer to take up the case."

His face clouded over. "Officer Farrah is one of my best. I can give her the leave of absence she needs," he assured her.

"At great inconvenience to you and the department," Viv said sweetly.

"Yes, ma'am," he said, nodding. "I let my irritation get the better of me. I have two other people on the force, only they aren't trained as detectives. But I can call in help from another precinct. Let me get on that and I'll get back to you."

He turned his swivel chair to face a small table that held his computer. "You can go now," he muttered over his shoulder.

The sound of fingers tapping on the computer followed her out the door.

Once outside the precinct, Viv took a quick breath. *It's nearly two o'clock. I have one more errand before going home. Maybe then I can answer my messages and get to my email. After that...siesta time.*

She felt drips of perspiration making their way down her spine. *It's so hot! Plus I'm getting impatient. I want this case solved before it gets swept under the carpet.* She felt her exasperation tightening her chest. *Okay, that's it. I'm not going to wait for the cops. Maybe it's time for me to get more involved.*

Irritated and hot, in that moment she decided to become her own investigator. It felt good to take charge, though she knew quite well she had no authority to do so.

On the drive home Viv considered the next step. *Sarah had a sister. I think she listed her as an emergency contact. I can start by calling her to see if there will be a memorial service.*

20

REX REDONDO

I could have slept better, but I kept thinking about Viv and the key and how she probably thinks I'm some kind of maniac. The way I pulled it out of thin air last night, just a ridiculous stunt.

This insecurity around women isn't my usual. Not that I'm bragging, understand, but in the past? Since I was in third grade and took my girlfriend out for an ice cream, I've known my way around females. I've always had good luck with the opposite sex, and if I say so myself, I've been pretty successful.

But with Vivienne Rose... Even her name makes my heart beat faster. I'm second-guessing myself all the time with that woman.

I usually don't have to try this hard. I mean, not that I'm as good-looking as some. Okay, I have aged well. I keep fit. Get a little Botox now and then. I'm in show biz and it's expected.

I know I'm vain, or at least I've been told that before. My last girlfriend accused me of spending more time in front of the mirror than she did. That was an exaggeration. She was twenty-two and believe me, she had a lot to appreciate when she took the time to get ready.

But back to Viv. I don't know what to do next. If I wait for her to initiate talking, it may never happen. She's got that polite aloof way about her, as if she's pretending I don't matter. Maybe it's not pretending. From her perspective I'm probably the lunatic neighbor and that's it.

I hear a knock. Someone's at the bedroom door.

"Come in!"

It must be Sutton.

"Here's your coffee and orange juice." She puts it on a table out of reach and then stands beside my bed. "I assume you want to have your usual steam after that—"

"Sounds good." I cut her off to admire her outfit.

Today Sutton wears short-shorts and a halter top, her hair tied in a bun at the nape of her neck. Her false eyelashes blink rapidly over bright blue eyes. Sometimes her eyes look more blue, depending on her contacts.

I sit up and rest against the headboard. "You having lunch with a cowboy?" I nod at her attire, including the pair of red boots with heels.

She smiles. "There's a horse show in town, a Palm Springs annual event."

"In this heat?"

"Oh they air condition the competition tents. Very chichi, with lots of Hollywood types attending."

"I didn't know you went for that sort of thing."

"I don't usually, but I met a guy last night who owns a thoroughbred and I thought I'd show up."

Sometimes I wonder how we have stayed together for so long. We met in the military, both of us marines. She was a lieutenant, an intelligence specialist like me. During the early years of Afghanistan, I worked with the intel team. We kidded a lot but kept our distance. Fraternizing between officers of a different rank is frowned upon. Plus if you're found out, you can be discharged.

As a major I had a little rank on her, but we got along instantly despite the rank and age difference. In case you haven't guessed, Sutton is sassy and very smart. And she's gorgeous.

The first time we worked together, I noticed that we had the same keen eye for detail and that we liked to laugh. She got me through those couple of years. Please understand, we never hooked up. Stayed in the friend zone and frankly, I'm glad.

Once we were both out of the military we decided to work together. I have enough dough to pay her a lot to be my personal assistant. A few boundaries and we get along great.

I yawn and stretch. "Maybe your interests will work in my favor. I wonder if my next-door neighbor would agree to going to the races in Del Mar with me. I'd welcome a weekend at the beach. A casual invite. Nothing fancy."

Sutton shakes her head. "Fat chance she'll say yes after last night. She didn't look that happy when you pulled her house key out of midair."

My heart plummets. "I saw her face. It was too much, me calling her down as part of the show. I should have known better. But you convinced me!"

I glare at Sutton and pause to think for a minute. It was fun to see the surprise on Viv's face last night. But it would have been better just to hand her the key and make an excuse. I found it on the ground. I put it in my pocket. I forgot about it until later. That would have been more reasonable.

Sutton smirks. "You couldn't pass up a chance to show off, could you? But now you're not on her good neighbor list. I'm pretty certain of that. Since you reported to the cops about that body in the pool. And you kept her house key and forced a private woman, most likely an introvert, to stand in front of a crowd as if she's part of the show."

I shrug. "What was I thinking?" I use a light voice and hold my hands up Lucille Ball fashion.

"Drink your liquids and take a steam." Sutton spins on her heel to leave the room.

Then she comes back. "I'll help you figure out what to do about Viv later. Right now I have to read up on horse shows. I want to impress my date with vapid chatter and my vast store of all things horse." Sutton turns and walks out, leaving the bedroom door open to the hall.

There's nothing Sutton cannot figure out, especially if she has access to the internet. She researches everything, spends tons of time doing deep dives into obscure topics. I can lose her for hours while she takes notes and types.

And I have to admit I've asked her to do a bit of research on my private clients for my psychic readings. I meet all sorts at the casino. Before I invest, I want a background check. You know it's not all legal, but we both can get in and out of a person's email so fast, no one notices. But then I have all the details, the names of relatives and lost pets. More importantly Sutton has a way of finding out who is having an affair or cheating on a spouse in some other way. Often it's financial.

"Sutton!" I call out to her.

She comes back again, this time sporting a cowboy hat with her outfit, dyed red to match her boots. "What's up, boss?"

"Would you check into the dead woman's internet history? Sarah Esperanza."

"Already did," she says calmly. "Like I said, I'll fill you in later. But before that?" She steps quickly, making way for a running ball of fluff streaking the distance between the door and the bed. Kevin leaps and then begins to dig at the covers. I lean over to give him a shove.

"Off the bed, mangy mutt. I paid five grand to have you trained and this is what I get?"

He spins around with a "bork, bork," as his comeback. He mocks me, ducking down over his front paws, his butt in the air.

"I'm not playing with you," I groan. Am I ever going to get out of this bed?

"Don't forget to walk the dog," Sutton tells me over her shoulder. "He's all yours until this evening."

"But I haven't even taken my steam."

When she doesn't come back, nor seem to care, I sit up, putting my feet on the floor. Kevin jumps off the bed to sniff my toes. I scratch behind his ears, so he sits at attention.

I have a lot of questions about Viv and the investigation.

Like is Viv more of a friend or a colleague with the dead woman? And why was Sarah at Viv's house all alone?

What was the actual cause of death? Maybe she tripped and hit her head on something hard and then fell into the pool...

And even if all of that can be answered, there is still the question that's most important.

Why would anyone want to kill a doula?

21

VIVIENNE ROSE

A steaming bowl of rice topped with ahi, ponzu sauce, freshly grated carrots, and broccoli sat on the kitchen counter. Viv smirked, noting her dinner looked very similar to Miss Kitty's one-dish meal. She poured herself a glass of Chardonnay. Taking the glass and the bowl to the table, she sat down.

Eight o'clock was her usual dinner hour. She used to eat earlier, but the desert climate dictated her appetite more than she'd like to admit. In August the sun began its descent after eight. The temperature would drop, but more importantly the oncoming darkness made it feel cooler.

She felt her energy return as the temperature descended.

After eating, Viv rinsed her bowl and put it in the dishwasher. She poured a little more wine into her glass and then opened the sliding door to the backyard. The pool illuminated the darkness; the palm fronds waved in the desert breeze, throwing shadows over the deck. Relaxing in her chair with her feet up, she pulled her phone from her pocket to check her messages. Her heart beat quickly when she saw the call she'd missed. She tapped redial and a woman's voice answered, "Hello?"

"This is Vivienne Rose."

"Hello, I'm Sarah's sister, Aida Rodrigues. I got your message."

"I want to say first how sorry I am for your loss. We, all of her doula family, will miss Sarah so much. How is everything going with you and the family?" Viv used her professional voice: calm, matter of fact, low.

"I'm okay, I guess. Such a shock. I never imagined my sister would die so young."

"Have you heard from your nephew?"

"Timmy is with his father. He came right over and gathered all of Timmy's belongings and took him away."

Viv heard her sniff.

"He'll let you see Timmy now and then I hope."

"George hasn't called me since her death. I hope he reaches out soon, before Timmy forgets that he has a family."

Viv took a minute to give Aida a chance to compose herself. Then she said, "I'd like to get information about any memorial service and to send a condolence card to you and... Did Sarah have a boyfriend by chance?"

"Oh, Zach is around now and then. They started a business together a couple of months ago. She wouldn't say what the business was about, but she was certainly stressed."

"Ma!" came a voice in the background.

"I have to go now. I'll text you those addresses." The phone clicked.

Viv sighed. She looked up at the stars filling the sky. One of her favorite things about desert living was the night sky. Cloudless, without a cover, the constellations glittered brightly.

She looked toward Rex Redondo's backyard. Through the fence she saw a glow, most likely from a firepit. Many people in the desert gathered around a pit in the evening to watch the stars.

A low conversation floated her way, but she couldn't distinguish who was speaking. *Maybe my neighbor has company.* Surprised at her own curiosity, she continued to wonder. *He won't go in to work for another couple of hours.*

Her thoughts drifted back to the phone call with Sarah's sister. Aida wasn't much help. *I wonder what kind of business Sarah started with her new boyfriend? I wish I knew his last name so that I could do an internet search.*

Her eyes drifted to the shimmering water in the pool. The faint smell of bromine wafted into the air. A slight ripple against the water's surface caught her attention. The filter gave a particularly loud slurp. *I hope it's not clogged. I'll have to call the guy.*

The ripples pulled toward the corner. A sucking sound reminded her of gargling. She stood up. *What's in that drain?*

Stepping closer to the edge of the pool, she saw a long leaf clogging the drain. She moved closer. Not a leaf, but a small lizard.

The lizard struggled, twisting against the pull of the water. Viv hurried alongside the pool toward the deep end. She bent over the side looking for the lizard. "There he is!" Floating toward the drain, his tail had separated from his body. Before she could reach into the water, both disappeared, sucked out of sight.

Her chest heaved. *I haven't really cried since Sarah was found. What's the matter with me anyway?* The pit of discouragement and sadness felt insurmountable, like a huge boulder lodged in her gut. After holding it back for days, the lizard's struggle brought everything back for Viv. Hands over her chest, she cried. *Poor Sarah. Isn't that the way. Sometimes no matter how hard you try, you just get sucked in and spiral out of control.*

22

REX REDONDO

I don't work Tuesdays, so my routine is a bit different. Without a gig at the casino, I'm feeling a bit restless. Usually by midnight I can turn off Netflix and get some sleep. Been watching the *Lethal Weapon* series and finally finished; don't want to start another show.

I see myself as a Mel Gibson type. His height and build and a whole lot of crazy. Of course my crazy can be shed like a cheap suit when necessary. I can also come off as a professor. A jacket with elbow patches, glasses, and a necktie. Wrinkle my brow and voila! We have Harvard or at the very least an uptight Berkeley vibe.

With the internet I've become a semi expert on nearly any topic. Sutton and I have gone down some real rabbit holes together, researching for my show. Enough of that. Time to go outside now that the temperature's dropping. I'll grab a beer.

The night's illuminated by a full moon. So peaceful out here; still hot though.

Sutton and I talked before we moved into this place about how we wanted to decorate and landscape. Most of the neighbors have swimming pools. I'm not a water fan, but I do like the night sky and a firepit.

If neither of us have plans, Sutton and I meet in the back-yard around the pit, put our feet up, and enjoy the silence. Maybe it reminds us of the old days, the nights we spent at Camp Shocker shooting the breeze.

I hear noises from the kitchen. Sutton comes through the sliding door. She has another IPA in her hand. "Want one?" she asks.

"Sure, and I'm ready for some intel."

When she returns she hands me the bottle and then sits down in a nearby chair. Propping her bare feet on the concrete fire ring, she takes a long pull off her beer. Her hair flows around her shoulders, over the light caftan she's put on. I don't suppose there's much underneath, but frankly I'm not interested. Sutton and I, like I said before, have never taken our relationship to that level. We're just pals. And colleagues. I don't know what I'd do without her intel for my mentalist act. She's way beyond capable.

"Anything on Sarah Esperanza?" I prompt her.

"Not much. I did hack into the police report with a little back-channel finagling."

"Gone rogue?" I made sure the admiration sounded in my voice. "What did you find out?"

"She fell and hit her head on the large boulder. There's a three-inch gash on the side of her head. After that, she may have fallen into the water or was pushed. They found the print in the sand by the pool shed. One flip-flop, that's it."

"Man- or woman-sized?"

"Size 11, could be either man or woman. No trace elements on the flip-flop. It had been doused with chlorine bleach."

"Like dipped in the pool water?"

"Except the pool uses bromine. The bleach came from another source."

I feel my gut twist. What a terrible way to go. "Did the killer leave any evidence?"

"They checked the pool carefully. After it drained they took samples and they cleaned the drain too. Lots of particles. The DNA was from Sarah Esperanza, the deceased, and Vivienne Rose."

"No one else?"

"Nope."

"So nothing in the report about Viv having a boyfriend or a girlfriend?"

"Really? We have a dead body here, boss. Maybe you should get your mind off the neighbor next door and think about that."

I feel Sutton's disdain. Not sure I can blame her. I am weak. Let's admit that I get preoccupied at times. I can't see Sutton's face clearly in the dark, but I can feel her irritation even more so. She's very intuitive. Sometimes I ask myself, who's the mentalist here?

"Okay, so I'm an inquisitive bastard."

"You're just obsessed."

"She's quite something."

"Don't you usually go for the younger ones?" Sutton knows me too well.

"Did she ever say thank you for the cat feeder?"

"Nope. Feelings hurt?"

I take a sip of my beer. "I took Viv for one of those old-fashioned kind of women who always says thank you. So yes, in answer to your question, I am slightly annoyed that she didn't say thank you."

Another swig of beer and I ask, "Do we need to send something else? Maybe a gift basket of gourmet kitty treats?"

"Stop trying so hard, boss. You've got to find another way."

The fingers in my left hand begin to tingle. I rub my forefinger and thumb together, remembering how I held the key in my hand the night of the performance. "I don't have her key anymore. Can't use it as an excuse to drop by her house."

But when I held the key, I got a glimpse into Viv. The key told me a lot about her emotions. They don't come easily to her, like other women. A few images came up. The cat, of course, but also of Viv huddling over the computer and on the phone at all hours. Burnout. It must have happened a while back. Viv is recovering. Maybe that's why she isn't dating. I tell Sutton what I felt holding the key.

Sutton sounds confused. "I didn't realize you actually got vibes from objects. I thought you were just acting, you know, playing a role."

To be fair I've always known that the mentalist persona was an act. I've perfected it over the years. But lately, now that I'm retiring, I'm wondering if I've acted for so long, I'm believing it myself, that I can hear voices from the dead, read people's minds, and get, as Sutton would say, "vibes."

"I'm retiring, remember?"

"You say you're retiring or that you're retired all the time. Yet you continue to work six nights a week, pop out double shows on the weekend. Is retiring part of your act, or are you actually going to toss in the towel and quit?"

Once again Sutton points out the obvious. "I can't get away with anything around you."

"True." She stands. "Want another?" She holds up her empty beer bottle.

"Why not?"

As she heads to the house, I think about what she's said.

I've been claiming retirement, but I'm still in the game. I guess I'm tired of people treating me like some kind of freak show. It's okay on stage, but it's hard to keep friends when they all want to be read. Or even worse, they tippy-toe around my feelings for fear I'll dig into their deep dark past in retaliation.

This detective thing, even if it's mostly in my imagination, is intriguing. With Sutton's help I can still be a mentalist by day and Sam Spade by night.

The flames from the pit shimmer in the dark. I lean forward to turn down the gas, sitting back in my chair. A *ding-dong* comes from inside the house. Who's coming over at this time of night?

It has to be nearly one a.m. I've been sitting outside that long. I wait for Sutton to answer the door.

A rustle comes from behind, as the door slides open. The scent of hibiscus drifts toward me, light and sweet, making my heart race. Could it be?

I turn in the chair. Sutton's one hand grasps three beer bottles by the neck. Her other hand gestures to the firepit. "Come on in. I'll get you a chair."

My dream manifests right before my eyes.

Vivienne Rose walking toward me, a gentle smile on her sweet lips.

23

VIVIENNE ROSE

Rex Redondo stood, teeth glinting in the darkness. "Hello, neighbor. What brings you here this evening?" He sounded delighted, more than an unannounced drop-in at one o'clock in the morning warranted.

These late hours may be normal for him. "I need some advice," she said at once. *No use beating around the bush. I'm not here to chitchat.*

She walked closer to the firepit, staring into the flames, gathering her thoughts. Looking up, she noticed Sutton. Face washed clean of makeup, her hair up in a high ponytail, she looked relaxed wearing a sheer fabric caftan. *Nice figure. Is she a live-in girlfriend? Why is my jaw tightening? Not like I care. Rex Redondo is as good as a Hollywood actor. Everyone knows what they're like.*

"Can I get you a beer?" Sutton asked.

Viv turned to nod and then noticed that Sutton already held three bottles in her hand.

"Here you go."

I guess I'm staying for a drink.

"Thank you." Viv took the bottle and then glanced around

for a chair. Rex, still on his feet, pulled one up to the firepit, closer to him than to Sutton. "Prop your feet up. Take a look at the stars. It's beautiful tonight." Not taking his own advice, he kept staring at her.

Viv noted that he no longer sounded surprised. *He's so calm and assured, as if women drop in unannounced all the time.* She sat down and raised her bottle. "To neighbors," she said and then took a sip. Sutton handed Rex a beer and sat down on Viv's right. Rex took the bottle and clinked Viv's before he took his seat.

"To neighbors," both Sutton and Rex echoed. Sutton closed her eyes, leaning her head back against the chair, the bottle hanging from the fingers of one hand.

Rex spoke up, his voice slightly teasing. "Did Miss Kitty get my gift?"

"She loves that thing!" Viv felt grateful to him for bringing up a safe topic. She'd come to pick his psychic brain, but it didn't pay to be unkind and rush right into questions.

"Is that why you're here, to thank me for Miss Kitty?"

She swallowed a sip of the IPA. "You read minds, so you must know that's not the only reason. I need help."

He cleared his throat. She watched the fire cast a light over his face. Even in the dim light she sensed that his body tensed.

"I just learned that the police have stopped investigating Sarah's murder," Viv started. "Officer Farrah took an unexpected leave of absence. I don't think they were going to tell me, except that I dropped into the Palm Desert precinct. The captain told me that he's looking for another cop to head up the investigation. Not enough people to go around, I guess."

"A government shortage," responded Rex.

"I'm not going to sit back and wait for the police. I decided to do some investigating on my own. And since you were there the night they discovered Sarah, I thought we could talk and see if we noticed any clues. You seem to have a knack for getting into other people's business, and I know you have that psychic gift."

Rex cleared his throat. "Despite what I do in my show, I don't consult with the dead. So if that's what you think you need, I want to be honest. I can't pull your friend out of a hat like a bunny and ask her what happened." He sounded disappointed in himself.

"Oh, I know that!" she assured him. "If you even mentioned talking to Sarah from the great beyond, I'd run right back home. I guess what I'm wondering, at least at first, is how you came to have my house key. That would be a good place to start."

Viv's question floated in the air. Sutton coughed as if to push back a laugh. Then she broke the silence. "He picked it up that night, when the cops arrived. They totally focused on you, giving Rex a chance to grab and go. I can't take him anywhere. He's always snagging small things and stuffing them into his pocket to use at one of his shows."

"What do you mean?" Viv asked, perplexed.

Rex explained, "It's called psychometry. People believe that the objects you encounter have stories to tell, or that the one who owned the object leaves a vibrational imprint. So I practice my act by picking up the imprints in unfamiliar locations. A matchbook here, a key there. I've done it for years. Nothing that fancy really, just a bit of imagination and a willingness to connect."

"But you must have known the key would be important to the police investigation!"

Rex shifted in his seat. "I figured the key was important to you." He cleared his throat again and then very calmly stated, "And I wanted an excuse to see you again. So it was personal."

She felt herself flush, feeling the full intent of his words. *I guess he's not going to disguise his feelings.*

"I hope you realize that could sound really creepy."

"I know, I know. I'd feel the same if I were you. But I returned the key, didn't I? You got it back in just a few days."

"But you didn't know I'd be at your show! How long would you have kept it had I not arrived that night?"

Rex cleared his throat, responding with less authority. "I get what you're saying. But just so you know," he said, shifting to the soothing voice often used for a small child or a frightened animal, "I regretted taking the key as soon as I got home. I was hoping the gift for Miss Kitty would lead to our getting to know each other. Then I'd come over and put the key back. You'd have found it eventually."

He did send over the gift before the show. Okay, so he may be speaking the truth. I just don't know what to think of him. But I'm not gonna judge him and write him off. At least not yet.

"My neighbors in the past were more conventional. Lawyers, doctors, tech traders. I've never lived next door to a charlatan and casino performer," she teased.

Rex laughed.

Viv felt relief as even Sutton guffawed. "Oh my God, you nailed Rex in one, and to his face. Beautiful." Sutton raised her beer bottle in the air.

"I am a charlatan," Rex admitted. "But rarely am I called one to my face. So now we know two things. I don't pull dead people out of a hat and I am not above taking a small item with me just for fun."

Viv felt more and more relaxed. *It may be the beer, but I think it's the company.* She turned her head to look at Rex through the darkness. "You're the real deal, only you're not. You're someone who tricks people for a living. But then a beer in hand, you tell them to their faces that you've tricked them."

"That's me," Rex admitted.

"That's him," added Sutton.

Loud barking came from inside the house.

"What's that?" exclaimed Viv.

Sutton stood. Viv heard her walk across the pavement. A door slid open, just in time for the patter of paws dashing across the patio. The dog leapt onto Viv's lap. She wrapped her arms around him, feeling a rough tongue lick her chin.

"Down, Kevin," roared Rex. "Where are your manners?" He stood and reached over to take the dog by his collar. He took the moment to stare at Viv. "Did he hurt you?"

"Just surprised me, that's all."

"Kevin is a gift from Sutton." He leaned over to pat the squirming dog, clutching his collar firmly in the other hand. "She thinks I need company. So now I have a hobby, which is feeding and walking Kevin." Rex sounded exasperated.

"Perfect for Rex. Low maintenance." Sutton defended her choice. "Especially since I do all the work, including picking up the poop. Kevin sleeps with him, but that's about all."

"Not true." Rex leaned over to pat Kevin on the head again. "I'm teaching him tricks. He's getting good too. Sit, Kevin."

The dog spun on his back legs and sat down in front of Rex.

Rex pulled something from his pocket. "I keep treats on me for impromptu training lessons." He held the treat in the palm of his hand. "Good boy." He lowered his hand and the dog quickly took it in his mouth.

"Hey, not so rough." Rex checked his fingers for damage. "At least he's getting the idea." He glanced at Viv. "Sorry he jumped on you."

She held out her hand. "May I have a treat?" Rex handed her one from his pocket and then dropped Kevin's collar.

She called, "Kevin," in a quiet voice.

The dog, raising his nose in the air, inched closer to Viv.

"Sit," she said.

He sat down at her feet.

She held her closed fist in front of her, then opened her hand to expose the treat. Kevin looked at her, drool dropping from the side of his mouth.

"Stay," she warned him.

The dog watched as she slid her thumb over the top of the treat and then lowered her hand in front of her knee. "Okay," she said.

He bounced forward to take the treat, sitting back down. He looked at Viv adoringly.

Viv turned to Rex. "It's all in the placement of the thumb. It stops him from biting on available fingers."

"I see." His voice, filled with deep consideration, sounded like a schoolboy who'd just been told the answer to an algebraic equation.

Kevin looked from Rex to Viv and then Sutton. Then he yipped, jumping up on his back paws.

"Not now," Sutton muttered.

The dog yipped again. When no more commands or treats were forthcoming, he took off running, disappearing into the dark. Viv heard him racing across the pavement around the yard, until he brushed past her legs, around the firepit, to disappear into the dark again.

"Time for zoomies," Rex said, sitting back down in his chair.

Viv's eyes followed the dog, appreciating his energy as Kevin ran around and around the yard. He came to a skidding halt in front of Sutton, plopping himself at her feet.

Viv watched, keeping her thoughts to herself. *Rex Redondo is a character. Sutton knew him well enough to get him a dog. Should I go now?*

If she stayed, then she could try talking about the case again and quite possibly open herself up to a deeper friendship. If she left, no harm no foul.

It had been ages since she'd made a new friend, let alone two who lived next door. It would be a risk. They may have a disagreement and then it would be awkward. They'd have to be polite afterward. But what if they got along...and what if Rex and Sutton helped her discover who murdered Sarah?

Viv took a deep breath. She stopped the internal debate by propping her feet against the firepit.

"So tell me, are you two all in for my whodunit?"

24

VIVIENNE ROSE

The next morning Viv's eyes gradually opened. She reached her hand over to grab her cell from the nightstand. It was nine o'clock and there were already seven text messages from clients. Getting a late start was Viv's idea of a bad day already unfolding.

She depended on her routine, rising at six a.m., swimming early, showering, and dressing. Then she'd answer her messages and talk to people. Sometimes she made appointments and scheduled with the doulas on her staff.

That was Viv's idea of a good day unfolding.

She hadn't always been so regimented. It was when she had the breakdown that she'd become more of a compartmentalizer. Part of that change was to downsize and move. Put her feelings aside instead of getting bogged down. The life coach helped her realize the importance of taking small steps in a timely way. It reduced her anxiety and she no longer felt like she was running without reaching the finish line.

All right, stop worrying. If you tell yourself it will be a bad day just because it didn't start how you wanted, then you'll most likely miss a good day because you aren't looking for it.

I need to get one thing done right away.

Instead of getting out of bed, she propped her head up on the pillow to text one client. She sent a brief hello and a promise to catch up in the afternoon. After pressing Send, she listened to her messages. *I can schedule those later as well.*

She didn't like answering her work messages from bed, but she could do it in a pinch. With one thing accomplished and her messages heard, she already felt better.

* * *

Tamara called right after lunch. "Any chance I could come over and hang out by the pool this evening?" Viv heard the fatigue in her voice.

"Everything okay?"

"Pretty much. I can tell you when I get there. I have an errand to do and then I can swing by your house. Do you want me to bring dinner?"

"Actually I have a date this evening." A smile came to her lips as she remembered Rex's invitation the night before.

"You have a date? Tell me everything."

"I'll leave the key in the usual place. We can talk later. Gotta go."

She knew she'd enjoy her evening more if she kept her phone calls short because it would give her time to swim and do laundry before her dinner with Rex and Sutton.

Shedding her clothes, she slipped into her favorite one-piece swimsuit. It stretched in just the right places and made her feel fast in the water. "Miss Kitty," she called down the hall. "Eat your breakfast from the new feeder. I'm going swimming. Tamara is coming over later. I have a date tonight." She pulled her hair up in a high ponytail. "But you won't have to wait up."

* * *

"Where are we going?" Viv sat next to Rex in the back seat of his Mercedes SUV. Sutton drove.

He wore linen shorts and a soft-blue untucked cotton shirt. His straw boater-style hat sat by his feet on the cleanest floor she'd ever seen in any car. Not a speck of dirt or a wisp of dog hair on the black carpet.

"You're quite tidy," she commented.

"Oh I keep things neat as a pin, as my grandmother used to say." He smiled at her and then added, "You're looking beautiful tonight."

She felt herself blush. "That's enough from you. I'm old enough to be someone's grandmother and I'm not easily taken in with compliments." *Except that's a big lie because I'm blushing. Geez, Viv. Get a grip.*

"You are nobody's idea of a granny," he commented dryly. "No matter how much you insist."

"Enough about me." She looked out the window on her side of the car, watching the desert landscape. Turning back to Rex, she asked, "Did you find out anything—"

Rex nodded toward Sutton's back. No wig, she wore her hair down this time. Straight and blunt cut, Viv approved. "You're looking great as well," she called over the back seat.

"Thanks, Viv. Are we done talking about how great we look?"

"Nobody commented on me," complained Rex. "My car gets more notice than I do. Tidy. Please, what about my linen shorts. Aren't they desert chic?"

"Oh very." Viv nodded.

"Très chic," added Sutton.

Both women laughed as Rex pretended to sulk. "I can't

believe I had to beg for attention." Then he leaned closer to Viv.

"To answer your question," Rex began, "we're going to the casino. I don't have a show tonight, but Sutton knows where people hang out. She's always on the prowl over there to pick up tidbits for my mentalist act." He pointed to her ear. "She has these nifty state-of-the-art earphones so that she can easily drop in on people's conversations. Since she never forgets a face, she knows who attends my shows and gives me the intel."

Viv's stomach knotted. "Is that legal?"

"It's not illegal," he commented. "It's a well-known practice in the trade. Mentalists have always had a front-runner who gathers information from the audience. Some put microphones under seats. Some dress as a part of the audience and take notes. It's the same idea, only we listen in to conversations earlier, at The Roadkill."

"That's how we knew you were coming to the show the other night," Sutton said over her shoulder.

Viv's stomach stopped turning. "Okay then. I suppose that falls under the tricks-of-the-trade category, at least for mentalists. Doulas have tricks too, only yours sound kind of...intrusive."

"Oh, we are intrusive," Rex said immediately. "That's why I'm telling you right up front. We try to use our ill-gotten information for good, not evil. Just so you know."

I guess my opinion matters to him. That must mean he has a conscience, even if he is a showman.

Sutton pulled the SUV into a space behind the casino marked "Rex Redondo" on the sign in front. "I have my own space," he explained, reaching over to open her door.

She slid off the seat, grabbing her purse by the strap. Dressed in white pants and a white linen top, she felt ready for an evening out. She'd given herself a quick pedicure after her swim, which showed off her white strappy low-heeled sandals. She felt oddly confident. *I guess I deserved his admiration.*

After Sutton locked the SUV, she spoke to Rex under her breath. Then she turned to Viv.

"We'll go in and walk around a bit."

"Then we'll do a slot or two," Rex added.

"All the while keeping our eyes and ears open." Sutton pointed to her ear.

Viv nodded. "So what are we looking for exactly? This seems a little like a needle-in-a-haystack situation."

"I think I saw Sarah Esperanza with a guy at the casino a few weeks ago. He always brings a small quilted cooler with him. It fits over his shoulder like a purse, only it's big enough for a six-pack of beer."

"You saw Sarah with him?"

"It's not just that I saw Sarah. I may have seen him hand off the cooler to another woman. I haven't checked the CCTV tapes yet, but I'm working on getting access.

"I've been watching that guy and the women for a few months now. At first I didn't pay a lot of attention. I mean there's a lot of odd stuff that goes on at a casino. But then I realized it was a regular thing, him bringing the backpack and someone picking it up."

Viv stopped to consider the information. "So you think the drop-off has something to do with Sarah? That's why we're here tonight?"

"I have a hunch about those drop-offs and our dead woman. There is some regularity, about two times per month, on Thursday around ten p.m. Maybe you will recognize the guy or the woman. It could be a lead," she added hopefully.

"Just so you know, casinos are not my thing."

"So this is a bad idea?" Rex looked concerned.

"Sensory overload," Viv explained. "Too many sounds and way too many people. It makes my nervous system jumpy and it takes a long while for me to calm down."

"My sis is like that," Sutton said. "Do you have trouble sleeping? She does."

Viv nodded. "I have in the past. But I can do this. I think it's important to our investigation. So I'll hang out and try to stay out of the way while I watch you two professionals at work."

The door to the casino swept open. A man dressed in a security uniform called out a greeting. "Hey, Redondo, what are you doing here? You're not workin' tonight."

"Yah, hey, Jones. I'm here to gamble with the ladies." Rex added a slur to his words as if he'd been drinking.

Viv felt herself perk up. *This may be fun. He's playing the role of man-about-town with a woman on each arm. I can play along.*

"Oh honey," she giggled, taking his elbow with both hands, "I do feel lucky tonight."

Rex looked down at her, his eyes lighting up. "Oh, you have no idea how lucky you're gonna be," he drawled, going along with her improvisational whim.

Jones's dry laugh drowned out any further comment.

They stepped inside the gambling area. The clang of bells and the smell of smoke stopped Viv in her tracks. She inhaled deeply, taking in her environment. She noticed people in bright yellow t-shirts labeled Pair-a-Dice Casino. They held trays aloft, filled with drinks, working their way through the crowd.

"Over there." Sutton nodded to an empty slot machine with one chair.

"You sit down first," Rex whispered in Viv's ear. "We'll hang around and see what happens."

Viv pulled a chair out and gratefully sat down. Her palms had begun to perspire and she felt an ache in her back. *The body keeps the score.*

"I've got this," Sutton said loud enough to be heard over the din. Then she made her way through the crowd, heading back toward the lobby.

Rex leaned over to speak into Viv's ear. "Don't worry. Sutton knows what she's doing. Let's just sit here and pretend to converse. If you see someone you recognize, let me know."

"I can't hear you!" Viv said, pointing to her ear.

She felt a wave of nausea rise to her throat. Drunk voices filled her ears. For Viv, casinos were pits of despair. Her father gambled and drank. She had memories of being dragged around as a child, spending lots of time in hotel rooms, with her best friend the television set repeating old sitcoms.

Viv turned toward the slot machine. Bright-colored fruits spun on a wheel.

Rex rested his hand on her shoulder. His breath felt warm in her ear. "This place is loud. But don't worry, Sutton is already coming back."

Viv turned to see Sutton wading through the throng of gamblers. She gave Viv a sympathetic glance and then leaned over to explain to them in a loud voice. "I was right. The guy showed up with his cooler that looks like a purse. I got a few pictures on my phone."

Rex nodded. "Let's look at the photos later. I think we can find a quieter place. Viv's had enough." His hand touched Viv's elbow. She rose to her feet, and then grabbed his arm when a wave of dizziness came over her.

"I can't wait to get out of here," she said loudly, pointing to the exit sign.

She held her breath. *The cigarette and vape smoke is getting to me.*

Viv was no longer concerned about waiting for Rex and Sutton. She rushed through the crowd toward the exit sign. Once outside she bent over to take a deep breath. The hot desert air scorched her throat. She braced her hands on her knees, waiting for the nausea to pass.

"I'm not the best in crowds," she explained to Rex and Sutton as they stood next to her. They'd followed her outside, both with concerned faces.

"I'm not either," Rex said, as if to make her feel better.

"You work here all the time."

"I work as a mentalist, where I control the crowd. I'm in charge. I'm not a casino kind of guy. I can't stand to lose money for no reason. It's against my grain. Plus the smell is awful, with the booze and the secondhand smoke."

"Back to the car then?" Sutton gestured with her head toward the parking lot.

"We can go to my place and sit by my pool to talk," Viv suggested. "I can put together some food."

Rex took her by the elbow with his hand. "I thought you'd never ask. I'll bring the beer."

25
_____

VIVIENNE ROSE

Viv stepped into her house. She'd regained her composure and steady stomach on the drive back. Rex and Sutton had agreed to come over in a few minutes. She called out, "Tamara?"

When her friend didn't answer, she put her purse on the table and sighed. *I wanted to include her in our sleuthing group. I guess she's not here yet.*

She felt her gut tighten and then realized why. *Don't panic. It's not like the last time. Tamara must be here somewhere.* When she didn't see her in the living room or kitchen, Viv felt renewed worry. It wasn't until she found three baskets of bright red strawberries on the counter that she relaxed. *Tamara's been here and gone to bed.*

When she returned to the kitchen she noticed a piece of paper tucked under the corner of one of the strawberry baskets. Viv read: "I got these earlier for our breakfast. I fed Miss Kitty her dinner. Let's catch up in the morning?"

She took a minute to empty the strawberries into a colander and rinse them under water from the faucet. Then she dried her hands and walked across the living room toward the hallway. One glance at the closed door convinced her that Tamara must be asleep in the guest room.

Kicking off her sandals in her bedroom, she looked at herself in the mirror, noting a smudge of mascara under her left eye. Applying coconut oil, she swiped with a tissue.

She turned away from the mirror and spotted Miss Kitty curled into a ball on the bed. The cat looked up, blinked, and then snuggled back to where she was. "I have company coming over. I won't be late," she told her.

Back in the kitchen Viv put together a tray of crackers, cheese, and olives on her charcuterie board. As she arranged the food she considered what had happened in the casino. *I wonder what Sutton's photos will reveal?*

Pulling a wicker basket from the shelf, she tucked a variety of crackers in a spiral pattern inside. Then she remembered the smoked salmon she kept in the refrigerator.

Arranging the salmon on the charcuterie board, she stepped back to take in the presentation.

"Meow." Miss Kitty stood at her feet.

"You want salmon?" Viv took a small bit from her tray and offered it to the cat.

When she didn't offer a second bite, Miss Kitty yowled louder, "Meow!"

"Nope, you aren't getting any more. You have to wait for breakfast."

Miss Kitty spun around, twitching her tail indignantly. Then a slight knock came from the door. Viv walked around the kitchen island, heading to the living room.

She looked in the peephole. Rex stood outside holding out a six-pack of IPAs in one hand. He was alone. She opened the door.

"I brought you these," he said, stepping past her.

"I have snacks," Viv added.

"Will I provide the entertainment?" Rex asked in his performer voice.

Viv giggled. "It's like you are always on. How is that for you?"

"Oh, honey," he said. "This isn't on. Just you wait. You will see me in all kinds of situations that will make your head spin. I can go from John Wayne to Boris Karloff to Fred Astaire in a matter of minutes." He looked a bit embarrassed as he shook his head.

"Good to know. This way to the kitchen." She nodded to show him which direction.

Walking ahead of him, she could feel his eyes on her back. Her neck grew hot. *He called me honey. It's been a long time since someone called me a word of endearment.*

She felt surprise. Not because it had been so long, but because she didn't mind.

* * *

Outside under the stars, Rex lifted his beer bottle for a toast. "To our first night of sleuthing," he said, leaning back in the chair. The darkness enveloped them. She could see his shape but not his eyes with only the pool to offer light.

"Like Tommy and Tuppence from Agatha Christie."

"Never read mysteries. I do watch TV. How about *Hart to Hart*? They solved crimes and were married."

"And very rich," she said.

"I'm pretty well off."

"I'm what you'd call comfortable," she murmured. "So what do you have to show me?"

He took his phone and flipped to the photo. "Give me your number and I'll send you what we've got."

Such a simple request, but it meant so much more. Once he had her cell phone number he'd be able to text and call. Doubt, like a small bug, made her hesitate. But then she slapped away the doubt to give him the number.

Ping went her phone. Viv opened it immediately. She stared at the photo, issuing a slight gasp.

"Is it her?"

There was a man and a woman in the photograph. The man handed the covered cooler to the woman, who slung it over her shoulder. It looked like a quilted handbag. The man wasn't smiling, neither was the woman.

He wore an LA Dodgers baseball cap, the brim covering his face. She wore a lighter blue Dodgers cap, also pulled down to cover her face. Viv knew who the woman was immediately. She inhaled her surprise.

"Are you going to tell me?" Rex chided.

"This is one of my doulas. We had lunch yesterday and I thought she seemed edgy. I figured it was because of her new relationship."

"I see. So you're worried for her..."

"I can't tell you why, but yes, I am. She's vulnerable and part of my team."

Rex took a long sip from his bottle. The pool filter gurgled loud enough to hear from where they sat.

"I've seen the guy before too," she said quietly.

His head quickly shifted as his eyes pierced the darkness. "Say more."

"He said his name was Zach. He works for my pool service; I saw him right after the murder. He came to clean the pool and I had to send him away because the cops had not taken down the investigation tape. When they finally did, I called the service back and they sent out a team. He wasn't with them that time."

"Maybe he had another assignment?" Rex sounded dubious.

"I have no reason to believe otherwise."

"So let me get this straight. We have two people: one woman you know quite well and a man you've briefly met in your backyard."

When he explained it that way, Viv felt a shiver up her spine. "I seem to be involved with this murder whether I like it or not."

Rex placed his beer bottle on the ground next to his chair. He linked his fingers behind his head, staring ahead.

"So, Redondo." She cleared her throat. "What do we do next?"

"So, Rose," he said, using her last name. "I'm thinking we get some more background on the pool guy. I'll assign Sutton that task. She has some guy who knows a guy who can get us into facial recognition of the police department."

Viv didn't want to ask if that was a legal process because she didn't want to know. "I get the feeling Pearl was holding back on me the other day. She's the woman in the photo."

"Will she tell you what she's up to?"

"Not if I say I got the information by spying on her and taking a photograph. I just hope she's not involved with drugs. What they're doing, exchanging a bag, looks illegal."

"I agree, and I think you may be an unwilling accomplice."

"I don't know a lot about illegal substances, but I do know that the town of Desert Hot Springs, right next to us just down the road, is the meth capital of the world."

"And how did that information come to your attention?"

"When I decided to buy this house I did some research."

"I figured Palm Desert was a really safe town," he admitted.

"Oh, Palm Desert isn't the problem, unless you count the area around the casino, which can bring all kinds of people looking for trouble. But Desert Hot Springs has a reputation."

He stood. "How about one more beer? Did you mention food?"

"I have plenty. No need for takeout." Viv rose to her feet.

Rex pulled out his phone. "I'll text Sutton and tell her to get on that research. She doesn't need to come over."

"Sounds good," Viv said, making her way to the house.

* * *

He held the bottle toward her for a toast. "To Redondo and Rose, neighbors in crime."

She smiled and tapped her bottle against his. After a sip she asked, "What about Sutton? Isn't she part of this team?"

"Sutton helps me out when I need it, but she lives her life and I live mine."

Viv swallowed. "Does that mean Sutton is a roommate without benefits?" She tried to sound disinterested even though she cared.

She held her breath waiting for his answer. *He could easily lie to me, since lying is his bread and butter. But why would he? It doesn't really matter about his relationship with Sutton. We just met each other.*

"Sutton is a friend." His voice sounded firm. "I met her in the military. Over the years she's become like family, like my sister." He didn't look toward her but kept staring at the night sky.

Her mind began to backpedal. *He may get the wrong idea. I was just curious. I'm too old for him; I'm pretty sure he dates much younger women. I can verify that by checking into his social media profiles tomorrow. I don't want to look like a fool, now do I...*

"It's good to know a little about my neighbors," she commented in a matter-of-fact voice.

26

REX REDONDO

"Stop whining. How can a man sleep with you pawing at his head?" As soon as Kevin hears my voice, he digs harder at the covers. Then he barks more and does an eighty-pound body slam on top of me.

"Knock it off, you big mutt!" I pull the covers away from his mouth. Why does he think waking me up is so much fun?

His tail thumps against my exposed arm. *Bam, bam, bam.* I snuggle more deeply into the mattress, blanket over my head, remembering last night. I said goodnight to Viv at the door. I leaned in ever so slightly and she leaned toward me... but she must have thought better of kissing me, because she leaned right back out, offering her hand for a shake.

So what could have been the best evening of my life took a slight turn.

I keep my eyes closed as Kevin pants above my head. I'm still thinking of Viv, the feeling of her sitting in the dark next to me, her sweet voice asking, "Does that mean Sutton is a roommate without benefits?" She's interested. No turning back from that question, not even with a handshake.

Viv isn't easy to read. She's not one of those women whose

natural inclination is to flirt with the opposite sex. She holds back, which makes things difficult because I can't play off of her energy. The keen intelligence and the way she cares about her doulas is kind of a turn-on. But I'm still way ahead of her in the romance department.

Until last night I wasn't sure if she cared about me even a little, you know, as a man. But she laid her cards down just for a second when she asked about Sutton. What was it again? *Roommates without benefits...*

I hear the bedroom door open. "Come on, Kevin," Sutton calls the dog. "Get off of him. It's lunchtime." Kevin bounds off my chest, his back legs digging into my gut. The door closes. He's gone and it's safe to get out of bed.

I slide my feet down to the floor and lift my arms over my head to stretch. Unlike most people, getting up by lunch is normal for me. Since I'm rarely in bed before two a.m., it works okay.

Standing in front of the mirror naked is the next step. It's there I assess my body, which may not be a wonderland, but I am in show business and I have to stay on a pretty strict regimen of exercise and low carbs. I turn to the side. Not much of a belly. I face front. Will Viv like my manscaping?

There I go again, wondering what will please her. She's a vixen, that Viv. I pull on some shorts and head to the exercise room. Half an hour on the elliptical will wake me up, and then I'll talk to Sutton about our murder investigation.

* * *

"Ham sandwich with Swiss, lettuce, and tomato." Sutton shoves a plate in front of me. She sits across the table, fork poking at her salad. "So did Viv know anything about the guy in the photo from last night?" She lifts the fork to her mouth.

"Viv recognized him. He's been to her house to service the pool."

As Sutton munches I tell her, "Viv also knows the woman. One of her doulas."

"Not Tamara?"

"Not Tamara. Which doesn't explain where I've seen her before. I wanted to talk to her, but she was already asleep last night."

Sutton shoves her empty salad bowl aside. "My facial recognition guy didn't pick up the phone yesterday. I'll follow up today." She grabs her phone from the table, scrolls on it, and then adds, "Got a few messages from Hailey and Cam. They tried to text you last night, but you didn't respond."

I must look blank because Sutton laughs. "You don't even know where your phone is right now, do you?"

"Haven't a clue." I hide my head, pretending to be ashamed. I was busy talking to Viv. Fortunately Sutton keeps up with any important messages. She has my password.

"You didn't even know where your phone was last night, did you? Never mind this morning." Sutton stands, her bowl in her hand.

By the time she returns to the kitchen, I've started the dishwasher. The counters have been wiped down, and I've filled a pitcher of filtered water with tea bags. "I'm going to put this out for sun tea, be right back." See how domestic I am? A good catch for some woman, don't you think?

When I return, Sutton is sitting at the table, her laptop open. "You have lots of messages from Hailey and Cam. They want to meet up in town for dinner. I told them you had a gig later tonight. They promised to keep it short and simple."

"Something not right in paradise?" I only ask because my honorary niece rarely has dinner with me unless she needs something. Since she married Cameron, she's had little time for me or her father. Her dad complained to me just last week.

"I never see Hailey anymore. And now with the baby..."

I could see the disappointment in his eyes. He's divorced and single and my age. A baby, especially one from his only daughter, means a lot to him. I suppose he has visions of teaching the baby things, like how to golf and grill a steak, plus putting potential suitors in their place. I mean, we don't know if baby will like boys or girls or both. Not that there's anything wrong with that.

Since I don't have children myself, I live vicariously through Greg. His first wife produced Hailey back in the nineties and I've been her honorary uncle ever since. She was a charming baby and every year she just got more engaging. It wasn't surprising, the modeling and then the acting. She'd held some fine part in indie films; that's where she met Cameron. Then they got married, a big deal destination wedding.

If I am to be honest? I'm a bit miffed Hailey and Cam haven't contacted me about being a godfather or something. No one in the family is religious, but these titles have a certain significance, even for those of us who don't have a faith life. I don't need a church blessing to be a godfather, just a healthy bank account and some time to mold and shape the baby. He may turn out to be a mentalist like me. It could be worse.

I take a look across the table. Sutton is typing. "What time and where?" She looks up, her face blank.

"Dinner in town..." I remind her.

"Oh! Six o'clock. Meet at The Roadkill so that you'll be close to your gig."

"That works." I can already feel my mouth watering. Their hangar steak is the best. No one in the desert grills a better one.

I slide my hand over to grab my phone. Looking at my screen I see the messages from Hailey, and then as I scroll, there is one from Viv.

Be still my heart, you ridiculous schoolboy. I open the text.

> Tamara is not responding to my texts.

An emoji with a puzzled look ended the text.

I start to text back and then stop. I delete what I've written. What can I say that will sound businesslike and not too eager?

I remind myself: we're on a case, Viv and me. That's my focus, at least for now.

I start to text again.

> Let's talk later. I've got a gig tonight. Any chance you want to come to the show? I can leave tickets at the box office so that you don't have to stand in line this time.

I select a happy face emoji and then hit Send.

Maybe she'll come by herself. We can have a drink. I can show her around backstage. Most people like to see what happens behind the curtain where the sausage is made. She could come to my dressing room before or after the show. I want my performance to be the best, at least the best she's ever seen.

27

REX REDONDO

Cameras click, some flashes go off. The paparazzi jockey for position outside of The Roadkill, trying to get a shot of Hailey and Cameron. She ducks her head, walking past the tables filled with diners.

I sit in the back booth, the one they save for me. When I'm not here Sutton occupies the space. I watch as Hailey darts past people who reach out to touch her. She ducks her head away from photos and requests for selfies as the paparazzi crowd into the restaurant close behind.

She's nearly to the back booth when Jake roars from behind the bar, "Get outta here!" He recognizes Hailey and nods to me. Unsatisfied with the paparazzi response, Jake leaps over the counter. He carries a baseball bat in his hand. Waving it in the air to get their attention, he yells again, "Get out of my bar!"

"Leave us alone!" Cameron calls out. Standing by the door, he sounds frustrated. As Jake comes forward, Cameron reaches for the bat and grasps it in his hand. Raising it above his head he turns, eyes bright with anger.

The paparazzi finally get the message, scattering out of the restaurant toward the street.

"I don't care who I hit!" Cameron shouts. Then he shoves a photographer with his elbow.

The man drops to his knees as if injured, the camera hitting the floor.

Jake puts his strong arms around Cameron's gut and pulls him away. He yanks the bat out of Cameron's hand and rolls it along the floor until it settles, hidden under the bar. "Easy, buddy. I'll take care of this. You go sit with your wife and settle down."

From the back booth I can see Cameron glare. Then people start to get up from their tables. Grasping a handbag, one woman runs toward the exit. Another picks up her to-go box, disappearing into the bathroom.

The rest keep their seats, leaning into the center of the table to gossip.

"That guy has a temper," I mutter as Hailey slides into the booth opposite me.

"But I appreciate him keeping the paparazzi off my back. I don't need any photos right now," she says primly, looking past the end of the table toward her belly, adjusting her top to drape over her lap.

Is this what they mean by body dysmorphia? She has no belly to hide.

With the paparazzi gone, the crowd goes back to eating and drinking, the usual hum of the dining room returns. Hailey fidgets in her seat, looking uncomfortable.

"You doing okay?" I focus my attention on her. Her face looks thinner and more drawn since the last time we were together. I remind myself she's just given birth a couple weeks ago. I don't know a man who won't admit he is clueless about that process. The truth is I'm never giving birth so I don't give it a lot of thought.

Hailey's eyes fill with tears.

"What's the matter, sweetie?" I reach across the table to take her hand.

"I'm so depressed," she sobs.

"Is it the baby? He's doing okay, I mean you're both doing okay?"

Baby...does he have a name? Instead of making a mistake, I'm gonna keep calling him the baby until Hailey or Cameron fill in the blank. I am a horrible person.

"You and baby doing okay?" I repeat.

Hailey wipes her eyes on her sleeve. She looks like the child I remember, the one who fell down on the sidewalk and skinned her knee. I'd taught her how to play hopscotch that day. Her wobbly young legs gave out. She cried every time she fell, just like this. Her face puffy, her eyes red, the same look of helpless distress.

"Don't worry, pumpkin." I use her childhood nickname. "We're going to make things better." Then I have this brilliant idea. "I know someone you can talk to. She lives right next door."

This could not have worked out better for me. I get to be the hero for my niece, I get to bring some work to Viv, and I get one more great excuse to call Viv and hear her sweet voice over the phone.

28

REX REDONDO

"Put the phone down," roars Cameron from our booth. He flips off a paparazzi who peers in the window, his phone raised to take pictures.

I can see Cameron is rattled, so I put my own cell in my pants pocket. Jake stands behind the bar looking my way. I nod. He puts down a glass he's polishing and makes his way toward our table.

"What can I do for you, Mr. Redondo?"

"Go wave your bat at the guy outside. He's annoying my dinner guests."

Cameron starts to his feet as Hailey puts her hand on his shoulder. He sits back down.

"Will do." Jake leaves our table. I can hear his voice outside the window. Whatever he said, the guy walks away.

I hand menus to Hailey and Cameron.

"Maybe a burger for both of you. Hailey, you look like you could use a good piece of beef."

"I can't eat," Hailey says, closing her menu.

Cameron shrugs.

Jake shows up, ready to take our order. When Cameron

doesn't say anything, I order burgers all around despite my craving for a steak.

"Sorry about that," Cameron mutters after Jake walks away. "I've been so angry at people since the baby came home. They shouldn't mess with Hailey."

As if overwhelmed with his chivalry, she buries her head in her arms.

I can tell when people are hiding something or lying or both. Cameron's sensitivity and Hailey's odd nervous behavior are activating my intuition. "Is there something you aren't telling me?"

Cameron leans toward Hailey. "You tell him, honey. It should come from you."

She raises her head from her arms. Face still thin, but carefully made up. Only the slight bit of puffiness around her eyes. She must use some kind of waterproof makeup.

She takes a long sip of water. "So Uncle Rex, I...I mean *we*...have a baby. But the thing is, I didn't get pregnant."

Bingo! Have you ever had one of those moments when the obvious is sitting right in front of you, only you failed to notice until somebody pointed it out? "You weren't pregnant..."

"We were not pregnant," Cameron corrects me. "We do have a baby, a biological child. But a surrogate carried the baby using our embryo."

"I didn't want to deal with the weight gain and everything else," explains Hailey. "So we froze some eggs and sperm and then got an attorney and a surrogate."

"Everyone signed a nondisclosure," Cameron hastily adds.

"Even the doula. No one is supposed to talk about us as parents or clients."

"So you're not having postpartum depression then? I know some pregnancy stuff. I've seen movies with pregnant women. In fact I've watched every season of *Call the Midwife*."

Hailey smiles, her face looking less tense. Gone are the on-demand tears. Her hands no longer nervously make fists. "I'm depressed because I told a lie to my followers. And I have to keep telling it for a while. I have to keep lying to my fans on social media and to the paparazzi, who are everywhere trying to take photos of my belly."

I realize I was too optimistic about connecting Hailey with Viv. They'd most likely want a nondisclosure from her too. Plus Hailey doesn't have postnatal depression. She has a crisis of conscience from telling lies and living with the consequences. She needs a priest, not a doula.

"How much longer will you have to lie?"

"What do you mean?" The indignation returns to Cameron's face.

"How much longer will you pretend you are postpartum?" I try to keep the disappointment from my voice.

"Only a couple more weeks," Hailey says.

"Then what?"

"I can stop wearing these disgusting tops and gradually start showing my body again."

"But that's not everything," Cameron adds. "She's been getting lots of hate mail about her body and the baby. Some of her fans want her to snap back right away. Others are whining that Hailey looks too good."

"People don't have to keep comparing themselves to me!" Hailey wails.

I'm going to set her straight on that one.

"Except that's what you ask them to do. You post on social media about your perfect life, your perfect husband, and now your perfect baby. Competition and unkindness are likely to follow."

If you could see the expressions on Hailey and Cameron, you'd know I said something they'd never thought about. Talk about a shadow. That's what Jung called the parts of yourself that you have no idea about. These two look stunned as if they'd never realized the fallout of putting their lives on public display.

I'm going to change the subject before I lose my temper. "What about the baby? Have a name yet?"

Hailey blinks.

"Not yet. He's good. Hanging with his nanny while we have dinner."

"Did you plan on getting caught by the paparazzi, you know, to enhance your brand?" I try to make my voice sound curious as opposed to furious.

"Kind of," Cameron admits. "We called our publicist and told them we were having dinner at The Roadkill with you." He gestures with his thumb toward Hailey. "She needs to be seen a bit before she comes back fully. We didn't think you'd mind."

Mind? Do I look like a guy who thrives on cameras taking my photo in restaurants with the flashing lights and the loud words and the near fistfight? Not to mention dragging Jake into the mix, tossing people out of the place. Why would that be a problem for me?

Big breath, Rex. They are spoiled children who have no idea how privileged they are.

"I want to name him Dondo," Hailey said.

"After you, of course," adds Cameron.

Okay then, I love my niece and her husband. At least they thought of me. But then again, I know better. They probably told any number of people they'd name the baby after them. They may change their minds, depending on who they want to flatter and please.

The food finally arrives. Cameron picks up his burger, while Hailey picks at her side salad. I passed on the hangar steak to have a burger like everyone else. Since I'm going to perform, I didn't ask if they want wine or a beer.

We eat in silence. People cruise by our table and slow down to look at the famous couple. I keep my eyes focused on eating.

I wait for the plates to be removed and for coffee to be poured. Cameron and I sip the dark roast together. My first question makes Cameron's eyebrows raise.

"Did you arrange for a postnatal doula?" I wouldn't have known to ask that question without Viv telling me there were such things as doulas who help out after the birth.

"How do you know about doulas?" Cameron asks. His eyes narrow as if he suspects me of some nefarious deed.

"I live next door to a doula."

Hailey's eyes grow wide. "I didn't think a doula could afford to live in your gated community."

"She's not just a qualified doula," I begin to brag. "She's the head of a doula agency called Desert Doulas. Heard of it?"

Hailey's expression freezes. I watch as Cameron's arm slides over to grip her leg under the table. He shakes his head fast. "Nope, never heard of them." He glares at Hailey, who lowers her eyes.

It doesn't take a genius to suss out that lie. Right in front of me they deny knowing about Desert Doulas, which they obviously have some connection with—why bother to pretend otherwise?

"I can talk to Viv and see if she has someone on her staff to help out."

"We don't need another doula!" Cameron says loudly.

"Okay then, calm down. It was just a suggestion." I hold up my hands, aware that everyone in the restaurant is staring at us.

Cameron's volatility bothers me. He's not the same guy he

used to be before the baby. Tonight is the first time I've witnessed anything like this. How he grabbed the bat from Jake's hand. And even he admits it was all staged. Not his anger though. That feels real enough.

"You need to calm down," I tell him. "You're upsetting my niece and making a fool of yourself." I want to add a few choice expletives to my advice, but apparently Cameron gets the gist.

He sits back in his seat, embarrassment flushing his cheeks. "You're right, Rex. I'm sorry. I'm on edge and I can't seem to shake this feeling."

Because you lied about your baby, you dumbass. I want to tell him this, but I don't.

I stare at the couple across the table. Hailey places a trendy pair of glasses on her face as if they'll help her avoid my glance. And Cameron, he smiles right at me, though his fingers keep tapping at the table. He looks over his shoulder. If I didn't know better, I'd assume he's feeling guilty and hiding something more.

From me or from Hailey?

29

VIVIENNE ROSE

Friday had flown by in a blur. She hadn't taken any work since the death, so her schedule was off and she knew there would be consequences if she didn't get back to a healthier pattern. *Saturday will be different*, she had assured herself. But then Saturday arrived, and she slept past eight a.m., a sure sign that her schedule was off.

Since her breakdown a year ago, she'd kept a close monitor on her daily habits. Mindfulness and taking solace in going to bed and waking up at the same time. Her exercise routine kept her mind clear and she ate her meals with the same regularity, except when dining with friends.

Even Miss Kitty thrived under a schedule. She was the one who most often reminded Viv when she strayed from her healthy way of life. "Meow" and a paw to the cheek woke her up this Saturday. Otherwise she might have slept even longer.

When she didn't open her eyes, Miss Kitty batted her again.

"Go away," she told the cat. "I'll get up in a minute."

Not taking her word for it, Miss Kitty laid her paws on Viv's belly and then kneaded her claws. She purred as an accompaniment. The claws bit into the blanket and then Viv's skin, causing her to yelp. "Stop, you crazy cat!"

Viv flung the covers over the cat and scrambled out of bed. *Eight o'clock. Not terrible. Better than yesterday. I think I can get back on my schedule if I eliminate unnecessary tasks today and then make sure to get to bed at the usual time.* Bathrobe wrapped around her body, she tied it in front.

Her phone showed the text she'd sent before going to sleep.

> Thanks for asking me to your show. I can't come tonight. Maybe another time?

She'd added a sad face emoji to let him know she really was sorry.

Tamara had sent another early morning text.

> Sorry I had to leave early. Maybe we can catch up next time?

The timing of the text was five a.m. *She was certainly up early.*

With Miss Kitty leading the way, Viv walked through the living room toward the kitchen. She pulled out her blender and then arranged ingredients on the counter. With the fruit and protein powder going first, she added orange juice and a banana to thicken the drink. The cat jumped on the counter to watch her work.

"You don't belong up there," she cautioned. "And you're not gonna like what happens next." Viv turned the knob, advancing the dial as the concoction began to whir in the bowl.

Miss Kitty cried an indignant meow and jumped off the counter. Her tail waved as she disappeared around the corner.

Once she'd poured her smoothie into a tall glass and

rinsed the blender, Viv sat down at the table. She checked her phone and found a text from Rex.

> Would you have time this morning for a professional consult? BTW Sutton has a report about our case.

"Our case" struck her as particularly charming. He did seem to care as much as she did about finding out who murdered Sarah. She wrote back.

> I would be happy to consult. Can't imagine what you'd want to know about birth work. This afternoon perhaps? I'm rushed this morning.

She pushed Send. Within a minute a text came back.

> Is 3 okay for you? I have to leave early because I have two shows tonight.

She texted him a thumbs-up emoji.

Okay then, I'm working my schedule more intentionally. That's a good thing. Plus I want to call the police to see if they've found a new detective. Then I can answer my doula hotline messages and get in a swim.

She finished the last sip of her smoothie. *I'll postpone the swim until this afternoon.* Viv pulled her computer across the table. She opened it up and clicked the Desert Doula hotline page.

Once she'd answered the messages, she closed down her webpage. Then she began to wonder about Tamara. *Are we just missing each other by chance or is she deliberately avoiding me for some reason? She initiated coming over, but then she left before we could talk.*

Aware that something had changed, Viv had to admit to

herself. *For years I've let Tamara dictate our comings and goings. She's the one with the busy schedule with one boyfriend or another who always gets priority. I haven't really dated since my divorce. So Tamara got to say when, where, and what time, since I was usually more available.*

Maybe I'm changing—I hope for the better.

30

REX REDONDO

Man, that was a long show. It took every ounce of my concentration not to think about Viv and to focus on the audience. Finally, I'm home.

I toss the keys on the counter and then hear the *thump, thump* of Kevin's tail. He's here to greet me no matter what time of the day or night. I bend over to give him a pat. He runs away and returns with a squeaky toy shaped like a dinosaur. He lowers himself down, back end up, front legs ready to spring. Growling, he begs me to play. I pat his head and straighten my back. I resist a groan.

Kevin squeaks the toy again.

"Maybe tomorrow, buddy. I'm tired." I turn my back on his hopeful face, feeling guilty as sin.

Even though my back hurts every time I stand up and sit down, I don't have to tell the world. Even when I'm alone I practice not groaning. It's just a way of announcing to everyone that I'm no longer twenty. It takes a lot of energy not to act and sound old.

Not that people don't notice by looking at me. I see them

staring, wondering how much work I've had done. I never talk about that. It's my business—and Sutton's, of course. She makes the appointments every couple of months.

Kevin, giving up on the toy, bumps his nose against my knee. "Okay, buddy. I'll get you a dog cookie and then to bed. I'm beat and you need your beauty sleep." I ruffle the fur on the top of his head one more time.

Turning the lights off behind me, I head to my bedroom. When we first moved in, Sutton ordered a lot of expensive furniture, but I only sit in the kitchen. I use my bedroom and sauna room, that's about it. I have no idea what Sutton's wing of the house looks like. She's very private that way.

Kevin leaps on the bed. He turns three times, and then plops himself down, his head on his front paws. "Just go to sleep," I tell him as I head to the shower.

He briefly lifts his face, then drops it. Eyes closed, it's as if he's determined to get to sleep faster than me. Everything is a game with Kevin.

Sometimes I actually hear the words in my head, like Kevin speaks English to humor me. Just so you know? I'm not that kind of mentalist. I don't talk to animals and they don't talk to me. That's a lot of jibber-jabber as far as I'm concerned. But I have been wondering lately if Kevin may be changing all of that...

Although Miss Kitty has her own opinions. Maybe Viv doesn't hear them, but I do, loud and clear. I'm not what you'd call a cat person, but even I can tell when MK wants to chat. The way she kept meowing this afternoon, for example.

That's probably just my imagination kicking in. Everyone knows cats don't talk. But you gotta admit, the cat wanted me to stay and help Viv. That's what I heard.

It doesn't bother me either, that Viv's a cat person. I think it's interesting that I love dogs and she loves cats. I wonder if anyone else notices that she smells like fresh hibiscus... Must be her scent. Whenever I'm near her I want to lean over and inhale more, maybe even get a quick kiss...

That Viv. What a fascinating human being.

31

VIVIENNE ROSE

Viv googled the address of Sarah's sister. *Aida Rodrigues. It will only take twenty minutes or so to get there. I have time to finish up some online business before I leave.*

Once she got on the road, she took the main highway out of Palm Desert, increasing her speed. Viv had a chance to think about whether Sarah ever talked about her sister. *Maybe Aida knows more than she's saying. Maybe their relationship was less than close since I don't recall Sarah mentioning Aida. Sisters do squabble.*

As she drove she pondered her new role as self-appointed detective. *I wonder if the professionals investigate family members first and then move on to other suspects...*

She let her thoughts wander as Vivaldi's *The Four Seasons* played in the car. By the time she found Aida's house and parked on the street, she got out and locked the car, taking a deep breath. She knew of this neighborhood. Where early California pueblo-style houses had been constructed right after WW II. People now enclosed their front yards with chain-link fencing, parking old vehicles in front. Ones that waited for repair.

Looking around, she saw bars in the windows. Aida's house did not have a chain-link fence across the driveway. This made it easier for Viv to step over the concrete toward the front door. She rang the doorbell.

A woman in her late forties opened the door.

"I'm Vivienne Rose. We spoke on the phone?"

"Come on in," she said, letting Viv walk ahead.

Aida looks like Sarah. She felt a pang in her heart.

Viv took a quick look around the sparsely decorated living room. Behind the worn fabric sofa, curtains had been drawn. She had to admit that the darkened room reflected the circumstances, a recent death in the family.

Only one chair stood in the room. Equally worn, with faded chintz fabric. It faced the sofa. Her eyes lifted and then stopped on the photos arranged on top of a small piano. She walked closer to the pictures, picking one up. "You and Sarah growing up?" Viv held the photo in her hands, staring at the young girls. They wore dresses made of identical fabric, holding bouquets of flowers. "You were flower girls in this one?" Viv wondered.

"My mom sewed. She made us lots of matching outfits for church. We were flower girls for our uncle's wedding that day."

Viv heard the catch in Aida's throat. She turned to face her. "Thanks for agreeing to meet with me."

Aida took the photo from Viv's hand, placing it back on the piano in front of vases of flowers. "Can I get you something? Coffee maybe?"

"That would be wonderful." When Aida walked through a doorway, Viv took the opportunity to look around the room once again. She felt and saw the grief, in the way curtains had been drawn and the candle had been lit on a small table next to the piano. This time her eyes stopped on a small plastic barrette, like a child would wear in her hair, along with a small vase of yellow flowers. Viv sniffed, eyeing the tall vase filled with lilies which stood behind the photographs.

Aida came into the room, holding a mug in each hand. "That's my altar for Sarah," she said, putting the mugs on the coffee table. "I'm not religious, but it helps. Once somebody dies, it's like they just vanish. I need the reminders that she was once alive."

Aida's bottom lip trembled. Then she turned around as if to keep her grief safe. By the time she turned back to Viv, she'd composed herself. "Do you want cream or sugar?" She gestured for Viv to sit down.

"Nope, this is fine. Thank you for letting me visit on such short notice."

Aida sat down in a chair as Viv sat close to her at one end of the sofa. "I didn't know how to tell you on the phone, but we're not having a memorial or anything. I wouldn't even know who to invite. We haven't been close for several years. What with the custody problems and her work, there wasn't time." Aida took a sip of coffee. Viv waited for her to continue. "She mentioned friends in the doula community, and then there was her boyfriend..."

Viv didn't want to appear too eager, so she just nodded. Fortunately Aida had led right where she wanted the conversation to go. Finally Viv said, "I never met Sarah's boyfriend. Had they been together very long?"

"Just a few months."

"Was he a good guy?"

When Aida didn't respond right away, Viv already had her answer. She took a sip of her coffee and waited for her suspicion to be confirmed.

"Not exactly a good guy. Not reliable either. She never let him come over to her house, because of her son. She'd tell me that he'd disappear for a couple of days and then he'd turn up without any explanation. I never heard from her when he was in town."

"Wasn't she concerned about his behavior?"

"He was always mad because she wouldn't let him come to her house. So he blamed her for everything. Sarah was ready to have a conversation with him, maybe break up. But every time she had a chance, he'd duck out and disappear again."

"Did he have a job?"

Aida's eyes narrowed. "You are asking a lot of questions about her boyfriend. Do you think he's the one?"

Viv took a deep breath. "I don't know. She never talked to me about him."

"That surprises me," Aida said. "Sarah really loved her doula community, you especially. She told me how you pulled her up when she felt really low and that you knew how hard the work could be."

Viv felt her eyes tingle with tears. "It had been a while since we'd spoken about anything personal. I didn't know she had a boyfriend, for example. Oh, we talked about schedules and referrals, but not anything real, you know. She kind of closed herself off."

"She could do that." Aida nodded. "I thought she'd gotten the idea for that certification from you. That's why she took those classes. It seemed like something you'd recommend, since it's doula related and all."

"Certification?"

"Something about learning to encapsulate..."

Viv put down her coffee cup. "Do you mean placenta encapsulation?"

"That's it! She took classes and got a certificate, all official like. Then she set up her kitchen for business. Kind of gruesome, if you ask me."

Viv was used to people's ick factor when it came to birthing work. Most men didn't want to hear let alone witness any details. As for women, there were still lots who wanted to check into a hospital and check out with a baby, leaving all of the placenta disposal to the doctors and nurses.

"The placenta is an organ, did you know that?" She put on her teacher voice, keeping it low and detached.

"Like a liver or a kidney?" Aida sounded shocked.

"That's right. It's an organ specifically designed to feed the baby as it gestates. Once it's expelled at birth, it's finished its function, or at least that's what most people feel. But some women keep the placenta next to the baby until the umbilical cord falls away. Some women will use the placenta to make capsules and then ingest the capsule as a part of their post-partum recovery."

"I heard that some cultures bury the placenta." Aida nodded.

"They do, but there are many people who believe there are considerable benefits from consuming the placenta, for the birthing mother especially."

"Don't tell me my sister was involved in that, consuming placentas!"

"I can see why Sarah may have been interested in encap-sulation. Being health-oriented and all. She wanted the best for her clients, especially nursing mothers.

"Some studies have shown consuming the placenta increases the milk supply and also builds the mother up so that she isn't susceptible to postpartum depression."

Viv took a sip of her cold coffee, giving Aida a moment to digest that information. *Now is not the time to tell Aida that the actual benefit of consuming the placenta has not been veri-fied and that's why I stay out of the encapsulation business.*

"It feels so weird to me." Aida sounded less incredulous, but still deeply skeptical.

"I don't know. Sarah never mentioned to me that she'd gotten the certification. I do know of doulas who have gone that route. It's not out of the question."

Aida shook her head. "It took over her life. She had three dehydrators in her kitchen. I thought she was making jerky to sell at the flea market. Is that where she put the placenta, in the dehydrator like a piece of beef jerky?"

She's way overwhelmed with this conversation. I'd better soothe her and give her some space. Instead of answering Aida's question, she nodded and then stood.

"It's been good to talk to you this morning and to hear about Sarah. She was well respected by her doula family. She had exceptional empathy for birth work, a quality I tried to emulate. Even though I run Desert Doulas, we were more like equal colleagues, but mostly friends. I will miss her so much." She smiled at Aida.

Aida stood up. "Who murdered my sister then? I know you aren't the police but I want answers. As you said, she was a good person. I can't imagine who would be angry enough to kill poor Sarah and toss her into a pool."

"It's unbelievable," Viv said. "I agree. That's why I'm going to do everything possible to find out what happened. We both loved her, and as her sister, you deserve to know the truth."

* * *

On the drive home, Viv sorted out what she'd learned from Aida. *So Sarah's boyfriend wasn't allowed to come over. That made him mad. And she was a placenta encapsulator.*

She took a right turn from the main highway, stopping in front of the gate to the Desert Tortoise Estates. A quick glance at the caretaker's booth told her that no one was on duty. So she leaned out the open window to punch in her code. The gate lifted slowly. As Viv drove forward she noted a small camera installed at the corner of the security hut. *I bet they keep track of the vehicles that come and go.*

She began to accelerate, heading to her house. Once in the driveway she decided, *I'm going to call the community hotline and ask to see the CCTV tapes for the night of the murder.*

32

VIVIENNE ROSE

Late Sunday afternoon Viv stood in her kitchen contemplating a snack. *I could cut up some of that baguette. Then have warm Brie along with apple slices.* Her stomach growled.

She remembered Sarah bringing up placenta encapsulation at a Desert Doula meeting nearly a year ago. Then the topic got dropped. Mostly because Viv didn't support the process.

She made it quite clear that the jury was still out on evidence-based science in terms of the benefits. After the one time, whenever the topic came up for the group, it was quickly squelched. Viv knew it was because of her and her adamant opinion. *Somebody has to remind people about the science.*

She assembled a small tray with her snacks, poured herself a glass of Prosecco, and walked to the living room. Placing her food and drink on a side table, she sat in her most comfortable upholstered chair.

One bite of cheese and baguette quieted her stomach. Cell phone in hand, she scrolled her contacts. The phone number for the Desert Tortoise Estates caught her eye. She held the phone to her ear as it rang. *It would help to know who came in and out of the community the night of Sarah's death.*

Voicemail picked up. "This is the administrator for the Desert Tortoise Estates. We're unable to come to the phone right now. If it's an emergency, please call 911. Otherwise call back during our usual business hours, Monday through Friday, nine to five o'clock." A click sounded loudly before she could even speak.

They don't seem too interested in residential calls after hours. I'll take care of that. She scrolled to Rex's number and texted.

> Want to come over?

She put the phone down and picked up another piece of bread. Before she could spread the cheese, her doorbell rang. She stood and walked across the room to open the door.

He wore an untucked turquoise-blue Hawaiian shirt, along with slightly fitted tan cargo pants. His hair looked recently brushed and his tan face made his teeth look very white when he smiled. "You texted?"

"You got here fast." She opened the door wider for him to come inside. As soon as he crossed the threshold, a meow floated down the hall.

"Miss Kitty," he said with a nod.

"You can go say hello later. I have snacks in the living room." She pointed.

He walked ahead of her, whistling quietly.

"Miss Kitty likes you," she told him brightly. "Sit there and have some bread. Do you want a beer?"

"What are you having?"

She reached down to pick up her glass and held it up to show him.

"Bubbly," he commented. "I'll have some of that." His intense black eyes looked at her appraisingly.

She ran her finger over her neck, right where her t-shirt stopped at her clavicle. *It's getting warm in here.* She turned on her heel, walking toward the kitchen. When she returned she had an open bottle of Prosecco and another glass in her hand. He'd already sat down at the end of the sofa, the seat closest to her favorite chair.

She put the glass and bottle on the coffee table, then filled each glass to the top, handing one to Rex. "There you go. Not expensive but lots of bubbles." He watched her sip before he raised the glass to his lips.

Viv set her glass aside to offer him the tray with snacks. "Brie, sliced baguette, and apples," she commented.

He eyed the contents as he took the tray from her. "This is how I eat before a performance. Bites of this and that. How did you know?"

"I like to nibble, so this is my preferred way of eating at home."

She watched as he put the tray down and spread cheese on apples and bread. "Good cheese," he announced after the first bite.

"The bread is from our local bakery, Just Desserts," she told him. *And why am I sounding like such a local know-it-all? He's lived here long enough to know way more than I do. This man makes me act stupid.*

He didn't flinch. Just took another bite of apple with Brie, smiling back at her.

"So I assume you have something to tell me about our investigation?" he finally asked.

"My first question is do you know who sits in the Tortoise security booth? If they have CCTV of that night..."

"I already thought of that," he told her. "And I ran down

the guy, who told me the camera is up but not running. Apparently appearances matter more than function."

Viv felt disappointed. "They always catch the bad guy with CCTV. I thought for sure we'd get a lead."

"So what else did you learn?" He picked up a piece of cheese, his gaze tracking her face so intimately that she turned away to gather her words. "Aida did tell me that Sarah got a placenta encapsulation certificate. But no one seems to know the name of Sarah's boyfriend."

"And what's that again?" Rex looked confused.

"The name of Sarah's boyfriend. She didn't say and I didn't ask."

"That could be a problem. But it's the other thing I'm wondering about. As soon as I heard the word 'placenta' I kinda tuned out. That's baby business, right?"

Viv sighed. Men were a disappointment when it came to birth. She'd never really gotten over her judgment in that regard. A guy could shoot a deer with a rifle, step closer, and finish it off with another shot. Drag away the body, blood everywhere, and not even flinch.

But when it came to something about women and their lady business, they turned pale and tuned out hearing some predictable word like period, menstruation, ovaries, vagina, and even placenta. She sighed again.

Rex stared at her over a raised hand holding his next slice of baguette and cheese.

She shrugged. "Placenta. It's an organ, just like a heart or a lung."

He nodded. And then he put the morsel back down on a napkin.

"Don't tell me you lost your appetite. Just because you heard the word placenta," she challenged.

His neck grew red. "You got me. I didn't know it was an organ, the placenta thing."

"Not a thing," Viv corrected him. "A vital part of gestating an embryo, which results in a fully functioning human being."

He nodded, putting on an interested face that didn't fool her for a minute.

"This is my work," she explained. "I hope I can speak freely about birth without having to tiptoe around you." *And every other man I've ever known.*

She watched his reaction. His jaw tightened as his lips drew a straight line. *Uh-oh, did I annoy the famous Rex Redondo?*

To her surprise he reached over for his napkin and dabbed at his lips as if considering her words carefully. Then he lifted the slice of baguette and put it in his mouth. "Duly noted," he said. "I'll work on my squeamish attitude as of now."

Viv knew this moment was a turning point in her relationship with Rex Redondo. She hadn't planned it as such. But she'd told him the truth about her work. And instead of backing off, he leaned in. He didn't belittle or dismiss her challenge. He'd taken a bite of food, and then Rex Redondo had done something quite remarkable.

He said he'd be willing to learn and change.

That was the moment when Viv knew they would become great friends.

* * *

The bottle of Prosecco stood empty as Viv sat back against the chair cushion, appreciating the buzz she felt and the company. They'd laughed and talked about words that made them each squirm, getting to a place of ease. A place, Viv admitted to herself, that she'd not felt with a man for a very long time.

"So I have an idea," he offered.

"About the investigation?" She sat up in her chair.

"Do you have your doula's address anywhere?"

"You mean Sarah."

"That's the one."

Her brow wrinkled. "On my computer. I keep up-to-date contacts for all of my doulas." Thinking about Sarah pushed aside any of the previous giddiness she'd felt. "I'll go get Sarah's address." She stood up from the chair.

"And I'll pick up the dishes." He stood next to her.

They both walked to the kitchen. She left Rex to rinse the dishes at the sink while she sat at the table and opened her laptop. A few clicks later and she had what she needed. "I've got the address here. What do you propose to do with it?"

He came around the island to peer over her shoulder. "I think we should go have a look at the place. If I'm not mistaken, it's near that trailer community in Desert Hot Springs."

"I do know the one. Some would call it a low-rent neighborhood."

"The real estate prices dip considerably once you cross the highway to the other side."

"So we go and case her place like real detectives?" Viv felt her excitement grow. "Why don't we have a quick bite and then..."

Rex smiled. "After dinner we'll go over the plan. Plus there has to be coffee."

"And we need to dress so we're not noticed. We can wear black t-shirts, you know, in case we're stopped by the cops, hanging out in a neighborhood not our own."

"Now you're really talking," Rex agreed.

"I'm on it!" she said brightly. Feeling energized by the proposition of investigating with Rex, she pulled the carafe from the coffee maker and filled it with water. Then she looked in the freezer for something to make for dinner.

"After dinner we'll brew the coffee and fill a travel mug," she called over her back.

"I'll drive. You can ride with me," he suggested.

"Perfect," she confirmed.

33

VIVIENNE ROSE

Viv sat in the passenger seat of his Mercedes SUV. The dashboard had every possible gauge and gadget, all lit up for nighttime travel. Despite their casual conversation over dinner, she felt surprised at how awkward she felt now that she was in his vehicle. *Actually he makes a delightful conversationalist. He helped with the dishes which was nice. But what now? Do I make conversation about his ride, like we're in high school? Do I ask him details to get him talking? Is this like a date?*

She quickly glanced at his profile. He still looked immaculate in his Hawaiian shirt and brushed-back hair. Sighing, she thought, *Not a date. Just part of our investigation. Keep it simple, Viv. Stay on topic.* When her jitteriness didn't go away, she wondered even more. *I've never played detective before. This is new for me. Very exciting if I can handle the nerves. I remember those old Thin Man movies with Myrna Loy. Maybe I'm her. Only older. Stouter. And less of a debutant.*

"So what do you hope to learn when we get to Sarah's house?" she asked.

Rex lifted his right hand from the steering wheel. Keeping

eyes on the road, he opened the cargo container between the seats. "First of all, I come prepared. I brought a few tools." He pointed inside. "I keep these for emergencies. Plus it's part of my work. You never know when an act will require a few adjustments with a screwdriver or a wrench."

Eyes still on the road, his hand came up with a credit card. "This is old-school but it works. I can jimmy a lock and get inside, especially if there's no dead bolt."

"You're quite the expert on home break-ins." She kept her voice dry, but inside she felt even more excited. *He's such a bag of tricks. Never a dull moment with Rex Redondo.*

She looked at her cell phone. The app announced, "Turn left and then the first right." By the time they reached the address of Sarah's trailer community, Viv had already turned off her phone.

Rex parked next to the curb on the opposite side of the street. "We can walk the rest of the way," he told her, turning off the ignition. "I don't want to be seen."

She opened her door, stepping onto the dirt pathway. A shiver ran up her spine. Only the stars and moon lit the neighborhood. Without sidewalks or street lights, it felt eerie and isolated in the desert quiet. Double-wide motor homes lined the street on both sides. Some in better repair than others. They walked side by side up the gravel path to the front entrance of Sarah's home. Viv felt her stomach tighten with nerves.

"I don't see any light on," Viv commented.

"Let's look around back," he suggested. "I'm hoping the place is empty."

Palms sweating, Viv said, "We could get arrested."

"Not tonight," he said calmly. "I'm feeling lucky tonight. We're going to go inside and get some information and then go home." He took her hand in his, making his way around the back.

Under any other circumstances Viv might have felt a bit giddy, holding the hand of a man she barely knew. But tonight she just felt terrified. "Have you ever done this before?" she whispered to him as he dropped her hand, bending closer to get a better look at the doorknob.

"Oh yeah, don't worry. I'm an expert at breaking and entering. Got some magician pals on the circuit who show me stuff. But I'm going to check the windows first. One may be open already." Standing up, he reached past her to test the screen on the closest window near the back door. "Locked," he muttered.

He held his finger to his lips. "Stay here," he whispered. Walking around the corner of the house, she heard the crunching of gravel under his feet. Finally he returned from the opposite corner to stand by her side. "All the windows are locked." Reaching his hand out, he jiggled the doorknob, which turned easily in his hand. "I didn't try it before." He sheepishly grinned. "She left the door open."

Viv couldn't believe Sarah would be so negligent.

"Wait here while I check things out." He disappeared into the trailer as Viv held her breath. In a few minutes he returned. "No one home so far as I can see. Come on in." Her heart beat wildly as she slid past him. With a twist of his hand he locked the door securely behind her.

"We don't want anyone walking in unexpectedly," he explained.

Once Viv's eyes adjusted to the inside darkness, she stared at what she assumed was the kitchen. Rex stood next to her, shaking his head. "Lots of dehydrating machines here. More than most people would have. Those are for the placentas, right?"

Viv sighed. She recognized the kitchen setup right away. The extra roasting pans, the three dehydrators, the two blenders, and the pill encapsulator set to the side...waiting.

She pointed to the roasting pans next to the dehydrators. "Sarah got her certificate and it looks like she went into the placenta encapsulation process in a big way."

He shrugged. "So this is when I tell you I think the overuse of the word placenta has desensitized me already." He held out his hands, palms facing down. "See? Not even a shake. No tremors. I'm all about facing my fears." He lowered his arms, watching her reaction carefully.

"You are a very quick learner," she said dryly. "But aren't we supposed to be gathering information about Sarah, not complimenting you?"

He snickered under his breath. "Yes, ma'am. I hear you loud and clear."

Viv looked behind her on the opposite wall, where an old refrigerator stood, humming loudly. She stepped closer to open the freezer door. Rows of plastic containers had been stacked, labeled with names and dates, along with the hour. She knew what she'd discovered without opening the lids.

"Come look," she called to Rex.

He stepped beside her to stare inside the refrigerator. "Someone is planning a big barbecue. Looks like a lot of steak marinating, ready to be grilled."

"That's not steak," she explained calmly.

He looked again. "I don't think it's chicken. Let me have a closer look."

"Stop," she said in a loud voice. "If I'm not mistaken, those are placentas, stored and ready to be encapsulated."

He dropped his hand, turning to face her. "You're not telling me that those..." He pointed behind him. "'They look like meat or liver or something I'd eat. There must be a dozen of them lined up, waiting for slaughter."

She patted his arm. Reaching behind him, she shut the freezer door. "They're only viable for forty-eight hours after the birth. If not dehydrated by then, they must be destroyed or frozen. They can be kept up to three months, but not much longer, especially if you want to receive any benefits from the capsules. Whoever harvested these will have to come back and finish the job pretty soon."

"It's illegal to use people's organs," Rex muttered as if to remind himself.

"But remember," Viv said calmly, "we're here to figure out who killed Sarah. She didn't put those in the freezer. If I'm right, the dates were marked days after her death."

Before Rex could comment, a light flashed through the curtained window. "Looks like we might have company," he whispered close to her ear. "We need to get outta here."

Rex took her hand for the second time that night and led her through a doorway, toward the living room. He crouched behind the sofa, pulling her down with him.

Viv heard someone rattle the back doorknob, then bumping followed by a string of expletives.

"We locked them out," Rex whispered. "While they're trying to get inside, let's make a break for it out the front door." He edged his way away from the sofa as Viv followed. As soon as they reached the front door, Rex unbolted the chain lock and turned the handle, right before a crash came from the kitchen.

"Someone is breaking the door down," she gasped.

"Run," Rex told her, gripping her hand again. Across the front yard they sprinted. Rex reached for the key fob in his pocket. She heard the beep. "Get in!" he told her, holding the door.

She hopped onto the seat and slammed her door. By the time he sat behind the steering wheel, he'd started the engine. "Lock the doors," she said, then heard them click shut.

One quick glance out her window showed a man running from the house. Arms over his head, he waved his hands, coming straight toward them.

Rex pulled away from the curb. Tires screeched as he drove onto the highway. Taking the first right onto a side street, he accelerated the SUV toward the main highway. Rex took a quick glance in the rearview mirror. "I don't think he's following us."

Viv held her breath as he turned onto the highway behind a red truck. She glanced over her shoulder and sighed a breath of relief. "Now that, Rex Redondo, has to be the most exciting first date I've ever had." She patted his thigh and then, feeling self-conscious, returned her hand to her lap.

He stared straight ahead as a slow smile came from the corner of his mouth. "I wanted to think we were on a date, but I dared not ask. You went out with me despite your best intentions."

"We broke into a house."

"Technically the door was already open."

She shook her head. "And considering what we found, you're getting much better about not flinching."

"Well, good for us then." Rex smiled. He looked in his rearview mirror. "Looks like we're in for some rain. Let's head home and pretend like we just had the most exciting first date ever."

"Pretend?" she said, her eyebrows lifting to accompany her smile.

34

VIVIENNE ROSE

"Meow," came Miss Kitty's greeting. Glowering in the hallway, Miss Kitty waved her tail at Viv.

"Is it breakfast time already?"

"Meow." Miss Kitty tiptoed forward. She wove her way around Viv's legs, stopping to gently sniff her right shoe. Drawing away, she sneezed, not liking what she smelled.

"I'll feed you a treat," Viv sighed. "Then I'm heading to bed." She dropped her purse on the table. Stepping over the cat, she walked slowly toward the catio, but not before casting a look of longing toward her own bed.

Viv opened one eye. "It's already noon." With a groan she sat up in bed. Swinging her legs over the side, Viv stood and then stretched her arms over her head. *No ill effects from the break-in and chase last night. I must admit I'm in pretty good shape for a woman of a certain age.* She walked past the doorway down the hall toward the kitchen.

Waiting for the coffee to brew, Viv checked her phone. It did not light up. She shook it in the air, resisting the urge to gently tap it on the tabletop. *With all of the excitement I forgot to plug in last night.* Plugging it in, she reached for her laptop.

To her relief only one person required a return phone call. She shut the laptop and stood. One look at her phone showed the battery was not recharging. *If I hurry I can take it to the repair guy in town. My first priority.* She looked longingly into the kitchen. *I could fix lunch here. I'm hungry but my stomach is in an uproar. I can't think straight. Maybe I can grab lunch while I'm in town.*

She quickly showered and dressed as Miss Kitty called out, "Meow." Grabbing her hat and a purse, she hollered back at the cat, "Try your automatic feeder."

The door slammed behind her.

* * *

After Viv left her phone at the repair shop, she walked down the street to Just Desserts. Voices from the crowded outdoor patio floated out to the street entrance. She asked the hostess, "Is there somewhere inside the cafe?"

"I'll find you something," the young woman assured her. She returned with a menu and a smile. "Go through the door and turn right. In the very back there's an empty booth."

Viv took the menu with a smile. She removed her straw hat, reaching out to open the door. Once inside she stopped to appreciate the cool air. *Even after a drenching the night before, it heats right back up to three digits.*

Viv walked quickly past several tables with people chatting, the sound of utensils tapping against plates. As she approached her booth, she stopped in surprise. A familiar woman dressed in a tank top, with a pink baseball cap pulled over her head, had taken her spot. *Why did she take my seat?*

"Hey, neighbor," came a voice from under the cap. Her head tilted up, revealing the steady gaze of Sutton Drew.

Viv sat down. "How did you know I'd be here?"

"In the first place, I know a bit about your routine." Sutton tilted her head.

"A bit?"

"Okay, so I know more than a bit. I've seen you drop in here on several occasions. Usually for lunch or later in the afternoon. Sometimes you meet with other women. I assume your doula colleagues. Sometimes you make calls and answer texts and email. At least that's what it looks like from afar."

"You've been spying on me?"

"I take care of Rex. That's what I do. I get to know everyone in his circle and I keep an eye out just in case."

Viv couldn't keep the skepticism from her voice. "So Rex is some kind of big deal?"

Sutton grinned. "He actually has a pair of socks that say, 'I'm kind of a big deal.'"

For the first time since she'd gotten involved with Rex and Sutton, Viv felt a bit insecure.

"Rex is a big deal in mentalist circles. I've been his friend slash bodyguard for some time now. He pays me. Quite well, I might add." Sutton reached over to hand Viv a menu. Viv opened it and stared, using the time to think.

I didn't realize that Rex required so much looking after. I guess he's a celebrity just like the rest of the Palm Desert crowd. All of the LA celebrities golf here and spend time. I don't know why I'm so surprised.

Sutton spoke up. "Rex and I started in the nineties, when he was an officer and we first met." Then she paused to add, "I bet he mentioned that already. Anyway you're here for lunch, right? I hope so, because I'm starving. What are you having?"

Viv swallowed back her urge to ask more about Rex. "I usually take the vegetable sandwich on sourdough with goat cheese. They put lots of sprouts and cucumbers."

A slight wave to a waitress brought her to their table. "Your usual?" she asked Viv.

"Yes, please. With a large iced tea. The passion fruit."

"Got it." The waitress turned toward Sutton.

"Large burger with blue cheese crumbles and a water," she said immediately. "Oh, and make the French fries extra crispy."

"Got it," repeated the young woman before she walked away.

"Are you waiting for your phone to be repaired?" Sutton asked.

Viv glared across the table. "You are uncanny. You knew about my phone too?"

"Only because I saw you walk into the shop. Do you need a new one or can they fix the old one for you?"

"They told me to come back by three o'clock."

"Great, we can have lunch and chat. Like girlfriends." Sutton looked quite pleased with herself.

Viv settled back into the cushion. She looked out the window onto the street. Tourists walked past in a variety of summer clothing, mostly wearing hats and shorts. "You'd think people would stay home in the summer heat," she mused aloud.

"Some of them only stay a couple of nights. They play golf and then go home to nurse the heat stroke. I think some of these tourists are day-trippers. They start at the top of the mountain in Lily Rock and then take a ride on that tram to Palm Desert."

"Have you ever been to Lily Rock?"

"A few times. Very quaint and a bit rustic for my taste. A good day trip, if you make a reservation at their famous restaurant. It's called The Refuge. Have you eaten there?"

"I've never been to Lily Rock," Viv answered.

Their food arrived quickly. The waitress placed the plates and drinks on the table and then hurried away for another order.

Viv lifted half a sandwich to her mouth, taking a big bite. She chewed, watching Sutton daintily pick up a French fry with her thumb and forefinger. "You wear fake nails sometimes," Viv commented after swallowing.

"I wear lots of different outfits. Makeup and nails change with my mood." Sutton dipped the end of her fry into catsup. "Even though I can look a bit outlandish, people don't recognize me because I rarely look the same two days in a row."

"That's interesting," Viv said.

By the time three o'clock rolled around, the women were finished with lunch and working on a piece of cheesecake with one fork each. Sutton cleared her throat. "So you probably haven't been able to pick up your phone messages today. Just a heads-up? The Palm Desert cops asked Rex to drop by for another interview. I suspect they may also want to talk to you."

Viv felt her stomach churn. "Does this mean their replacement finally showed up?"

"That's exactly what we figured. His appointment is for five o'clock today. When you get your phone back you might want to check your messages."

Viv reached over to pick up the check the waitress had already left. "Lunch is on me," she told Sutton. "I'd better get that phone. I already feel behind."

Sutton slid across the cushion and stood up at the end of

the booth. "Thanks for lunch, good talking to you. Maybe we'll run into each other at the station." Sutton walked ahead as Viv followed her out of the cafe into the blazing-hot sun.

35

VIVIENNE ROSE

Viv wasted no time pulling up her cell phone messages. Name after name appeared on her screen, some texts, some email.

She scrolled the list, scrubbing it for messages from Desert Doulas. A business request caught her eye.

> We are looking for a prenatal doula beginning as soon as possible…

I'll read that later.
Viv continued to scan. A message from Tamara was next.

> I want to see you face-to-face. We've been missing each other and I have to get a few things off my chest.

I'll get back to her when I can. Viv scrolled to the next. Pearl also texted.

> Can we talk asap? Dereck found out where I live. Big fight. What should I do?

How about not get involved with the partner of a client

next time? You're still picking up the pieces a year later. He was obviously unstable.

Her thumb continued to scroll. She stopped on the pool service reminder.

> We'll be in your neighborhood tomorrow for our regular service. Text us the code for the security gate if you won't be home.

Viv sighed. *I live in a gated community, yet I'm constantly giving out my code and keys so that people can get in. How safe is that?*

The next one brought a smile: a text from Rex. Two, actually.

> Cops got in contact. Will I see you at the police station? Five o'clock.

Followed by a shrugging emoji.
Then his second text.

> It seems my niece is in some kind of trouble. It involves her surrogacy. Help!!!

His niece? I wonder if that's the Hollywood woman who was on television a few days ago? Hailey and Cameron Steward, the celebrity couple. Actors. At least I think they are. Interesting...

Finally the message from Chief Wilson.

> Got our new detective. Come in this afternoon at five for an interview. Thx.

Viv checked the time on her dashboard. *Nearly three thirty. I hope they have some leads on the case.*

* * *

She got a twenty-minute swim, a quick shower, and her hair blown dry. Dressed in shorts and a soft t-shirt, Viv had deliberately not gone overboard with her outfit. Her thoughts scrambled as she admitted her own impatience. *It's taken them forever to interview me.* She glared at herself in the mirror. *Okay, so it's only been a few days, but still. I'm frustrated that they dropped the case.*

Maybe the cops will reveal what they've learned from the forensic investigation. That would help. Viv held the hair dryer in her hand and then she froze. *Stop it, Viv. They aren't going to tell you things. It's not like anyone asked you and Rex to join in the investigation. For all you know, you're both suspects.*

Finished with getting ready, she walked back into her room to select a purse to go with her outfit. Tote in hand, she returned to the kitchen. Her watch read four fifty-five. *Better get going.*

Driving to town, Viv had time to wonder about Sarah. *She'd been so distant these last months. Apparently she had a new boyfriend. Did he find out where she lived and break into her house? Maybe he was the guy we ran from that night.*

With little traffic she made good time. Viv parked in front of the police station. She popped out from behind the driver's seat, stopping to use her Tesla app to lock the car. Taking the steps quickly, she flung open the glass door to escape the heat and get back into air conditioning. The officer behind the reception counter greeted her immediately.

"You are Ms. Rose?" he said.

"That's me," she replied crisply.

"Mr. Redondo is just ahead of you. Go through that door," he said, pointing, "and then walk down the hall. Interview room one."

Viv headed toward the door. Her breaths came quickly as

thoughts filled her head. *Rex is here. Interview room one?* The nagging question returned. *Does that mean we are both suspects, now that they've finally decided to solve Sarah's murder?*

Interview room one was clearly marked. The door stood ajar. Viv walked in, feeling her stomach twist in a knot.

The first thing she saw was Rex's back. Then she heard his familiar laugh. The female police officer on the other side of the desk smiled, as if she were flirting with him. *Look at him, oozing his charm all over the place.* "Hello," she said.

The laughter stopped as Rex turned around.

"Hey, Viv. Glad you're here." He nodded to the empty chair next to him. "Take a seat and I'll introduce you to the new detective on the case. She's come down the hill from Lily Rock on loan."

"I'll take care of the introductions, Mr. Redondo," came the woman's now serious voice. She stood from her chair, walking around the end of the desk, and extended her hand toward Viv. She wore a navy-blue blazer and tan slacks, a white shirt tucked in, snugged in by a brown leather belt. Her hair was smoothed back tightly in a bun.

Viv shook her hand, feeling the detective's eyes assess her.

"My name is Janis Jets," the woman said.

Viv looked her over and wondered. *Lily Rock must be missing their police officer. Such a small town. The captain has two people just hanging out in the front. Maybe he thinks this woman will get the job done. I certainly hope so.*

Viv nodded. "You already know who I am."

"Please have a seat. Mr. Redondo has been telling me about how you broke into the victim's house and were chased out by an unidentified occupant. It seems you've both broken the law and nosed your way into my investigation." Her voice sounded mild but her face looked grim. Officer Jets walked back around the desk to sit down.

As Viv sat next to Rex, he turned to her, his eyebrows raised. "I think we've already annoyed the officer," he said calmly.

Jets thumped the desk with her fist. "I am an officer of the law. But I'm also a detective and that's what the Palm Desert police need right now." Her eyes narrowed.

"You wouldn't be the first to underestimate the ability of trained professionals to do the work necessary to bring a culprit to justice.

"Just to make myself clear, your butting in won't help. I've seen people like you before. Thinking you know more than the professionals. On the one hand, people complain about police inefficiency. But on the other hand, the same folks don't want their taxes raised to pay for qualified officers."

Viv wanted to interrupt the officer, but Jets kept talking.

"In all my years of policing, there's only been one exception when it comes to amateurs."

"One exception?" Viv looked interested.

"That would be someone up the hill. You don't know her. But she has this weird thing. Every time she sings, somebody confesses. It took me a while, but I realized she can just be sitting in a room and people open up. Some kind of psychic gift."

"There is no such thing as a psychic," Rex said on cue.

"That's what you think, fella. I know because I've seen it happen. Plus she's not even aware of her gift. Anyway, enough about that. Like I was saying, Olivia is the only exception. The only amateur sleuth I will ever work with and that's a fact."

A knock came at the door. Rex and Viv both turned

around. "Want some coffee, boss?" a young uniformed man asked.

"Not now. I have to figure out if I'm going to arrest these two do-gooders or just chew them out."

The young officer disappeared, closing the door after him. Viv and Rex turned back around to face Officer Jets. "Now that you've done your duty and chewed us out," Rex remarked in his calm voice, "let's hear Viv's opinion."

"I think it's the pool guy," Viv chimed in. "Rex has a photo. Sutton took it at the casino and she identified him already. He was handing off a quilted cooler to one of my doulas." She took a deep breath, the words tumbling out. "We went to Sarah's house to gather more information—the back door was unlocked, by the way, so it was only trespassing instead of breaking and entering—and while we were there someone broke in. Of course we hid and then got out of there. So I think the pool guy's our killer." She sat back in her chair.

Rex turned to stare at her, eyes shiny with what she assumed was admiration.

She assumed he was proud until both he and Jets burst out laughing.

"Now that was some tale," the officer said, covering her mouth with a fist.

"I'd already told her most of that," Rex admitted.

"And if you'd bothered to ask me," Jets continued, "I would have explained to you, just like I told him. That was one of my team. We've been watching Ms. Esperanza's trailer for days."

Viv felt her heart drop. Her fists balled up with exasperation. She looked from Rex to Janis and in one final sigh, she folded her arms over her chest in a huff.

36

VIVIENNE ROSE

Jets laced both hands behind her head. She appeared to be thinking. Neither Rex nor Viv said a word. Rex looked slightly bored while Viv felt she'd already talked enough.

When Jets's phone went off, she pulled her hands away, reaching over the desk and answering it. "What is it, Brad? ... Really? ... I'll do some background as soon as she gives me a name. Tell her to stay in bed. Get over there and watch their house. Grab the mayor while you're at it. ... What? ... He's been seen again. No matter. You go. That's an order." Jets clicked off the phone.

She looked at Rex, then back to Viv. "A personal call," she explained. "The mayor of Lily Rock has been seen riding in the back of a lime-green VW Beetle, right through town."

"A political ploy," Rex said.

"Maybe he's campaigning for the next election," suggested Viv.

Jets snorted. "I would say that were true, if the Lily Rock mayor were a person. But he's not. Our mayor is a labradoodle named Maguire. He never rides in strange vehicles. So this is puzzling and requires an investigation."

Viv looked at Rex. He shook his head slightly as if to say, we have a whack-a-doodle in our midst.

"Are we done here?" Viv asked.

"You are done when I say you are done," barked Jets. "I have a good mind to put you two in a holding cell just to keep you out of my hair."

She glared at Rex. "You seem like a reasonable kind of guy. Why don't you take her and go have a nice dinner somewhere? I've got the investigation from here. When we get some information that I can share—it may take a day or two—I'll call you back in. Just don't go rogue on me again. I'm warning you. I have plenty of cell space in the back and it won't be fun and games."

Viv watched Rex. The way he sucked in his cheeks and rubbed his forefinger over his lips. *Apparently he thinks Janis Jets is joking.*

She looked over at Jets. *She strikes me as a woman who follows through with her threats.*

Rex stood abruptly and placed his hand on the back of Viv's chair. She took the move as an invitation and stood. Viv cleared her throat.

"Before we go, I could tell you more about the dead woman. She was my colleague. A doula. One of the best." Viv felt tears threaten, realizing she was letting her emotions get the best of her. Rex took her elbow with his hand as they waited for the officer to reply.

Jets's face softened. "I can see you really cared about Sarah Esperanza. I get that. It's kind of odd, but the word doula never crossed my lips until the last twenty-four hours. And now it's doulas everywhere. Even my Lily Rock friends are talking about hiring a doula."

Rex cleared his throat. "I don't believe in psychics, but I do pay close attention to coincidences. It seems to me the whole doula business is at the heart of Sarah's demise. I don't know the details, that part is up to you." He nodded to Jets as he dropped his hand to open the door. "We're going to have dinner now. That was a very good idea. Good luck with your investigation." He waited for Viv to head out the doorway.

As they walked the short distance down the hall, Viv said, "Are we really..."

He held his finger to his lips. As they passed the reception desk, he nodded to the officer.

Outside the station, Viv exhaled. "I was holding my breath," she told him. "I believed her threat." The heat of the sun pounded on her head. "It must be over one hundred now," she added.

"It's always about the weather here in the desert," Rex said mildly.

"So are we gonna just give up our investigation?"

"Please, we're not giving up a thing. We'll have dinner first. I know a little place with air conditioning and an indoor waterfall. Very chic. We'll talk and figure out our next move over a good meal."

"Oh, I am so glad. I thought she had you buffaloed."

"Nah, she's just asserting her authority. I respect that, but I don't have to follow her rules. No one wants to fill up the jail with innocent citizens who are trying to help out. Plus there's another coincidence I want to talk to you about. It got lost in the search of Sarah's house. I was going to tell you, actually ask your advice.

"It's about my niece. She's actually hired a surrogate, but for the sake of her brand, she's pretending that she gave birth to her baby. Surrogacy, isn't that something a doula gets involved with?"

"Oh, yes it is!" Viv nodded. "Sarah was a doula for surrogacy cases. She'd been a surrogate herself years ago, so she was an excellent resource for other doulas." It felt good to point out Sarah's expertise.

Rex nodded toward her car, then his cell phone rang. He held it to his ear.

"Hi, Sutton. ... Sure. Is she okay? ... I'm just finishing up here. I'll ask Viv." He touched his screen and shoved the phone in his pocket.

"My SUV is still in the shop," he explained. It looks like we'll have to postpone our dinner. My niece, Hailey, showed up unexpectedly and is in kind of a state."

"She's the one who just had a baby?"

He nodded. "Like I said, she used a surrogate. She tried to fake her postpartum with the media, but they've gotten wind of the truth. That was one thing I wanted to talk to you about."

"No worries about dinner. Let's get you back home." She pulled her cell phone from her purse. Using an app, she unlocked the Tesla. "Have you ever ridden in one of these?" she asked him, walking closer to the car.

"I've always wanted to." He opened his door. "All electric, right?"

"That's right, just push that strip and the handle will pop out." She walked around the car. Once they were both inside, he ran his hand over the dashboard. "A very streamlined interior. Just the screen and a couple of stick levers on the steering wheel."

She tapped the screen, adjusting the air conditioning. "I always say to people, it's not really a car. It's a computer that happens to be a car."

"It depends on your perspective, I guess." He watched her back out of the parking space.

The word *perspective* gave Viv pause for thought. She

drove along and then began to wonder. *Maybe I need to look at Sarah's death from another perspective...*

I saw Sarah as experienced and competent. She was always my first call for doula work. Never mind me, I always thought she was the doula to die for."

Truthfully I never saw her as needing my help. She was the one I took for granted, the capable one, never weak and always strong.

But maybe for once Sarah was in trouble and didn't know how to ask for help. She may have gotten in over her head personally or professionally or both. Maybe she overestimated her own strength, only to find herself underwater, sinking to her death.

.

37

REX REDONDO

By the time Viv drops me off, I am plenty mad at Hailey. Viv and I almost made it to dinner, just this close, and Hailey had to show up and ruin everything. Viv didn't seem too disappointed though. Maybe that's what's really bothering me. I wanted her to be just a bit more disappointed when I had to postpone our meal together.

I walk toward my front door and Sutton opens it. She must have been looking out the window for me. "She's in there." Sutton points to the solarium side of the house.

Before I moved in, I had a glass-sided room added to the back. It's where I spend a lot of time ignoring the desert. I spray my jungle of plants in the morning, water and feed at night. It's a ritual. Kevin sleeps on his chair, one eye open. He thinks he's my bodyguard, protecting me from the likes of a Sansevieria or a Pothos.

I find Hailey sitting on the rattan sofa, dabbing at her puffy face with a polished pink-nailed forefinger. "Oh, Uncle Rex!" She bursts into a flood of tears. Leaping from the sofa, she runs toward me, wrapping her arms around my neck.

I pat her on the back, just the way I used to when she was

a tike and had skinned a knee. She'd never been very good on roller skates. Nor did she have the balance for skateboarding. I tried over the years to bring age-appropriate gifts but was informed that she wasn't a tomboy. That happened right after I'd bought and installed a tetherball pole for her backyard. The first swing, she rammed her hand into the pole and broke two fingers.

"Jewelry, makeup, and salon care gift certificates," her father advised me after that. "Those are the gifts from an honorary uncle to a princess niece."

"It's okay, sweetheart." I put my hands on her shoulders, moving her back from my chest to look at her face. She sniffs as I hold her steady for my inspection. "You need to sit down right over there. Uncle Rex is here and we'll sort this out together."

I lead her back to the sofa. Plumping the cushions, I gently guide her to sit down. She sighs, bestowing upon me the grateful smile of a queen.

Okay, so I'm good with distraught females. It's part of my charm. I trained to be that guy every woman wants, the one who puts all of his problems aside at the drop of a hat to listen. That's the persona I use in my show when I want to call a woman from the audience. That's the persona I bring for Hailey right now, even though I am highly annoyed about missing the almost date with Viv. I sit down in the chair opposite her.

"Sutton?"

"Right here, Rex." I turn in the chair to see her standing in the doorway.

"Could you bring us drinks? I'll take a beer. What about you, Hailey?"

"A dry martini, one olive, shaken not stirred," she says immediately.

When Sutton leaves, I turn to Hailey. "So what's going on?"

"It's Cameron. He's acting so awful!" Her bottom lip begins to quiver.

Brace yourself, Rex. It's gonna be a long night.

"Tell me about everything." I smile, waiting for her to begin.

It didn't take long.

"He's told me to butt out of his business, that he's handling the logistics. I mean, how can I let it go when it's about my baby and our private life?"

The hair raises on my neck. "Has someone kidnapped your baby?"

Hailey sniffles, her shoulders begin to shake. Her face remains beautiful, despite the slightly swollen eyes.

"Baby is home with the nanny," she finally tells me. "That's not the problem. He's safe."

I take a deep breath. "So tell me what made Cameron so mad. Was it a legal problem with the surrogacy? You did get good representation, I hope. Documents by lawyers who deal in this sort of thing."

For a quick moment I wonder. What might happen to my niece's fragile mental state if the surrogate should all of a sudden want to keep the baby?

"We had plenty of legal counsel," she assures me with another dramatic sniff.

"No name yet, just 'baby'?" I ask.

"We don't have a name yet." She looks at me, her eyes wide. "You realize that baby comes from my egg and Cameron's sperm. The process was long, but they did get our embryo fertilized and then implanted it inside the, you know, surrogate. She just carried it around for nine months."

My mind takes that information and I honestly feel more

than just a little irritated. Hailey and Cameron have no idea how privileged they are. Getting someone else to carry their baby for cash. It's not like Hailey was infertile or unable to conceive herself.

I bet Cameron probably didn't want to deal with the ups and downs of a pregnant wife. So he was more than happy to let someone else carry the load. Call me old fashioned, I know my opinions aren't always politically correct.

I also know better than to speak my opinions to just anyone. Especially a woman on her own body business. Since I'm not the one who has to be pregnant, I'm not sure I deserve an opinion. But I do have them. My chest feels tight right now. I am stressed.

"You paid her lots of money, right?"

"Oh lots! Tons, in fact. We paid for all of the surrogacy expenses and then another fee on top of that. Then we paid for the doula and the attorneys who did the paperwork."

I feel a niggle at the back of my mind. Then it hits me. "What was the surrogate's name and did she have a doula?" Please realize, Hailey tends to speak of people using their profession instead of a name. She calls people surrogate, doula, baby, uncle. Everyone's named in relation to the job they do for her.

"Alice M. is the surrogate's name." Hailey pauses. "She did have a birth doula, but I never met her. Wait a minute. I think her name was Sarah E. The attorneys wanted to keep things impersonal, so we didn't get the full names of all of the birth workers."

Sarah E. That could be Viv's doula. She did just tell me that she considered Sarah Esperanza as the doula to die for...

My heart pounds. "I thought birth mothers stayed in contact with the babies and the parents."

"Some do. Not us. We have a career to consider. I didn't

want our surrogate to be harassed just because she gave birth to a famous couple's baby."

Oh, so she's protecting the surrogate, not herself. Why don't I believe that?

This disingenuous assessment almost made me choke. Hailey probably feels very proud about that rationalization—saving the surrogate from too much scrutiny. Unfortunately I don't see it that way. I see Hailey and Cameron wanting to take credit for all of the baby, including the pregnancy. They don't want the complications of another person involved. Plus they have plenty of dough to pay for whatever they want.

This is just another role for Hailey. She made quite the show on social media of being seen with her baby bump these past several months. It's a role for her, pretending to be pregnant and "recovering" from her pregnancy. Telling that story brings her more followers. The truth is she's saving herself by dismissing the surrogate.

"So if Alice M. doesn't want to keep the baby, what could possibly be the problem?"

"She's threatening to out me and tell the press that I was never pregnant." Hailey's lower lip protrudes in a pout.

"But she signed a nondisclosure for that, I assume."

"She did, but her boyfriend started harassing us a couple of weeks ago. He's threatening to expose us to the media."

I watch Hailey. She fidgets, adjusting herself against the cushion. She's still holding back something. I just know it. I can tell by the way she's crossed her arms—that's her tell.

"There's something more. Give it up now, or I'm going to withhold your martini and send you to your room." My playful exaggeration brings a slight smile to her face. She releases her arms.

"The legal documents left something out. The lawyers never thought about it, nor did we."

"And what was that exactly?"

"The placenta. The surrogate's boyfriend told Cameron that he'd encapsulated Alice's placenta and that we needed to pay up or he would sell the capsules to the highest bidders on the internet. 'Celebrity placenta pills will bring quite a price.' Those were his exact words."

So for the second day in a row, I'm hearing about placentas. Some might think that a coincidence, but not me. I may not be a psychic, but I do pay very close attention when I hear something unusual two times, from two different sources. First Viv and now Hailey.

I hear the door open behind me. Sutton walks in holding two drinks on a tray extended in one hand. My mind swirls like it does when I need to look at something I've been avoiding. So if Viv is right and I really do have a problem with lady business talk, that may be the reason.

Yet I live with a woman, love them, respect them, uncle them, if that's a thing, I'd better man up and get over my nonsense. Sutton sets the drinks on the table. She looks over at me.

"I've got this," I tell her. She doesn't need any more persuasion. She backs away and turns to walk quickly out the door.

I hold the beer glass to my lips, watching Hailey sip her martini. I let my gaze rise upward, taking in the indoor forest behind the sofa, feeling calmer at the sight of the dwarf palm swaying slightly in the breeze from the fan. After another sip I lower my eyes, feeling much better, at least ready to continue the conversation.

"So the placenta is the problem. Maybe you'd better tell me more about that."

To give her credit, she doesn't start crying again. Her eyes narrow as she glares. "Like I just said, they didn't get rid of the surrogate's placenta after the birth. They kept it. Turned it into capsules and some kind of tincture and then threatened to sell it on the internet to the highest bidder."

"So Alice doesn't get her own placenta?"

"Technically it belongs to us," Hailey explains.

I wonder if that's true. Maybe another loophole in the legal documents.

"Who would buy a placenta on the internet?"

Hailey huffs. "Nutters who think they can get beautiful skin and push away aging. You know, look like us. Maybe they want to play with it in a lab or something, create new Haileys and Camerons."

"So your DNA, not Alice's, can be extracted from the placenta?"

"That's not the point, Uncle Rex," she tells me firmly. "Even if the capsules are made of ground-up vitamins, people will buy them if they think they came from us. People believe anything you tell them. And money can be made before anyone figures out it's a scam. Our reputation would be ruined either way, and we'd most likely get cancelled."

Am I living in an alternate world or something... Who's heard of such a thing? Didn't Viv just tell me a placenta is an organ? Why would people think they could buy them off the internet and use them for their own purposes without being arrested?

I look closely at Hailey. Setting aside her queenly demeanor, I think she's really upset. Maybe for herself, but maybe I've not given her enough credit. Selling the placenta may have repercussions for her child. They can't even name the kid; what would they do if his DNA became a must-have all over the world?

"I'm glad you told me about this," I say using my calmest voice. "Now it's time to tell me more about Cameron. Has he gotten involved with these scammers, and if he has, do we need to call the police?"

"Cameron has just gone ballistic. He's bought a gun and stays up all night connecting with people on the dark web. Now he's not at home for most of the day. He says he's tracking down the culprits, but I don't know where he goes."

Like any woman asked to describe her husband's bad temper, Hailey is just warming up.

"And on top of all that, he's irritable and he doesn't even hold the baby. It's all up to me and nanny to keep things together. I'm just a wreck!" More sobs, more rubbing of eyes, and then finally another sip of martini as she takes a breath.

I force myself to look up again, doing my best to concentrate. But Cameron's personality change has not escaped my attention. I noticed he was not his usual cool and calm self at The Roadkill. If he's half as angry as Hailey tells me, he might not even think twice about bashing a woman over the head and shoving her into a pool. Especially if he thought she had anything to do with the placenta nightmare.

What if Cameron planned to meet up with Sarah and her boyfriend that night at Viv's? A little internet research might have revealed my connection to Hailey and then my location, right next door to the owner of Desert Doulas. Where I live is public information.

Sarah probably told Viv she was coming over for a swim. But the reality was far more sinister. If Sarah and her boyfriend were trying to get the money and hand over the placenta capsules, Viv's backyard would be the perfect place. A gated retirement community, in the house of a respected doula, no less. I shift my focus to Hailey's red face.

"I need to talk to Cameron as soon as possible. And he needs to call his attorney right away."

38

VIVIENNE ROSE

Viv woke with a start.

Before falling into bed, she had sent a group text to Tamara and Pearl.

> It's time for us to talk. I will send you a link for a Zoom meeting tomorrow morning at nine o'clock. Cancel any other plans.

Her cell phone lay on the table next to the bed. She picked it up to check if her text the night before had brought results.

Okay, came the response from Pearl.

I'll be there, Tamara replied.

After showering and getting dressed, Viv fed Miss Kitty. She sat down to watch the cat circle her food dish, taking a moment to think about what she would say to her doulas.

Lifting a dainty white paw, Miss Kitty poked at her food. With the curl of her claws, she tipped a chunk of tuna out of the bowl and onto the floor. She pawed it again as if it were a toy.

"It's not a mouse, you silly fluffer. Eat your breakfast," Viv teased her cat, who looked up at her and then quickly back to the clump of wet food. Miss Kitty tried one more swift pass with her paw. When the food didn't fight back, she bent over and took a bite.

Not for the first time, Viv took the clue from her cat. *I'm going to emulate Miss Kitty when it comes to my doula team. I'm going to gently but firmly bat them about to see if they will reveal what they've been hiding from me these past months. Good call, Miss Kitty.*

Viv suspected Tamara and Pearl weren't being forthcoming. In hindsight she'd known something was up even before Sarah was killed. She'd been alerted when their posts on social media showed them together more, having drinks. She had been too busy to feel left out.

But the other night, when Tamara said she had to do an errand before coming over and then she didn't make time to sit down and talk, Viv's suspicions bubbled up. She started forming a story around what she'd been unwilling to admit.

When she saw Sarah's kitchen, she knew immediately. Not just she but *they* had gone behind her back to encapsulate. Encapsulating placentas was supposed to be an occasional service offered by select doulas, not a full-on business with several dehydrators and a freezer full of organs.

She poured a strong cup of coffee and looked at the clock. *Five minutes before nine.* She sat down at the table and opened her laptop. It only took a couple of minutes to send Pearl and Tamara the meeting link.

We're going to get to the bottom of this right now.

39

VIVIENNE ROSE

Tamara's and Pearl's faces appeared on the screen. To Viv's eyes, both looked like deer in headlights. Her irritation slid away at the sight of their tired expressions.

"Let's just jump in, shall we?" She used a no-nonsense voice she often brought out for her son when he was younger.

Tamara nodded an affirmative. Pearl looked down, avoiding Viv's steady on-screen gaze. She didn't wait for anything from them before she began.

"You've been keeping something from me. It seems you're in on it together. And I'm afraid your lack of disclosure may be holding back the police investigation." *Good thing I'm not above inflicting a bit of shame now and then. It's a gift that I use with great precision, like a skilled surgeon with a sharp scalpel.*

"But you've gotta understand," began Tamara. "Unlike you, the three of us—me, Pearl, and Sarah—got together to figure out how to get out from under our debts. Doula work doesn't pay that well and we needed money for living expenses. I also have my daughter. Heather decided to go back to school—remember I mentioned she needed fall tuition? She got accepted to Cal Lutheran. She wants to start over and try again. And I promised to help her out.

"You know doulas aren't rich. I mean, we're all driving old cars and living in small places. Sarah had been living in a junky mobile home."

"I saw where she lived," Viv said quietly. A look of surprise came over Pearl's face.

"Anyway, we all thought getting qualified for placenta encapsulation would bring in necessary money. That's what attracted us. One more way to get solvent and help our families."

"It was a class and we all went together," interjected Pearl.

"And all three of you got the certificate?"

"We all qualified. It didn't take long to convince the mothers we worked with. Once we explained the advantages of ingesting their placenta, they were on board. We mostly did the work in each mother's kitchen."

"If that didn't work, we used Sarah's kitchen," added Tamara.

Viv's eyes narrowed. "I saw Sarah's kitchen: the freezer, the dehydrator, the roasting pans, and the blender. She even had the machine that makes the capsules."

Tamara and Pearl stared straight into Viv's eyes. *They may be surprised that I've not only been to Sarah's but I've seen the whole operation.*

"And you both knew my thoughts on placenta encapsulation." *Put it right out there. That's my motto.*

"We know your opinion," muttered Tamara.

"You told us often enough," added Pearl.

"Like I've said before, I keep up on the research, and scientists are still out when it comes to the benefits of placenta ingestion. This is not a service I have added to Desert Doulas as of yet."

Pearl ignored her. "So we went out on our own because we figured there wasn't any harm. Even if the capsules acted like a placebo, the mothers would feel better. Four hundred dollars per placenta, that makes a difference to my budget. It pays for my electrical and air conditioning at least."

Tamara nodded. "As I said, Heather's going to college, and it's expensive. Everyone knows that student loan interest is astronomical, plus she has another year of tuition. I don't want her dropping out her last year because she doesn't have the money. I'm doing my best to pay for college for her."

"How many placentas per month?" Viv's stomach clenched waiting for the reply.

Probably two or three a month, for me at least," Pearl said.

"About the same for me," admitted Tamara.

Viv took a deep breath. "What about Sarah? How many for her?"

"Well that's the thing." Tamara's face dropped. "Sarah got so busy, she barely had time for new doula clients."

"How is that possible?"

"Her boyfriend got involved. He became very interested in the process, offered to help out. He paid for the necessary equipment. Then one thing led to another and he said he had a way to bring her fresh placentas from other birthing women."

"Did she meet the mothers?"

"Not really, but when she asked questions, he brushed her off. But the money was nothing to sneeze at, so she continued for a while anyway. Then recently, when she threatened to stop encapsulating, he started bullying her."

Viv's stomach dropped. "Sarah had a history of domestic abuse. I thought we'd worked through that. This is just tragic."

Tears rose in Tamara's eyes. "She was trying to get away

from Zach. I think that's why she came to your house that night—to think things over."

"Was he violent?"

"Zach shoved me one time when I was helping Sarah in the kitchen with an encapsulation. He pushed me hard from behind, and my stomach hit the edge of the sink. I was sore for days." Pearl looked down at her hands. She didn't explain any more so Viv asked the next question.

"Do you know his last name?"

"Zach Young," Tamara said immediately.

After another deep breath, Viv said, "Okay, then you two have to talk to the police about what you know. I think you may even be held accountable for breaking the law. You know from your accreditation program that you can't just buy a placenta from someone and give the encapsulations to another. It's the same as trafficking other organs in this state."

"Yes, but we weren't involved with where the capsules were going. We only used the placenta for practical purposes. The fee was for the capsules. That's legal," Pearl said defensively.

Tamara looked angry. "Don't be a dummy. We knew he was up to something illegal with all the drop-offs and pickups. Zach was making big money on this. He must have been charging a higher fee, keeping it for himself. Plus he got defensive every time we asked him."

"He got mean," Pearl agreed. "And he kept bringing more and more placentas."

Viv looked down at her hands. She shuffled her notebook to give herself time. Once she raised her eyes, she found Tamara and Pearl staring at their screens.

Viv tapped her fingers on the table. *Do I tell them the police have been staking out Sarah's trailer? I wonder if Officer*

Jets only has eyes for Zach... Maybe she doesn't know about Pearl or Tamara. Maybe it's not too late.

"How many times did you two work in Sarah's kitchen?"

"Not that often," Tamara admitted. "More frequently toward the end, before she died. The placentas just kept coming, so we kept working. Kind of an assembly line."

"Did you sterilize all the equipment?"

Pearl looked startled. She was the most germ conscious of all Viv's doulas. "Of course we did! I made sure everything got boiled and steamed. We never used the same butcher block or knife without taking sanitary precautions."

A sense of optimism came over Viv. "So I'm thinking your natural tendency to keep a sterile environment may be in your favor. If your fingerprints aren't on the equipment, the police can't arrest you."

"My fingerprints are all over Sarah's kitchen!" Tamara exclaimed.

"That can be explained," Viv told her calmly. "You were friends and colleagues. You fixed each other coffee and some meals. You chatted together at the kitchen table. That explains why your fingerprints may be found."

"But not on the encapsulation equipment," Pearl insisted.

Looking back and forth at her doulas, Viv felt her gut tighten. Her hands made a fist. *How did they hide this from me? I thought we were all on the same page as friends. Doulas of the heart, so to speak. Yet they had their own inner circle, leaving me out because I had an opposing opinion and wouldn't understand?*

She inhaled deeply to keep from blurting out her feelings. "Tell me more about the night Sarah was killed," said Viv.

"We were both at the Freebirth Rising event at Coachella," Tamara jumped in. "Like I told the cops, Pearl came by your house so that we could drive together."

"Did you let Pearl in the gate with the code?" She tried to use a calm voice to hide her concerns.

"I did. Used your intercom. She drove over and I hopped in. Sarah came later. I left her the key."

"We wanted her to come with us," Pearl said, "but she refused. She thought hanging out by the pool would give her a chance to think."

"If only..." Tamara sighed. "If only we'd waited and taken her with us, then none of this would have happened."

We'll have time for regrets later. I need to get to the bottom of this.

"So what happened to Sarah's car? Weren't you even curious?" Viv asked.

"I figured she parked on the street because she forgot the gate code," explained Tamara. "You can park on the road and then slide past when the gate opens for another resident. I told the cops that when they asked."

Viv took a moment, again fiddling with her notebook. *Did Zach find Sarah and try to persuade her to come back? No wonder Jets is surveilling Sarah's trailer.*

"Are either of you taking over with the placenta encapsulation process?" Viv tried to sound calm, but her stomach tied in a knot.

"Not me," came Tamara's reply.

"Me neither," Pearl said.

Realizing her trust in her doulas had been seriously eroded, Viv's jaw tightened. It would take some time to build back their relationships to the place they once were. "Okay then. I think you'd best stay out of that business, at least until the murderer is found. You'll look less involved and hopefully you won't be considered suspects."

They both nodded.

"I'm ready to get on with my day," Viv said to the women.

"But I do have one more question. Do you think Sarah was meeting anyone at my house that night? Could she have let Zach in the gate, for example? Did either of you give him my address? Maybe he called her in an attempt to change her mind?"

"I didn't talk to Zach. I was gone before she arrived," Tamara stated again. "I don't know what she was up to."

"I'd never give out your address to anyone." Pearl bit her bottom lip.

"Okay, you two. That's about all I can handle right now. If you want some advice? Stay out of trouble. Do your jobs and distance yourself from the encapsulation business, at least for now."

Viv clicked the button to end the video conference. Her head was pounding. Holding her fingertips to her temples, she willed the headache to go away. As she rubbed and pondered it occurred to her.

I forgot to ask Pearl about Dereck. Viv sighed. *But this headache... No wonder I forgot.*

40

REX REDONDO

I polish a bar glass, looking over The Roadkill dining room. People are chowing down food and hoisting drinks. The two televisions blare from opposite corners. Installed high over-head, they give the place a sports bar vibe. One screen shows a tennis match, the other a local news station. I pretend to be the bartender, a little exchange I managed with my pal Jake who is the real Roadkill employee.

It's the news station that catches my attention. A familiar face fills the screen. The anchor reports, "It couple Hailey and Cameron Steward have good news for their fans. The new baby's name will be released by the end of the week. Hailey told reporters..."

The screen shifts to Hailey standing in front of their house. She wears tight-fitting yoga pants and a form-fitting top; her hair bounces in a high ponytail. No more tunic for her, she's back to her before-baby weight. Of course I know the truth. She never carried that baby inside her body.

Hailey's perky voice rises above the din of the bar. "Now that we know our baby better, we're ready to name him this week."

The local anchor continues. "We've had photographers outside their home looking out for any possible view of the infant. So far he's been kept out of the public eye. But look at Hailey! She's back in shape already, heading to her yoga session only ten days after giving birth."

The anchor blinks, holding her finger to her ear. "Breaking news, everyone. Sources tell us there's more to the story than meets the eye about the Steward celebrity baby. Stay tuned for the late-night report to find out more on Hailey and Cameron and their untold birth story."

I feel my heart drop. I do love those two, even if I get impatient at times. Actually they make me nuts nearly all the time. This breaking news has to be about the surrogacy. Did someone in their inner circle blab?

I put down the glass on the rack behind the bar. Glancing at myself in the mirror, I pretend to straighten my collar. I want an excuse to stare at Sutton. From the mirror I can see her sitting in the usual booth. She's changed into a red wig with fluffy curls. My eyes drift to the pink spangly crop top, past the hot-pink short-shorts, to her knee-high white go-go boots.

In any other place she would have stuck out. But at The Roadkill in the Pair-a-Dice Casino she looks quite ordinary. No one stares at her besides me. That's how Sutton goes unnoticed. She's good at deciding what to wear and who will notice, long before I even have a clue.

She's already spotted me looking at her in the mirror's reflection. A slight nod tells me she knows I'm watching. It's getting late. Maybe we'll have a drop-off tonight. If not tonight, I'll be playing bartender until we do.

The other thing about Sutton? She doesn't give up. If she doesn't have time right away, like a dog with a bone, she'll bury a project until she can get back to it. I bet she's been sitting in that booth, wearing one kind of an outfit or another, every night since she realized something was up with that cooler exchange. She's been waiting for them to show, gathering information, patiently setting her trap.

I wouldn't want to get on her bad side. Just sayin'.

* * *

"What can I get you?"

Sutton stands across the bar. She slides onto a stool. "A whiskey, neat," she says, and then adds, "the good stuff."

I pour her a shot of Jake's best, my eyes glancing over the room.

"Is tonight the night?" I ask her, sliding the shot glass closer.

"I have a good feeling about this." She takes the glass in her hand. A lift and a tilt of her head make the liquid disappear.

"Another?" I ask innocently.

"Not yet." She pops the glass back on the bar. "Are you ready for your part?"

She refers to our plan, developed earlier. Once she spots the guy with the cooler she will text me to come over. I'll leave the bar and walk into the casino lobby. She'll start shooting the video, blending in with the other people no problem.

Then I'll leap into action to stop the people, and then Sutton can show them the video. We can demand an explanation right then and there. Not a complicated plan but effective if the timing is just right.

Earlier Sutton told me she thought the cooler would be filled with cash. "What a great way to exchange money right out in public."

"Yeah," I told her, "but I'm thinking they could just stand in the parking lot to exchange money. Do it old-school. Slide it into a newspaper and tuck it under the arm kind of deal. Why use a backpack in the middle of a public area like the lobby of a casino?"

"Maybe that's the point," Sutton said. "It doesn't look that wrong, two people in a crowd handing off a backpack. Plus there are at least a dozen security people looking out for anyone handing off money and drugs in a parking lot."

"Not so many inside the casino?"

"Oddly that's true," Sutton agrees.

While in the lobby, people don't notice that much. They're on their way to the floor to play blackjack or the slots. Other people are heading to The Roadkill. And nearly everyone has a drink in their hand.

"How did you figure out these handoffs were happening?"

"It wasn't that easy. It took me several surveillance sessions. After I gathered the information you needed for your show, I'd hang out in the lobby. Just for kicks, to people watch and drink a beer. Then I began to recognize them; they were more furtive than the usual crowd. They showed up two to three times in a month and always around ten p.m. Always on a Thursday."

There you go. Sutton amazes me. She never gives up. She goes on her instinct and keeps at it until she's proven right or wrong to her satisfaction. If only I were like that...

A guy in sweatpants and a comb-over slides onto the stool next to Sutton. "Buy you a drink, hot stuff?" He leers at her. This is going to be fun.

A slow smile comes over her face. "How about this instead? You pay for the drink I just finished and we'll call it even." She eases herself off the stool, giving him every opportunity to disagree.

But he just watches her, his jaw slack with appreciation.

She walks away, swinging her hips, adding a precise tiny extra wiggle for effect.

I hand him the bill. He looks at it and draws out a credit card. "It was worth it," he tells me, sliding the card across the bar, "just to see her walk away."

I process the card in the small machine, and as I hand it back to him, my cell phone buzzes. A text from Sutton.

He's here. Come right now.

I smile at comb-over guy and untie my apron. I duck around the bar. Dodging left then right to avoid chairs, I half stumble across the room. I hurry past the inside entrance to the casino and do a spin to avoid a guy with a beer in his hand. Whirling back the other way, I look for Sutton.

I see her right away. Standing close by, she's next to the guy in the LA baseball cap. He holds the cooler to his side, looks around and then taps on his phone with his thumb.

Maybe the pickup person is late.

Impatiently balancing from foot to foot, he shifts the cooler to the other hand. People walk around him. Just as Sutton said, they barely stop to look his way, jostling each other and laughing, haphazardly stumbling through the crowd.

Holding the phone next to his side, he puts down the cooler to tug at his cap, keeping his head down. It covers most of his face.

You may have figured out by now that I can be impulsive. It's a flaw, really. Gets me into lots of trouble. Also gets me into some fun, like falling for Viv. Do you believe in love at first sight? Anyway, impulse takes me away right now. I break from the original plan. Shoving the cell into my pocket, I hurry toward the guy with the cooler.

I dash the final few feet, push against an overdressed woman in high heels, and do a zig and a zag to avoid her falling on me.

No time to help her out. I dash two more steps. Reaching over, I snatch the cooler and then duck under a guy's arm to make a right. Sprinting toward the entrance of the main floor, I hear bells ringing, the noise of people yelling. Someone must have won a lot of dough at the slots. Perfect timing—I can get lost real quick in this crowd, which is what I do.

In the dimmed lighting I slip toward the edge of the room. Making my way farther into the gaming tables, I stop in front of the restrooms to catch my breath. That's when I see him. A guy coming right toward me. With a slight jump I turn from the wall and dive back into the crowd. Lowering my body, I shift left then right.

I can't see the exit because the cigarette smoke is so thick. Right in front of me a group of people cheer on an old lady at the slots. This looks like her lucky day. The tokens start to tumble into her outstretched hands. I slide next to the guy in back and shove my way toward the front.

"Look out, buddy," a man voice growls.

"Don't push," a woman warns me.

I move one step back, only to make a small step sideways. Lurching around another elbow, I lunge to the front where I can hopefully stay hidden. No one stops me this time.

Mingling with the crowd around the slots, I hold the cooler to my body.

I can smell liquor on the breath of the guy next to me. On the right is a woman, her hair in a bun. She looks like a dealer, wearing tan pants and a white shirt. I do a double take. Hey, wait a minute. I know this woman...

"Thank you very much, Mr. Redondo." I feel her snatch the cooler from my hand. "I'll take that. You can turn around.

These cuffs will fit quite nicely. Don't try one of your mentalist tricks on me. No magic or wiggles will release you from my custody."

As she speaks in my ear, she finishes slapping the hand-cuffs on my wrists. With a firm hand on my elbow, she pushes her way through the crowd. "Excuse me, please," she says loudly. When a guy tries to ignore her, she gives him a steely eye, nodding to my handcuffs. He moves real fast after that.

She keeps shoving people aside as we approach the far wall. Now I see the exit. Too late. I hear her say, "I'm arresting you for stealing property. You have the right to remain silent. Anything you say can and will..." Her words fall away, drowned out by the opening of the exit door.

The outdoor heat hits my face. My heart leaps at the sound of the door slamming behind me. Before I know what's happening, I feel two strong hands push me against the side of the building. The stucco stings the side of my face. Jets stands next to me. She holds the cooler in front of her and unzips the top.

We both look inside. It might have come from my own freezer, a bit of steak or kidney in a plastic bag. Jets sniffs.

Wait a minute. Kidney? I look again. A bit of blood oozes out of the ziplock. I know right away what we're dealing with.

That piece of meat isn't someone's dinner. Not by a long shot.

41

VIVIENNE ROSE

A text from Sutton interrupted Viv's evening.

Rex arrested at casino. Can you help?

Viv texted right back.

I'll come over asap.

She put Miss Kitty down on the ground, receiving a disgruntled look, the cat's tail swatting her leg in protest. "I'll be back," she told her.

Once in her room she changed into a pair of shorts and added a linen top from the unfolded laundry pile on the bed. Hair brushed, lipstick on, she grabbed her purse and headed to the car.

Fifteen minutes later the lights of Pair-a-Dice flashed *Welcome.* She found a parking space just as her phone pinged.

Back entrance. Hurry.

She flung open the door and slid out from behind the driver's seat. Tapping the lock on her screen, she heard the accompanying chirp from her car. Walking rapidly past cars and people, loud voices spilled from the casino.

Purse slung over her shoulder, she cut across the lot, making her way to the back of the building. People lingered, many with beer bottles in hand.

Once around the corner she could see a flashing light on top of a police car. The familiar back of Rex's head showed through the rear windshield. *What has he done now?* Viv picked up her pace. *Why would the cops pick up Rex?*

"Hey Viv, over here," called Sutton. Viv followed the voice and then saw Sutton standing at the corner of the building. Sutton stared at her phone, leaning against the gate that separated the large trash bins from the rest of the parking area.

Next to her was Janis Jets, whose face looked grim.

"I'm here," Viv called out.

Jets turned around. "What for? He doesn't need you, he needs an attorney," she said matter-of-factly.

"What do you mean?" Viv's breath came quickly.

"I caught him red-handed with the backpack that turned out to be a cooler, no surprise there, with the placenta right inside. He was trying to get away through the back entrance."

"Rex? He's not the one dealing in placentas. I can vouch for that."

"And how is that exactly?" Jets's right eyebrow raised.

"It's all he can do not to gag every time a placenta is mentioned."

Jets's eyes hardened. "That may be true, but it's not going to stop me from arresting your pal."

Sutton broke in. "Did you let the other guy go? The one who brought the backpack into the lobby?"

"For your information, Ms. Know-It-All, he's already in a

cell. He claims having placentas is no big deal. Just something hospitals toss in the trash. But I'll interview him as soon as we get back. Interviewing is my specialty."

Jets fingered the large gold badge pinned to her shirt.

Viv spoke up. "Well, he would say that, wouldn't he? Just so you know, as a doula I'm very informed about placentas. But most people aren't, so he could be telling the truth as he sees it."

It was Sutton's turn. "They look like they know they're doing something wrong. At least from my perspective. I've been tracking them awhile. That's why Rex and I were here tonight. The casino has CCTV of him and a woman exchanging a backpack. They look similar in build: both wear LA Dodgers caps and keep their heads down. One is a bit taller and skinny. I tracked the exchange for the past several months on tape. This isn't his first dropoff."

"You don't say?" Officer Jets said caustically. "I haven't had a chance to look at the CCTV because it's taken time to get a warrant. This is not government territory, you know. I have to get permission to be here let alone arrest someone since it's not in our jurisdiction. But apparently a rando female in a pink spangled crop top can look at tapes where I cannot."

Sutton smirked. "I have a network of friends at the casino, plus Rex and I are family. Did you get permission to arrest the casino's most famous mentalist?"

Jets did not back down. Her eyes narrowed. She thrust her chin out. "You're not the boss of me so don't forget it."

Sutton, who also thrust her chin out, said, "Just tell me, why is Rex in the back seat of your cruiser?"

Jets rocked back on her heels. Viv watched her shift her posture to look less intimidating. The move felt intentional to Viv.

She must be appreciating Sutton; maybe she doesn't have a

leg to stand on. "Rex obviously stole that backpack. I doubt that the tribal authorities will want to get involved with something so small but you never know."

"You cuffed a guy for taking a backpack..." Sutton looked skeptical.

"If you must know, I cuffed him for other reasons."

"And of course you put him in the back of your car, making a big deal about arresting him." Viv offered.

Jets glanced over her shoulder. She lowered her voice. "Unless security tells me otherwise, I'm going to keep your guy safe in my cruiser. Once we get back to the station, I can get your story and then let him go. I'm hoping the other people involved in this will think I've made an arrest and maybe, just maybe, get overconfident and make a mistake.

"I want the identity of those two Dodgers fans. Once I get my facts straight I can get a warrant and I'll use proper police procedure! Now we know what's in those coolers. For your information the illegal transportation, sale, and handling of human organs is covered under the National Organ Transplant Act of 1984." She stopped reciting to look up. "Breaking the law because you are stupid is still breaking the law."

"So this is a false arrest?" Surprised at the tone of her own voice, Viv realized in an instant she felt protective toward Rex. *He's a big personality covering a vulnerable heart.*

"More like protecting an idiot amateur from himself," Jets said dryly.

"Okay then." Sutton took Viv by the elbow. "We'll meet you at the station."

Viv nodded in agreement, letting herself be led away.

Once they were out of sight of the police, Sutton dropped Viv's elbow. "See you at the station. I'm driving Rex's SUV." She sprinted across the parking lot, the spangles on her top illuminated by the light on the police vehicle.

* * *

Twenty minutes later Viv parked next to Rex's SUV in front of the Palm Desert Police Department. *Sutton must already be here.* She slipped out of her car and locked it behind her.

Inside the precinct, she looked over at the front desk.

"Officer Jets said you can walk back to interview room one," the officer behind the desk said. "Door's there." He gestured with his thumb. Viv nodded and pushed open the door, arriving in the hallway that smelled like disinfectant and old linoleum. She found Sutton and Rex in interview room one.

Both of their backs faced the door. "May I come in?" she asked politely.

Rex turned first, standing. "I'm so happy to see you. It's been quite a night."

Viv blinked. "What happened to your face?"

He reached his hand up to run a finger over the scraped skin on his cheek. "I ran into a wall," he explained. "You won't believe my arrest. It got quite interesting. There were cops everywhere, some roughing me up, and I even got cuffed." He held out his wrists. She could see red marks around both.

"He was detained," Jets said, standing behind Viv. She walked around to point at Rex. "I told you not to get involved in my investigation. And what did you do? Not even a day later you're staking out my suspect, pretending to be the bartender. With your pal dressed like a go-go dancer listening in to every conversation, you couldn't have been more obvious."

Sutton ran her hand down her bedraggled spangled top. Sequins along the shoulders were missing, and one of the straps slid over her arm. "I think my outfit looks rather nice. At least no one stopped to take a second look, and that's saying something at The Roadkill." She gave Rex a side-eye.

Officer Jets pointed to an extra chair in the corner. "Why don't you take that chair and have a seat. I want all three of you Musketeers on the opposite side of the desk, where I can keep track of you."

Rex headed across the room. With one hand he lifted the chair. "Let's put you in the middle," he told Viv. Sutton slid her chair over, and Rex plopped Viv's next to Sutton. Viv sat down as Rex moved his chair to sit closer to her, on her right side.

"A rose between two thorns," Viv commented. "I've been waiting to say that for some time."

Jets groaned. Sutton smiled politely. Rex raised his eyebrows as if appreciating the pun.

Jets cleared her throat. "That's enough musical chairs and metaphors. For your information—not that I have to tell you any of this—I have Dereck Simmons in the next interview room. I told him I'm booking Redondo for transporting illegal organs." She nodded across the table at Rex.

Viv's stomach clenched. *I thought she'd be arresting Zach the pool guy. I wonder if that's Pearl's Dereck, the one I met at the cafe the other day.*

Jets continued to explain, "I thought he'd give us more information if he thought he wasn't our prime suspect."

Sutton spoke up. "Once the casino accesses the CCTV tapes from the Cloud, you will have plenty of evidence. You might as well just book him before he gets away again."

"That's not your business, and that's not how it works," Jets said calmly. "But what about you?" She looked at Viv. "As a placenta expert, what do you think is going on here?"

"Just recently my doulas shared information that I know

will be relevant. But I am fairly certain they figured everything they told me was confidential."

"You're not a shrink or a lawyer or a doctor, right? So far as I know doulas don't have a confidentiality agreement," Jets scoffed. "So tell me everything and I'll let you know if it's useful. If it's just shoptalk, then it won't go any further. Do you want me to ask these two to leave the room?"

Viv looked from Sutton to Rex. "They've been in on this since Sarah's death. We're a team."

"Neighbors in crime, if you will," Rex added, looking at Viv for approval. She stared straight ahead.

Viv began a halting summary of what she'd learned from Tamara and Pearl. How they'd formed a team and taken classes. How Sarah used her kitchen for the encapsulation and the others helped. How they worked legally with birthing women, encapsulating their placentas to promote better postnatal health.

"Everything was going fine," she continued to explain, "until Sarah's boyfriend got involved. He showed up with placentas and refused to reveal the sources. Pretty soon there were several a month. The doulas kept making pills and tinctures, appreciating the extra cash."

"At first no one asked where he got the placentas. If they tried to ask, he told them it was none of their business. Until finally Sarah got scared. She ran away from her boyfriend and came to my house to figure out what to do. And then she was found dead.

"So there you have it. That's what I know," Viv sighed. "Except for one other thing. The guy you arrested may be Pearl Overmann's boyfriend."

"Pearl, one of your doulas?"

"That's correct," Viv answered.

Jets tapped her fingers on the desk. Then she pulled out

her iPad and began to type. "Just let me get this down while it's fresh," she told them.

When she finished typing, Jets looked up. "It sounds like Dereck Simmons is our guy. I may need to pull out a few of my tricks to get him to talk. First I want the name of his accomplice, which you may have provided. See how it works when you tell me everything?" She glared at Viv.

"And then let's see if Dereck has an alibi for the night Sarah was murdered. You three sit tight." She stood and walked around the desk, heading toward the door to exit the room, closing it behind her.

Rex gave a heave and stood. "Unlike Officer Jets, I think we may know more than we realize. Just in the last few minutes Viv has brought us new information."

"I didn't realize dealing in placentas was even a thing," Sutton interjected. "Let alone an illegal operation. They must be selling placentas and the encapsulation products on the black market." Her eyes narrowed. "I bet they were making a tidy profit."

"I'm pretty sure my doulas didn't see any of the big money," Viv added.

"Couldn't the cops check bank accounts or something?" Rex asked. "You could see where the money came from and where it ended up."

"The police are probably already on that," Sutton said. "They'll need a warrant to dig into accounts. Even without that, if Dereck gets cornered he may give up his accomplice. But the thing is, even if Jets has uncovered an illegal placenta gang, we still have a problem."

"Who killed Sarah Esperanza?" Viv sighed.

"You thought Sarah was having boyfriend troubles, that's why she came by your house that night?" Rex asked.

"That's what Tamara told me. I didn't actually hear from

Sarah. I do have an open-door policy for all my doulas. But she texted Tamara not me. Probably because I was with a mother in labor. Tamara must have told her to go to my house."

Viv glanced over at Rex and was surprised to see him staring at his lap. If she didn't know better, she'd think he was up to something. Before she could ask, Janis Jets came back through the door.

42

VIVIENNE ROSE

"I'm transferring you to a bigger interview room," Jets barked.

Ushering the three down the hallway, she pointed to the end of the corridor. To-go cups of coffee and bagels sat in the center. Viv's stomach growled.

"Time for a snack," Jets explained.

Rex smirked. Viv came closer, reaching for the cream cheese. She slid the container to Sutton, who helped herself. Rex spread cream cheese on his bagel thoughtfully and then closed the top of the box. All three took a seat around the table.

Jets sat down on the opposite side, glaring at Viv. "So tell me the names of the doulas and where I can find them."

"Pearl Overmann and Tamara Teasdale," Viv said. "I can send you their contact info."

Jets took Viv's phone. "Here's my number. Text me what you've got."

When Jets was finished, she handed the phone back to Viv. "So using my usual means of deduction, I found out the name of the other guy."

"Usual means?" Sutton smirked.

"I am a professional," Jets explained yet again. "I brought in a box of bagels and placed them on a table. He started whining right away. I showed him my bagels and coffee and suggested that he'd better give me the name or he wouldn't be eating."

"Is that legal?" asked Viv.

"On the one hand, it's not strictly illegal," retorted Jets. "But on the other hand, I'm not obligated to offer up my best snacks to just anyone. He had water."

"So do you have the names of the two guys who keep swapping that cooler back and forth?" Sutton prompted.

"Dereck Simmons is the guy we arrested at the Pair-a-Dice. We know him actually. He's on our radar for meth dealing. He has a long arrest record and holes up in Desert Hot Springs. He claims to be Pearl Overmann's boyfriend."

"And the other person, you got them too?" Rex asked.

"Not yet, we're working on that. But Dereck told us everything, including some interesting information about your doulas." Her eyes darted to Viv, then she stared at Rex. "Dereck also had a lot to say about Hailey and Cameron Steward. I believe you're related to them?"

"My status is mostly honorary. I'm not really a biological uncle." His face grew pale underneath his tan.

Before she could say more, Jets's phone pinged. She looked at the screen. "My guys just picked up Zach Young and they're bringing him in for questioning."

"Is he the guy in the CCTV videos? Medium height, kinda skinny, hat pulled over his head?" Sutton asked.

Viv perked up. "Zach may be the guy who pretended to service my pool, right after Sarah's death."

"How about this?" Jets said. "We'll put him in a lineup and let you guys identify him on the CCTV."

"Good idea." Sutton did a quick glance downward. "Any

chance I could go home and get a change of clothes? I'm feeling a bit overdressed for this occasion."

"You're not under arrest. Why don't you take Mr. Redondo with you? And Viv, you can go too. Just get back around seven tomorrow morning. A few hours' sleep will help keep you sharp. A few hours' delay in a cell will give our guys opportunity to get more anxious. I want to have everyone together to get that confession."

"I could help with that," Rex suggested. "I'm kind of good at figuring certain things out. I can stage a medium circle. Add some candles and a bit of flimflam." He looked hopefully at Jets.

"You doubt the ability of the professionals?" Jets sounded angry, but there was a spark in her eye. "Not this time, Mr. Redondo," she said emphatically. "Once we have them all in the same room, I'll step in with a couple of swift questions and then we'll find out who killed Sarah Esperanza. Is it a plan?" She looked at each of them.

Viv swallowed her last bit of bagel. "I'm in." She held her arm out, her palm down.

"I'm in." Sutton put her palm on the back of Viv's outstretched hand.

"And so am I," announced Rex, putting his hand on top.

"Oh what the hell," Jets exclaimed. She put her hand on top of Rex's. "One for all and all for one. See you three Muske-teers at seven a.m. sharp."

* * *

Once outside the station, the three stood on the sidewalk.

"I'm going home," Viv said. "I'll follow you back." She used her key fob to unlock the car and then opened the door.

Viv followed Rex's SUV down the street. It only took five minutes to arrive at their neighborhood.

Sutton reached out the window to punch in the code. As the security barrier rose, they drove past the Desert Tortoise Estate sign. Viv didn't need to reenter the code; she slid in closely behind the SUV.

Viv turned in to her driveway, reaching for her purse to grab the garage door opener. She pressed the button and the door began its ascent.

Before she could drive into the garage, Rex appeared and knocked on her window. She rolled it down.

"You're not gonna believe this." He held up his cell phone.

She glanced at the screen and blinked.

Hailey Steward, dressed in an uncharacteristic baggy sweatshirt, spoke to a reporter. "No comment," she said into the camera.

"Is it your baby?" a reporter insisted.

"Of course he's our baby."

"But did you give birth to your child?"

Hailey shrugged. "He's our baby. That's all I'm saying for now." She turned on her heel, walking away from the camera.

A journalist spoke next. "We are following up on an anonymous report that Hailey Steward did not carry her own baby. After some research we think we found her surrogate. She cannot confirm or deny that she carried the Steward baby because she's signed a nondisclosure agreement. But our crack team of investigators was able to find another reliable witness, someone who is willing to come forward."

Viv's stomach clenched as she watched the screen.

Rex snatched back his cell, clicking it off. "So who do you think the informant was?"

"I have a pretty good idea," Viv admitted.

"One of your doulas?"

"Could be." She rested her forehead on the steering wheel. Then she looked up. "You looked worried when Officer Jets was talking about my doulas. Is that because you think Hailey and her husband may be involved?"

"Who's the mind reader here?" He quirked his eyebrow at her, then he nodded. "Suspicions about the double-crossing doula aside, I have a feeling Hailey and Cameron will be at the station tomorrow. They'll be part of the police interview."

Before she could speak, his cell phone lit up. He lifted it to his ear. "You saw the breaking news? ... I was just telling Viv the same thing. See you tomorrow." He disconnected with a click.

He shrugged and pocketed his phone. "So we have two doulas and two guys in LA Dodgers caps called Dereck and Zach. And two internet stars who happen to be my extended family. It sounds funny when we say it like that..." He looked away.

"It should be quite an event," Viv said calmly. "It's best to know the truth, don't you think?"

Running his hand through his hair, he stepped back from the car. "You are most likely right. See you tomorrow."

Viv closed her window and drove into the garage. *He's worried about his niece and her husband, and I'm worried about my doulas. This is all so confusing.*

43

VIVIENNE ROSE

Rex and Viv arrived early to the precinct. By the time they were greeted and ushered down the hall, they sat at a table with their backs to the door. At five after seven the interview room door opened behind them. Jets came in quietly.

She sat opposite them. "So we have six suspects to consider." She gazed across the desk. "Are you ready for the truth and nothing but the truth?"

Instead of waiting for their affirmation, Janis kept talking. "I'm seeing this crime, or should I say set of crimes, as kind of a relationship thing. Two by two I'm calling it, like the animals on Noah's Ark. When I call in the suspects, you'll see what I mean."

Rex gave Viv a side-eye, then said, "I've spent most of the night wondering how I'm going to explain to Hailey's father that I helped send her to jail." He shook his head, his mouth a straight line.

"Do you really think Hailey would kill someone?" Viv asked Jets.

"'This isn't about what we think and feel. It's about what

we can prove. As mentioned, I have three sets of suspects. But first I'm going to lay down a timeline and show you some videos. When we're done, we'll adjourn to the larger interview room to meet all the suspects and see what I can shake out."

"Since we're just amateurs, why do we need to be there?" Viv asked innocently.

Rex gave her another side-eye.

Officer Jets thought a moment. She clicked on the laptop and turned it toward Rex and Viv. "I think being in the room will help suss out the connections necessary to put this investigation to bed. Here's interview number one." She pointed to the screen.

Hailey spoke earnestly into the camera. "Our surrogate hired Sarah E. to be her doula. Our attorneys told us that she signed a nondisclosure and that it's in our file."

Cameron spoke next. "We had maybe four conversations with her over the phone. Never met face-to-face."

Jets's voice came from off camera. "So tell me how you happened to be at the house the night of the murder. Give me time and context. No detail is too small."

Hailey began, "We had baby home with us, maybe a day or two. Then Cameron gets a call. It's some guy who starts talking about the birth mother's placenta. He wants to know if we'd pay to have it encapsulated."

"That was not a fun conversation," Cameron added. "I kept asking more questions to figure out if he was for real. A lot of tricksters try to shake down celebrity couples. But he kept talking about the placenta. I got really upset because it occurred to me that the placenta may have our DNA material. I mean, we are the biological parents.

"Finally he got real mad. He threatened to put our placenta on the internet and sell it to the highest bidder. I was furious, as you can imagine. I had to think fast. I mean, he wanted a hundred grand in cash right away."

"He knew our surrogate," Hailey continued. "He used her name and everything. He also knew her doula. That's how they got the placenta. Plus we never told anyone about hiring a surrogate. Not even Uncle Rex, at least until a day ago."

"So you've been lying to your fans," Jets said dryly.

"It's to protect the baby!" Hailey exclaimed.

"Let's get back to the conversation with the unknown caller."

"So we agreed to meet the guy to talk and discuss a price," Cameron continued.

"He mentioned the Desert Tortoise Estates and said to bring the money. He seemed to know we had the code to get past the security gate. But he refused to give me his name."

"The address he gave us was right next door to Uncle Rex," Hailey interjected. "That seemed really odd."

"I was also surprised," Cameron agreed. "So I asked the guy some more questions about why he picked that place. He said our surrogate's doula had seen us at Rex's house a couple of times. That sounded plausible. I mean, we've seen lots of women coming and going over there, so they probably saw us. We are celebrities."

"What happened that night?" Jets asked.

"The guy told us to meet him around ten thirty. He said once we got in, we could go around back and open the side gate, which is unlocked. So we did."

"I was really nervous," Hailey said, her cheeks turning pink. "At first we didn't see anyone."

"Everything was really quiet. You could hear the gurgling of the pool filter. That's all," Cameron added.

"I heard a cat meow," said Hailey. "I looked over and saw

her in the window. She was sitting on one of those indoor cat castle thingies."

Cameron reached over to take Hailey's hand. "While she went over to talk to the cat, I wandered a little closer to the pool. That's when I saw her head floating in the water." Cameron's eyes grew wide.

"And I came right over," Hailey said.

"The rest of the body hung beneath the surface. Only the head—with her hair floating around, and maybe her shoulders —were out of the water." Cameron shuddered.

"You didn't think to call the cops?" Jets asked.

"I had my phone out," Cameron said, as if he wanted to be seen as the good guy. "But then I put it away. We were in a real fix. If we called in the police, then our whole story, including the surrogate, would probably come out."

"And I was terrified that we'd be blamed for killing the woman," Hailey added.

Viv looked at Rex. His eyes were glued to the video.

"Did you see any signs of conflict? You know, blood..." asked Jets.

"Not a thing," Cameron said. "Everything looked pretty normal. There was a table with four chairs and a couple of chaise lounges. Come to think of it, I did detect a strong smell of chlorine, probably from the pool."

"I thought it would be okay if we left," Hailey said. "I figured I'd call the police when we got home. The woman wasn't going to get any less dead."

"And then as we were leaving, we saw two guys running up the street," Cameron said.

"They didn't have a vehicle?" Jets asked.

"Nope, on foot," he confirmed. He spoke faster. "So we ran to our car. It was parked in Rex's driveway. Then we ducked our heads, hoping they wouldn't notice us. Once we heard them open the gate, I put the key in the ignition."

"He waited for what seemed like forever," Hailey said.

"Then I sat up and drove down the street, past the booth, then around the block, onto the main street as fast as I could go."

"So if those were the two guys trying to blackmail you, they probably saw the dead body just like you did," Jets mused.

"I think that's why they didn't chase me," Cameron said. "They were scared too."

Jets reached over for the laptop and turned off the video. "So according to Hailey and Cameron, they were at the scene. They had access to the gated community because they'd visited Rex. And they supposedly found the dead body floating in the pool."

She nodded toward Rex. "Anything you want to add?"

"They are two scared, overly privileged kids with a new baby. I don't think they have what it takes to kill someone."

Jets scowled. "But they had motive. They were angry about the placenta extortion. He even said he was worried about DNA complications if they sold the placenta. Maybe the two of them shut Sarah up." Jets's eyes gleamed. "It's possible."

Rex glared back at her. "It's not them. They may be self-centered, but as far as I know that isn't a crime."

Jets did not give in. "They walked away from a person floating in the pool. They could have pulled her out and tried to resuscitate her."

Rex nodded, his face a mask of disappointment.

* * *

Jets cleared her throat. "Okay, here's another interview, this time Viv's two colleagues. We have Pearl Overmann and Tamara Teasdale. I got them in here late last night after you told me they had a placenta encapsulation business." She tapped again. "Here's what they had to say."

Tamara sat in a chair, her back straight, her eyes bright with what looked like defiance.

Viv swallowed, feeling her heart thump in her chest.

Jets's voice spoke first from behind the camera. "Could you tell me what happened the night of Sarah Esperanza's death?" When neither spoke, she prompted them. "Ms. Teasdale, you said you arrived at Vivienne Rose's house at what time?"

"I got there around nine that evening. Sarah wasn't there. She'd texted me earlier that she was coming. I dropped my stuff in the guest room. Since Pearl was coming by ten, I put out the key for Sarah, under the rock, where Viv leaves it for us."

"So I'm wondering, how did Pearl get past the community gate to pick you up?"

"We all have the code. Sometimes Viv has to change the code, but she always gives it to us. We're part of her company, Desert Doulas. She invites us to come over when we need to unwind. We sit by the pool, get some self-care. Doulas work hard, you know."

"What time did Pearl arrive?" Jets asked.

"Like I said, Pearl showed up around ten and we left together."

"And your car...where did you park it?"

Tamara blinked. She looked startled. "I parked my car in Viv's garage."

"You have a garage opener?" Jets's voice trailed off.

"Viv keeps an extra one in the hall table, which I grabbed."

Tamara paused, as if to think. Viv watched the video closely. Tamara's eyes looked up and down. Viv heard Jets clear her throat.

"What was your relationship to the victim?"

"We were doulas and friends."

"Is that all?"

"We also ran an encapsulation business together, along with Pearl. Like I told Viv earlier. We took the class and got certified."

"How often do you encapsulate placentas?"

"It wasn't often at first. And mainly Sarah did the work in house, you know, after the birth, right in the mother's kitchen. But then her boyfriend got involved, started bringing us other placentas. He kept bringing more and more, so we did the extra work in Sarah's kitchen."

"How many placentas did you encapsulate?"

Tamara sat up straighter. "About ten every two weeks. We got $300 for each placenta. Less than if we worked with the mother. It helped me, the extra money. It helped Sarah and Pearl too. Doula work doesn't pay that well."

Jets cleared her throat again. "We looked into your cell phone records. It seems you've been making regular payments to a Heather Teasdale."

"My daughter. It's money for school. She's had a rough time—dropped out, used drugs. She's sober now. I told her I'd help out. That's why I was grateful for the extra income."

"One more question before we take a break. Ms. Overmann, did you think you were picking up Tamara and Sarah that night?"

"At first I did," came her crisp reply. "But Tamara told me that Sarah was too tired to go to the festival and that she'd be coming over to Viv's later."

Jets reached across the desk to turn the laptop around. She stopped the video.

Viv turned to Rex. "I didn't realize how under-resourced my doulas were. It sounds like they all needed money. We talked about finances at our monthly meetings, but I had no idea about the extent of the situation."

Jets commented, "I did some research. Normally the charge of encapsulation barely covers the time and materials. But if you are selling a placenta on the black market, then the prices can go as high as fifty grand each, sometimes a lot more. Money in live organ donations is a real business. It's illegal of course, at least in this country."

"Once Sarah's boyfriend got involved, all they had to do was encapsulate and make the tincture." Rex looked thoughtful.

"More about that in the next interview," Jets said.

* * *

She clicked on the computer. "Ms. Overmann. Could you tell me more about how Zach Young supplied you with placentas?"

"He approached us one day when the three of us were out having dinner. We agreed that his offer of $300 to each of us, per placenta, was pretty good. Most encapsulations pay only $200 to $100 per person.

"And did you ever ask Mr. Young where the placentas were coming from?"

Pearl's mouth drooped. "Not at first," she whispered. "But when the placentas came more frequently, I got suspicious. After a while I asked Zach right to his face."

"What did he say?"

"He told me to shut up and stop asking questions. He said

if I knew what was good for me, I would mind my own business." Pearl's eyes teared. "I found out that Zach would punish Sarah if I asked too many questions."

"How did you find that out?"

"A week before she died, she called me in the middle of the night all hysterical. He'd been yelling and he hit her. That's most likely why she went to Viv's to calm down. To think about things." Pearl sniffed.

"So describe Zach Young to me," Jets said.

"He's around five eleven. Kinda thin, wears his hair back in one of those buns."

"In a scrunchy?" asked Jets.

"Usually. And he has a Dodgers baseball cap. He wears it all the time with his bun sticking out. Kind of disgusting, it's so dirty-looking."

Viv sat up. *So the pool guy is...*

Jets slid the laptop back, clicking the video to pause. She looked at Viv. "I think Zach Young is your pool guy."

Rex spoke. "So we have Pearl's account. The same approximate timing as Tamara. They are each other's alibi."

Viv interjected. "Zach looks guilty to me. He used Sarah to make a profit on placentas. He has a temper. And he came to my house the next day, pretending to be a pool maintenance worker. Isn't that it? Can't we let Pearl and Tamara and the Stewards go?"

"Not just yet," muttered Jets. "I have two more interviews for you to see: Zach Young and his accomplice Dereck Simmons. Watch me come right at them," she said, a look of pride on her face.

She pushed the computer around to face them. "Just so you know, we've already filed charges on Zach Young and Dereck Simmons for trafficking human organs and selling on the black market."

"Did you ever find out why they dropped off the placentas at the casino? That puzzles me."

"It's all in the next interview."

Viv felt her heart drop. "And the doulas...are they also in custody?"

"Not officially, but we're looking into charging them. They didn't know they were encapsulating illegal placentas, and they did try to stop it once they suspected. At least that's what they claim. That goes a long way in my book. So I'm back and forth about charging them officially. But it would be a good idea for them to hire an attorney," Jets advised. "Two attorneys would be best. Tamara and Pearl may not be friends after all of this is over."

Viv held her head in her hands. *I've been so blind. All of this going on right in front of me and I had no idea. I thought Pearl had some relationship issues. I figured Tamara was just a bit distant and that Sarah only needed a couple of days of self-care. I am so stupid!*

* * *

With a click Jets got the video running.

It only took one glance for Viv to confirm her suspicion. "That's him." She nodded to the screen.

"My girlfriend was a doula," Zach said on the screen. "I picked up placentas for her to help out. She did all the work. I'm just her transportation guy." He sounded precise and innocent.

"Do you exchange placentas and capsules and tinctures at the casino?"

"We do it for our women." He pointed to Dereck sitting next to him. "The two of us contact potential donors online, we set up the encapsulation, and then get the capsules back to the owners. I do a lot of the connecting. We share the dropping off. We have this plan."

"So you don't drop and pick up the placentas at people's houses?"

"Do you think I'm stupid? I don't even mail the capsules. The placentas require ice and are only good for forty-eight hours. Otherwise we freeze 'em. I only deal with people in a hundred-mile radius. We pick up the placentas and then hand them over to Pearl or one of the other doulas."

Dereck butted in, "It's not illegal. Hospitals just toss the placentas anyway. The Cahuilla tribe doesn't care what we have in backpacks or even coolers. We were smart that way, in case anyone wondered." He leaned back in his chair with a slight smile.

"The casino is an interesting choice," Jets said.

"We exchange everything in a neutral place, the most convenient way. We don't hide, we do it right in front of everyone. We thought about using hotel lobbies but the casino seemed even better. Hiding in plain sight. You've heard of that?"

"Plus we get a few beers and play the slots while we're there," Zach added. He smiled into the camera.

Jets shook her head. "I have to say you two may be the dumbest crooks I've come across lately. You could have kept things on the down low but you thought a casino would work better? You didn't know that placentas are body organs? Placentas are no different under the law than a human liver or heart. There are regulations that protect their trafficking."

Dereck shook his head while Zach sat back in his chair.

"No way," Zach insisted. "We're not trafficking. Placentas are just weird stuff that comes with the baby. The placenta isn't a person. I'd never traffic a child."

Dereck kept silent. Janis Jets addressed him immediately.

"You knew, didn't you, that it was illegal? I mean, why use the black market if it's on the up-and-up?"

He shook his head. "Sarah and Pearl told me but I didn't believe them. I mean, who cares about a placenta? Just a bunch of lady business."

Viv felt the anger constrict her throat. She swallowed hard to keep from screaming at the video. Inhaling deeply, she told herself, *Calm down, Viv. Let the cop handle this. Ignorant men.*

Jets's voice, from behind the camera, sounded angry. "That story may fly if you didn't use the black market. I'm not buyin' your excuses." Her voice shifted to ask the next question.

"Where were you on the night of Sarah Esperanza's death?"

"We planned to stop and see Sarah at the house where she was staying. She invited us over for a swim and just to hang out and play cards."

"At Vivienne Rose's house?"

"She's the Desert Doula boss. Not exactly a secret," Zach snapped.

"Did either of you have the code for the security gate?"

Zach sat up straight. "I had it. Got it from Viv a few days ago. It was all on the up-and-up."

Viv's eyes grew wide. *I gave him the code because I thought he was the pool guy.*

"We walked around to the back from the side yard." Dereck paused. "Never went in the house."

"So you spoke to Sarah that night?"

"Not exactly." Zach looked at Dereck.

"What did you do exactly?" Jets insisted.

"We found Sarah all right," Dereck said. "She was floating in the pool. Her face looked kinda blue."

"I knew she was dead," Zach said. "We didn't stay. Ran straight out of there."

"Once we got to the street where we left our car we drove to the casino for a few drinks."

"Neither one of you thought to call the cops?"

Viv stared at the laptop screen, looking from one man to the other. Neither appeared concerned, as if it were perfectly natural to leave a dead woman floating in the pool without calling anyone.

"So here's what I want to know." Jets's voice hardened. "If all of you had the code to the security gate, then why did you two and Sarah park your cars on the street outside the neighborhood and walk in?"

Zach's lips formed a straight line. Dereck glared at the camera. Jets turned off the video.

44

REX REDONDO

Jets is good, I have to admit. Very organized. I watch her pull the laptop back again, closing it down with the glint of satisfaction in her eye.

Now Viv...she's a mess. She looks sheet-white and she's holding her stomach as if she's going to throw up. I know she's taking all of this personally, about her friends, as if she could have stopped them.

It doesn't take a mentalist to know Viv's problem. She sees the best in people. Because she works so hard to do her best, she never thinks other people aren't just like her. But I know better. I've seen lots of people not trying at all. They get stuck in their own stories, play the victim card, and then dig a hole so deep they can't get out.

"So far we have a timeline," Jets says. "Sarah arrives at Viv's place after Tamara leaves with Pearl. She parks her car on the main highway."

Viv interrupted. "I actually saw her car that night. I knew I recognized it but didn't think it was Sarah's. I was so tired."

Jets makes a note on her iPad and continues, "'Then Sarah uses the key that Tamara left to get in Viv's house."

I watch her tap her fingers on the desk. Now we're getting somewhere. I speak up. "So Sarah arrived closer to ten?"

"Not sure about that," Jets admits. "The window when she died is between nine and midnight. You discovered her by one a.m."

"Then Cameron and Hailey came next?" Viv asks. Her voice sounds so tired.

"They said they got there around 10:30." Jets nods. "They say that Zach and Dereck were coming down the street, and that's why they jumped in the car and drove away. According to Zach and Dereck they came earlier, found the body, and left."

Jets looks at me. "Maybe she argued with one or both of them. One thing led to another and Sarah got bashed in the head and tossed into the pool."

"That would explain why Zach and Dereck got out so fast, and why they didn't wait for Hailey and Cameron to show up."

Jets nodded. "But that doesn't explain why they'd double back if they had already killed Sarah."

I jump in. "Hailey is innocent. She may be part of a pretentious social media couple, but she's not a murderer." Look at me deflecting away from Hailey, yet leaving out Cameron. I'm not sure he didn't kill Sarah. He's got the temper *and* the entitlement. But I'll let Jets figure that one out.

"So you're thinking that Sarah was killed by Dereck and Zach," Viv speaks up.

"It looks that way." Jets taps her finger on her chin.

She looks at me and I put on my bland face.

Here's my problem: Viv will be heartbroken if one of her doulas is the killer. I'll be heartbroken if Hailey or Cameron are arrested and charged for the murder. I look over at Viv. Even when she's upset she's just adorable.

So small and kind and really pretty. It's her smile. Makes my heart race. It wouldn't surprise me if her doula friends envy her. They may not say so, but I bet they do. In my experience suppressed feelings can erupt and not always in a good way.

"So I have one more thing." Jets turns the video back on, pushing the screen to face us. Zach Young is speaking.

The speaker blares. "I'm not saying another word. I want a lawyer." Arms fold over his chest as he sits back with a huff. The video flutters. No more images.

Jets reaches for the laptop and closes it down.

I feel Viv's eyes on me. In her silence I hear the plea: *please do something.*

I want to comfort her, but I can't—not quite yet. I have to keep my head clear for the next part of the morning. Jets really needs a confession. And I can make that happen.

45

VIVIENNE ROSE

Viv and Rex waited in the hallway as Jets opened the door of the conference room. Mirrors lined one side. All of the suspects sat around the oversized table. "This room's usually reserved for mob family stuff," Jets told them, as Viv and Rex stepped inside.

Hailey and Cameron sat on the opposite side of the table. Cameron looked nervous. He fidgeted in his chair, refusing to give Viv eye contact and barely acknowledged Rex.

"Uncle Rex," Hailey said, as if surprised to see him.

Rex nodded. Viv felt his tension in the way he held his body. He'd excused himself earlier. Jets had followed him, leaving Viv by herself in the interview room. She appreciated the time alone to collect her thoughts.

Once Rex had returned he carried an expensive leather briefcase by his side. Jets had stuck her head in the door to tell them, "The big conference room will be ready very soon. Hang on and I'll come back to get you."

Now that they were standing in the conference room, Rex broke away from Viv's side to sit at the head of the table. Jets, leaving the door to the hallway open, pointed to the other empty chairs. "The doulas will be brought in next, followed by Zach Young and Dereck Simmons."

To Viv's surprise Jets did not ask Rex to move. So she picked the closest empty chair to sit down across from Hailey and Cameron.

She turned her head when she heard voices. Pearl and Tamara came next. An officer in uniform watched as Pearl looked at Hailey. Tamara's eyes stopped on Viv. "You too?" she said, her voice sounding surprised.

"Have a seat," commanded Jets. "I want Ms. Teasdale next to Ms. Rose, and then Ms. Overmann on the other side of the table with Mr. and Mrs. Steward."

With only three chairs left, everyone waited. No one spoke as Janis Jets remained standing in the corner looking at her iPad.

The door opened again, revealing the same officer with two men this time. Viv recognized Dereck and Zach immediately. Zach's eyes darted back and forth, while Dereck kept his gaze down.

"Sit there." Jets pointed. Another man entered the room, wearing a tan suit with a black tie. He sat in a chair next to Dereck, pulling out papers from his briefcase.

I bet he's the attorney.

To Viv's surprise, Zach's shoulders slumped toward his chest. He assumed the posture of a victim. When he raised his head and glared at her, Viv flinched. *He's not acting as confident now.*

Jets nodded to the chair opposite Dereck, next to Cameron. Zach walked around the table and sat down. Then Jets glanced at the officer. He stood with his back against the door. Eyes staring straight ahead, he flicked his jacket aside to reveal a weapon holstered at his side.

Viv looked over at Rex, who seemed unperturbed. He

didn't return her glance but gazed above her head, a slight smile on his lips.

Rex looks like he's in performance mode.

Viv shifted in her seat, aware of anxiety coming from Tamara. They'd been friends for so long, she knew Tamara's body language. She wanted to reach over and pat her hand, but she resisted, keeping her eyes averted.

A chair scraping across the floor brought all eyes to Rex Redondo. On his feet, he clasped his hands in front of his belt. "Though I haven't been asked to consult on this case, I feel I must offer my services," he explained.

Jets, still standing, did not interrupt.

Rex continued, "Due to the sensitive nature and complexity of this situation, I've consulted with Officer Jets and she's agreed. A quick confession and a closure to this case would be best for all concerned." Rex looked at Viv before he glanced at Jets.

Viv felt surprised. *They must have cooked this up when they both left the room earlier.*

Then Rex spoke again. "We owe this to Sarah Esperanza. Shall I begin?"

At the name of Sarah, Viv's stomach clenched. She felt Tamara's knee jiggle under the table. Across from her Pearl wiped at her eyes. *Just a month ago we were all friends, laughing and sharing stories...*

Jets pulled out the remaining empty chair and sat down. She looked at Rex with an unwavering stare.

Rex brought his briefcase up to place it on top of the table. He opened it and reached inside, pulling out a plastic bag that held white pillar candles, all five inches in length. He set them down, reaching into the bag again. He lifted a box of sturdy wooden matches, removing one. With the flourish of his wrist he struck the red-tipped match against the box, and the flame ignited.

Holding the candle with one hand he placed the remaining matches on the table. Then he handed the candle to Tamara while choosing another. "Just pass it along," he told her in a quiet voice. "Everyone will have one in a minute."

As he lit and passed candles to Tamara, he began to speak with a calm cadence, low volume, a confident and confiding voice. By the time everyone held a lit candle, he was the only one without.

Viv paid no attention to what Rex was saying. Because it was the sound of his voice that enthralled her. *So relaxing.* She felt her shoulders loosen, followed by her breath becoming more regular. Her eyes drooped slightly, as the fingers her free hand untwisted, laying open on the table.

As Rex continued to speak she became aware of her own breath, in and out, steady and constant. No longer distracted by the people around the table, her thoughts drifted, as she willingly gave in to the wave of Rex's intoxicating voice.

"All of us are gathered because someone killed Sarah Esperanza. It's not surprising really, why Sarah was killed. She was in over her head. She couldn't continue to encapsulate if the placentas were illegally obtained. So she finally said no.

"One of you knew that it was only a matter of time before Sarah would go to the police. She was a woman with upstanding character."

Viv found herself repeating Rex's words in her head verbatim. She knew with certainty that Rex was right. *Upstanding character.* Her jaw dropped slightly as Rex continued.

"No matter what our connection to her death, the people around this table hold up the light. We've all, in one way or

another, been touched by her caring and upstanding character. The candle is our connection with her."

He continued, his mesmerizing and calming voice
explaining, "There is one of us who hasn't told the entire
truth. You know you want to tell us the entire story. It's
weighing on you and you now realize, as you hold this light,
that it's time."

Viv inhaled deeply as Rex's voice continued.

"Keep holding the candle. You are protected by the
candle's glow; know that you are in a safe space. This could be
your living room. Just a bunch of folks who knew Sarah, who
miss her, who regret that things got so out of control."

Viv looked across at Zach. He blinked, holding his
candle in front of him, eyes staring into the flame. Rex
moved around the table, walking slowly toward Zach. He
stopped to tap his shoulder. "You are protected by the
candle's glow; know that you are in a safe space." He tapped
Zach's shoulder again and moved on to Cameron, repeating
the same pattern. He tapped everyone individually, not in
order, but stepped past Viv to speak to Tamara. He
repeated the words with the taps. Then he went back to the
attorney, who also held a candle. His eyes closed as Rex
tapped.

Finally Rex stood next to Viv. He leaned closer to tap her
shoulder and then instead of speaking so that everyone could
hear, he leaned in to her ear. She felt his breath brush against
her cheek. "You are protected by the candle's glow; know that
you are in a safe place."

Instead of pulling away he kept his mouth close to her ear.
His warm breath caressed her cheek with more words. "I love
you," he said, and then he tapped her shoulder and quickly
moved away.

Viv heard the words, but they didn't register. The deep

sense of calm tingled over her entire body. Her skin felt alive yet completely relaxed.

On the way back to the head of the table Rex stopped to speak to the officer. Viv couldn't hear what he said. Then Rex walked back to the head of the table, standing behind his chair. He nodded to the officer, who reached over with one hand.

The lights went off.

Ten candles glowed in the dark. Viv stared into the flame as Rex began to speak. "It's all right. You can tell us now. We're all safe in this room. Mistakes have been made and no one blames you."

As the silence deepened, Viv could hear a low hiss in her ears. It got louder and louder. She opened her eyes, aware of Tamara shifting in her chair.

Viv glanced from one person to the next. The hiss got louder, as if a snake had been caught inside her head. As everyone stared into their candle flame, she noticed their illuminated faces. They could be mistaken for worshipers at a vigil, not suspects for a murder.

But then, Viv felt a cool breeze drift past her face. The hissing in her ears stopped as suddenly as it had begun. Her eyes rested on Rex, who waved his elegant fingers in front of him, as if conjuring something into being.

Soon her candle flame wavered and then all around her the candles began to flicker, one then the other. Tamara shifted again. Viv waited, still wanting to take her hand. *She'll forgive me. I know she will.*

She felt Tamara take a deep breath. On the exhale her candle flickered and then went out. Tamara held it in front of her, blinking her eyes as if unsure what to do. Everyone in the room, aware that Tamara's candle had extinguished, now stared at her face.

"It's me," she said quietly, her voice thick with emotion. "I'm the one, I killed Sarah." Then she flung the candle on the table, wax spraying across Viv's arm.

Feeling the hair singe from the wax, Viv brushed her arm with quick strokes to relieve the pain.

Rex sprinted toward the door to flick on the lights.

The police officer caught Tamara in his arms as she bolted toward the door. He turned her body around, cuffing her hands behind her back in one swift motion.

Viv rubbed her arm as the wax began to harden. In the light everyone looked to Officer Jets. She clenched her jaw, her face stiffening with shock. *How could she do this, betray me and everyone else?*

Viv shook her head as her thoughts returned. While Rex sat calmly in his chair, he gazed at his briefcase on the table, not giving her eye contact.

He mesmerized all of us into thinking it would happen, and then...it did!

46

VIVIENNE ROSE

The armed officer sat Tamara, still in handcuffs, back in her seat. Though Pearl hovered by her friend, Janis said, "You can wait by the front desk. We'll let you know when you can go." She didn't leave any room for discussion.

Then Janis Jets instructed the officer to take Zach and Dereck to their cells. She also excused Hailey and Cameron. "You two can go," she told them. Surprisingly, she turned swiftly to Rex and then Viv. "You two sit next to me," she instructed.

They both obliged, one on either side of Officer Jets.

"So tell me how it happened," Jets said calmly. She had her iPad ready to take notes. She looked up at Tamara, while Viv and Rex sat quietly.

Viv's mind was so full of remorse that she had trouble concentrating on what Jets said. All she could think was, *Tamara killed Sarah. I never saw that coming. I thought I knew her so well. I can't believe this.* The shock was wearing off, leaving a keen sense of betrayal underneath. Her head spinning and her heart sinking, she didn't want to believe it was Tamara but it was necessary to hear why she'd done such a terrible thing.

Tamara appeared almost eager to tell her story. In a clear voice she began, "When Sarah told me she was going to tell Viv and the police about our illegal placenta business, I knew I had a problem. I needed the extra money, and my daughter needed her second chance at life.

"Sarah had a habit of going to Viv. She needed her approval. It just made me sick. She was such a goody two-shoes."

Tamara glared at Viv, her eyes bright with anger. "I am so tired of you telling us what's right and wrong. You're so haughty with your money and perfect life and perfect son, the doctor. You don't need things like I do, like regular people."

Viv cringed at the tone of her voice.

"Anyway, everything started out okay that evening. I lied about when I left. I was there when Sarah arrived. I let her inside and we got in our suits to sit by the pool. We were drinking wine from Viv's fancy glasses." She glared across the table once again.

"Sarah kept drinking. She was obviously upset. When she told me she was going to talk to Viv I just got furious. I screamed at her, how she let another man take advantage and how Zach made most of the money. I tried to tell her that we didn't need him, that we could do everything ourselves.

"Sarah started to cry, and then she began to yell at the top of her voice about how I wasn't a good friend and I always got her into trouble. How I'd tricked Viv into letting us use her house.

"Sure, I told the guys they could use the pool to meet up with Hailey and Cameron. Nobody had to know. Viv was at work. And I, the usual cat sitter, was left behind to pick up her pieces.

"So I told Sarah, 'You embarrass yourself. The guys think the same. They just use you because it's convenient.'

"We'd finished the bottle of wine, so she was wobbly when she stood up. That didn't stop her from walking over to smack me across the face. I was shocked. I mean, pathetic Sarah hitting me. I felt like I did all those years ago, when my mom would smack me around. So I didn't let her get away with it. No one gets to treat me with disrespect anymore. I smacked her with the back of my hand really hard, right across her jaw.

"The rage just overtook me. I kept yelling at her. I shoved her, but she lost her balance and stepped backward. Down she went. *Boom*, her head bounced against that boulder.

"It was self-defense. She hit me first. I reached out to help her just as her whole body went limp." Tamara leaned forward, her wrists straining against the handcuffs. "I tried to save her. Did some CPR. But then I saw the blood on the rock and I knew I'd never be able to explain. She was unconscious by this time. I realized no one would believe me. I'd be arrested.

"I checked her pulse but didn't feel anything. So I made a quick decision. I tucked her arms next to her body and rolled her over the pavement into the pool. She sank right away. A few bubbles rose from her mouth. She looked kind of peaceful, floating in all that blue water.

"It didn't take a minute to find the bleach under the sink in the kitchen. I grabbed a towel and the spray bottle and rushed outside again. The blood stains came up really easily on both the rock and the pavement. I had to hurry because Pearl was due to pick me up any minute.

"So I ran to my room with the spray bottle and the towel, and I put them in my large tote. It wasn't until then that I realized I needed to leave Viv's house key as if Sarah had let herself in. After some searching I found the key at the bottom of my wallet. I put it back on the table by the pool basket so that Viv would think Sarah had let herself inside.

"On the way back to the bedroom to get the tote I worked on the timing. I'd have to convince everyone that I'd left before Sarah got here. I didn't want them to think we even crossed paths. I looked at my phone and decided to leave it in my room. Without the phone I wouldn't have to talk to anyone once they found Sarah. It would give me time to get solid on my alibi."

Tamara shrugged. "The rest was easy. I left the phone and my small purse but shoved all the evidence into my tote and took it with me. By the time Pearl got there I remembered to take the extra garage door opener from the drawer. That way I'd be able to get back in the house the next morning.

"We drove away, and I felt pretty confident that no one would connect me with Sarah's death. I just kept repeating to myself that I never saw Sarah. She must have arrived after me. I left her a key under the rock. Over and over until it felt like the truth.

"Once we were at the festival, I emptied the tote contents into the trash. Then I dumped the tote across the field. It felt so freeing. I had a great time that night."

Tamara looked down at the table. Her shoulders drooped as her body seemed to sink into itself. Jets typed as Rex's head dipped into his hand.

Jets looked up. "Well, that's it then. I've got it all down. We'll type up a confession for you to sign." She nodded at the police officer who stood at the door.

As he escorted Tamara from the room, Viv blinked, feeling tears fill her eyes.

47

VIVIENNE ROSE

After Tamara had gone, Officer Jets sat back in her chair. She looked calm, yet the circles under her eyes told a different story.

Even Rex looked fatigued. "I thought it was her, you know. That first night she looked familiar. I'd seen her the few times she picked up the placenta at the casino."

"I thought Zach and Dereck might have killed Sarah," Jets admitted. "But Sarah was dead and Hailey and Cameron were already gone when they discovered the body. They didn't want to admit they found her body, so they just ran."

"But why did they circle back?" Rex asked.

"They probably thought they'd dropped something. It was too dark to really see, so they took off. You know they must have been scared."

"They ran right to the casino to drown their fear," Rex said.

"Zach did come back the next day," Viv reminded them.

"He knew the cops had already combed the area. It just made me suspicious once I realized he was also Sarah's boyfriend," Jets said. "I suspect that Zach, like a lot of greedy criminals, came back out of curiosity, not for any particular reason."

Jets continued, "On the one hand, we got our guy. But on the other hand, I broke my own rule. I've never done that before, called in a mentalist to get a confession. I'm not sure I can forgive myself."

Rex smiled sheepishly. "'I was just helping. We closed the case. Just be happy."

Viv swallowed, willing to bring the conversation to a close. "Okay then, I'm going to stop blaming myself for not seeing things sooner. Thank you, Officer Jets."

Jets turned to her, a serious expression in her eyes. "You are not to blame. Tamara lost her temper and then doubled down by shoving Sarah in the pool instead of calling for help. That's not you. Get that in your head."

On cue Rex stood. "Time to go." He made his way behind Viv's chair, placing his hands on the back as if to help her stand.

"I'm sensing a goodbye here," Jets muttered. "I don't like goodbyes. Just go home, you two. Sit by the pool and use lots of sunscreen, the kind without that cancer-causing chemical. One of you is overly sensitive and the other highly manipulative. The perfect couple."

Jets began to read on her iPad, flicking her fingers in the air as a dismissal.

* * *

"I brought Kevin." Rex stood at Viv's front door. It was seven o'clock, and Viv had invited him over for cocktails. He dressed in a bright Hawaiian print shirt. Kevin had a matching collar. "I thought he'd help cheer you up," Rex offered.

Viv opened the door wider. The truth be told, she wasn't

ready for company. Her punishing sense of remorse kept her mind whirling with thoughts of the investigation. "I'm not really ready for company," she told him.

"How about considering me not company but a friend," he said in a kind voice.

She sighed. "Okay then. Consider yourself forewarned."

Once he stepped inside Viv began to speak. "I still can't wrap my mind around how wrong I've been. I didn't see Tamara clearly, let alone my other doulas. How could I be so ignorant of their unhappiness?" She looked at Rex as if he might have an answer. When he didn't respond, only looked sad, she felt worse.

"You don't need to come up with any answers for me." Tears threatened, which she wiped away with her finger. "I'm just overwhelmed. Give me some time?"

"Of course," he said at once. "Since you're so hard on yourself already, it's up to me to provide some distraction. Kevin came to meet Miss Kitty." He closed the front door.

The dog sat right down. "I told him to behave." Rex nodded to the dog.

Maybe he's right. Dry your tears, Viv. "And does he always do what you tell him to do?" Her voice sounded hollow. Tears threatened again, but she wiped them away, determined to stop overthinking.

"If he doesn't, it's back to Sutton's obedience academy," Rex said dryly.

Viv smiled. "I have a charcuterie board all ready. I distracted myself by cutting up vegetables."

"Oh yah, that sounds good."

She glanced over his shoulder. "Let's take Kevin to the catio first." Viv led the way down the hall as Rex and Kevin followed. The dog walked briskly next to Rex, as if he was looking forward to a new adventure.

"Meow," came a call.

"Look out, Miss Kitty, we have a visitor." Viv opened the door and stood aside. Rex unhooked Kevin from his lead. The dog trotted in with Rex following. Viv quietly closed the door and turned to walk into the room.

"Meow," came the call from near the windows.

Kevin looked up and then spotted Miss Kitty perched at the very top of her cat castle. She stared imperiously at him, her tail wrapped around her body.

"Bork," came Kevin's reply. He stayed close to Rex, his body wiggling from the effort it took to stay put.

"Meow." Her tone suggested that she didn't appreciate having to remind him of her presence more than once.

"Take it easy, Miss Kitty. Be polite," Viv said, using her softest voice.

Rex bent his knees, placing his arm around Kevin. He tapped the dog's head with his finger and then leaned in to speak into his ear. He whispered something that made the dog lick his face.

Rex rose from his crouched position and smiled at Viv.

"What did you say to Kevin?"

"I told him to be cool. And that Miss Kitty needs to get used to his presence. Oh, I also told him that he's a good boy."

"I can't believe your mind tricks work on dogs." Viv shook her head.

He shrugged. "Frankly I can't believe it either. Why don't we sit over there and chat and watch what happens."

Viv pointed to the corner of the sofa. He sat down and smiled gently at her without speaking.

She felt her stomach relax, then her shoulders. *Maybe he's right. I do need distraction.*

She started as Kevin took a big leap, landing in the middle

of the sofa between Rex and Viv. He turned his body and then lay down, placing his chin on Viv's knee.

"You are a good boy," she told the dog, scratching behind his ears. Then she turned to Rex. "I am having trouble wrapping my head around all that happened. Some of the details got lost once I realized Tamara was the killer. Does that ever happen to you, your ears get a loud whooshing sound and you can't make sense of anything you hear?"

"That hasn't happened to me, but I have been overwhelmed with powerful feelings that render me helpless." He looked at her, his eyes twinkling.

She felt his meaning as a ping to her chest, a sense of instant insight. *He has feelings for me.* She looked up at him, wondering what to say.

Rex reminded her, "Don't forget Jets's lecture. You are not to blame. I can say the same thing in a lot fewer words: what goes around comes around."

She swallowed hard, willing herself to let go. "I didn't realize how Tamara would feel, comparing herself to me all those years. Once I got the divorce settlement, I just worked harder. Then I stepped away from the practice and formed a business so that I could take a few select clients. I figured she was happy for me.

"She watched me and never said a word. But apparently with all of her financial problems, she was in deep trouble. Plus she knew I didn't support the encapsulation process. It hasn't been scientifically authenticated and it just feels very iffy to me.

"Tamara was right, you know. I would have stopped referring her and Sarah once I knew about their side gig; I'd have told them to find another doula agency."

Rex nodded. "I know this must feel like a betrayal in so

many ways. You probably didn't realize she held any resentment, never mind when it turned to outward hostility."

"She did distance herself over the past several months. I just figured she had her clients and was busy." Viv shrugged.

"I've observed over the years that people usually get in trouble one decision at a time. Once Tamara lost her temper and slapped Sarah, things went from bad to worse. Then she cleaned up after herself."

"Did Jets ever say if they found the towel and spray bleach?"

"I bet it's too late. Must be in a landfill somewhere. I don't think Tamara will be convicted for premeditated murder. Does that help, knowing she won't get a life sentence?" When she didn't answer he added, "Her attorney will figure this out. He'll get Tamara the best deal."

"I suppose you're right. After all that worry about money, she'll be buried in legal fees."

She thought for a moment. "It will take some time for me to let myself off the hook. When I think about Janis Jets's perspective, I have to agree. She's quite convincing."

Before Rex could respond, Miss Kitty called from across the room. She'd leapt from the top of her castle, clawing her way down the carpeted post to land on the floor. With careful steps she came closer. Kevin growled, springing to all fours, still in the middle of the sofa. He bounced up and down on his front paws, ready to play.

Miss Kitty sprang onto Viv's lap. She sat possessively, eyeing Kevin and Rex.

"Kevin," Rex warned. "Don't even try it..."

The dog began to sniff the cushion, coming closer to Viv's leg. Miss Kitty pulled back a paw. With claws extended, she swiftly struck his nose.

Kevin yipped, backing away from the cat. Then he turned to lift his sore nose as if asking for comfort.

Rex patted his head. "Gotta watch out for those claws," he warned the dog.

Viv took Miss Kitty from her lap, placing her down on the floor. The cat scurried away, zipping toward the cat castle. Rex held his arm around the injured Kevin.

Then Viv heard her phone from the other room.

"Go ahead and get that." Rex ruffled Kevin's fur with his hand.

When Viv returned and sat on the couch, she had a smile on her face. Kevin and Rex still sat together, with Kevin curled into a ball in the center of the sofa. "He's okay," Rex assured her. "Probably a good first round. Now he knows Miss Kitty isn't amused by his playful attitude nor his good looks. But he'll try again, just you wait."

"So would taking a swat at you work the same?" Viv asked innocently. "Will you still come back?"

"Every time," he assured her. "And I don't mind being compared to a dog either. In case you wondered."

"Ever been to Lily Rock?" She changed the subject, appreciating that the genial conversation was working. No longer preoccupied, she felt better and if she had to admit, finally hungry.

"That's Janis Jets's town." His surprise turned into interest. *He wrinkles his forehead when I have his attention.*

"I've been there but it's been years ago," Rex added.

"It's kind of a problem, at least for me. Pearl had a job in Lily Rock; I got her a cabin and everything. Then she had to come back for a few days, for the freebirth women's circle in Coachella.

"The client is on bedrest so her sister was glad to help

until Pearl returned. But now Pearl won't be going back. What makes matters worse, they liked her."

"And..." He let his voice drop.

She patted her knees with both hands. "I may take the job. The mother's name is Sage. Her sister is Olivia. If they'll have me, of course."

"You're ready to get back to work?" he asked gently.

"It would be good for me to take another job. I've been too busy with the investigation."

His face lit up. "I thought you'd never ask. I'll bring Kevin along. He loves a good car ride. I hear they have a dog mayor. An odd little town, Lily Rock."

"Well that's settled." She felt the knot in her stomach relax. *He's good for me. I feel safe around him but I also feel...* She scooted closer to him. "You are by far the most interesting man I've ever met."

His look of surprise made her laugh out loud. "Don't let that go to your head now." She patted his leg. She felt a niggle in her gut, realizing there was a feeling underneath. Instead of pushing it away, she focused. Then she asked, "And one more thing I have to ask. Did you put a spell on me yesterday during the interview, one of your mentalist tricks?"

A slight grin started at the corner of his mouth. "Ah shucks. I thought you'd forget all about that. It was just for fun."

"I see." Viv leaned in to whisper in his ear. "Just so you know, I'm completely under your spell."

He took her hand, turning it over to brush his lips against her open palm. "Just so you know, I don't do spells. No amount of pretend magic could explain my feelings right now."

She felt his lips move against her hand, a shiver rolling up her spine.

Then he placed her hand back on her knee, giving it a pat. "How about we get that drink in town that we've been talking about? It would do us good after all that investigating."

"Bork," came from across the room. Kevin, on all fours, stared at Miss Kitty, who hid at the top of her cat castle, her tail swishing.

"May Kevin come along?" Rex asked. "We might as well take him with us before he gets another swat on the nose."

"Of course," Viv laughed. "But I think you may be wrong. Now that Miss Kitty has established her boundaries, there may be no more swats. It may take some time but they'll be friends before long."

Rex's forehead wrinkled. He stared at Viv. "We're still talking about Kevin and Miss Kitty, right?"

Instead of answering Viv laughed, walking toward the door.

* * *

Thank you for reading *A Doula to Die For*! For the latest news join my VIP newsletter. PS signing up also gets you a copy of *Meadow's Hat*, a short story set before *Getaway Death* :).

Sign up on bonniehardywrites.com/newsletter

Start the Lily Rock Mystery series with *Getaway Death*

Prologue

Overheard in Lily Rock

"I love the town of Lily Rock. Their lies are so authentic."

Fog rolled over the mountain road. Despite the poor visibility, the woman drove as if her life depended upon it.

A sharp curve to the right—her squealing tires issued a warning.

Tentatively removing one hand from the steering wheel, she kept her eyes on the road, her fingers reaching down for her windshield wipers. *Swish.* The blade on the glass moved to the left, then the right. Her gaze remained fixed on the road in front of her. Reaching over the steering wheel, she swiped with her hand at the thick condensation blocking her view from inside the car.

Veering into the next curve, she felt her stomach lurch. Brakes squealed again as the car catapulted into an unexpected second hairpin turn. Her head lolled to the right. As she came out of the curve, she pushed the button on the foggy driver's side door and rolled down the window, revealing clouds of fog.

Another vehicle rumbled behind her car, close to her bumper.

"I guess somebody's in a big hurry," she snapped to the empty car.

The window slid shut as she looked out of the front windshield to the right, then the left. No turnout lane yet. Tightness stiffened her neck as her hands began to shake on the wheel. *Stop tailgating me. Please.*

She felt the tires slip on the road, the car floating for a moment. As she slammed on the brakes, her body heaved against the seat belt, her neck and head rocking forward then back. Her stomach came up to her throat.

As her car skidded toward the cliff, she only had one thought:

I finally know how I will die.

End of Sample
To continue reading Getway Death, pick up a copy at your favorite retailer.

GET A FREE SHORT STORY

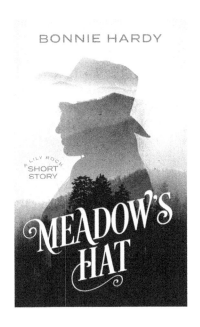

Join my VIP newsletter to get the latest news of Lily Rock along with contests, discounts, events, and giveaways! I'll also send you *Meadow's Hat*, a Lily Rock Mystery short story.

Sign up on bonniehardywrites.com/newsletter

NOTE FROM THE AUTHOR

I started listening to a podcast by a group of doulas two years ago, and I found myself fascinated by their stories. I loved the unpretentiousness of the women and couldn't get enough of their laughter and genuine compassion for themselves and those in their care. They soothed my soul during the isolation of the pandemic for surprising reasons. The least of which is that I am decades away from childbearing age.

I wondered about my interest in doulas, so I started to do more research. I read books and scholarly articles for months. Still unsure why I was so fascinated, I continued to listen to the podcast and to my amazement after one episode, I began to cry.

I sobbed for a while, grabbing for tissues, so surprised at my emotional response. At this point I allowed myself to remember the birth of my first daughter. Decades later, feeling so accepted and understood by this unknown group of podcast doulas, I felt safe enough to remember my first birth experience.

She weighed three pounds and arrived nine weeks early. After weeks of hospital care I brought her home at a whopping four pounds, all of the emergency birth drama swept aside in my concern for keeping her alive. With no experience and no female family member to rely upon, I was determined to help my daughter thrive.

After sleepless nights, nursing every two hours, I barely made it from one day to the next. Two months went by before

I stumbled into my local library. Convinced my baby would be endangered if exposed to the public for more than ten minutes, I grabbed the first best seller at the entrance. My library card poised, I hurried to the checkout counter.

The librarian smiled at me. She slid the book under the scanner and asked about my baby, who was fast asleep in a corduroy sling on my chest. The more I talked the closer the librarian looked at me, listening carefully. Most likely sensing my new-mother anxiety.

I was ready to go when instead of waving me on, she walked around the counter. She took me by the hand. "Come with me," she said. "I have just the book for you."

We walked through the center of the first floor, past readers and students studying, to the farthest corner where she halted in front of the stack on the back wall. She stood on tippy toes. Selecting the only book that actually had a spiral binding, she turned and handed it to me.

On the cover was a grandmotherly looking woman holding an infant smiling into the camera. Very 1950s. To say I felt no confidence would be putting it mildly. But I was desperate and even then respected the ability of good librarians to match a person with a book.

The next day I began to read. After that, the spiral copy went with me everywhere. I'd put baby in a front pack, hold the book with one hand, and move about my daily tasks reading from the pages. While she napped, I made notes on three-by-five cards, knowing I'd eventually have to return the book.

Finally I went to my local used book store and ordered a copy for myself.

I've kept that copy to remind myself that books matter. In fact, over my lifetime it's often been a book that's gotten me through very challenging times.

My First Three Hundred Babies by Gladys Hendricks changed the trajectory of my life. The book included wise counsel and lots of recipes from a woman who worked with young families just like mine. She wasn't a professional midwife or a doula. She didn't have any credentials. Her name was shared by happy families whose recommendations filled the back of the book.

Gladys Hendricks believed in schedules, both for mothers and babies. Much of that wisdom is not embraced these days, but my baby and I thrived under her tutelage. Gladys's matter-of-fact written voice instructs the reader to keep one step ahead of baby and not to forget to feed yourself and the rest of the family along the way. Her most famous saying? "It's not what the child will do, but what you will do about it."

When it came time to create the character of Officer Farrah in *A Doula to Die For,* I fully expected her to stay the course and help solve the mystery. But once she entered the scene and started talking to Vivienne, the story went in another direction.

It only took a casual chat with Viv, a compassionate professional doula, for Officer Farrah to be overwhelmed with emotion. She remembers her past, her own experience giving birth, and she knows it's time to pay attention and take care of herself.

Before closing I'd like to thank Christie Stratos from Proof Positive. She's maintained my sanity on more than one occasion, with her quick wit and turn of phrase and a deep knowledge of the *Chicago Manual of Style.*

And thanks again to Kate Tilton. She advises me on how to publish and get my books out into the world.

And thanks to Ebook Launch, with yet another eye-catching front cover design.

And finally thanks so much to you dear readers, for supporting this new series.

Please drop me an email if you want to chat or ask questions.

Keep on reading!
Bonnie
2023

ABOUT THE AUTHOR

Born and raised in Los Angeles, Bonnie Hardy is a former teacher, choir director, and preacher. A lover of libraries and literacy, Bonnie directed a literacy center in her home town.

Bonnie has published in *Christian Century*, *Presence: An International Journal for Spiritual Direction*, and with Pilgrim Press. She's written numerous short stories some which can be found on her Facebook page.

When not planting flowers and baking cookies, she's sitting at her computer plotting her next cozy mystery.

You can connect with Bonnie at
bonniehardywrites.com

facebook.com/bonniehardywrites

goodreads.com/bonniehardy

bookbub.com/authors/bonnie-hardy

amazon.com/author/bonniehardy

Made in the USA
Las Vegas, NV
20 May 2023

72317156R00177